P9-DDM-226

WAHIDA CLARK PRESENTS

THE BLACK
SENATE

CHASE BRANCH LIBRARY
17731 W. SEVEN MILE RD.
DETROIT, MI 48235

BY

ZAID ZA'HID

DEC   2017

This is a work of fiction. Names, characters, places, and incidents either are the product of the author's imagination or are used fictitiously, and any resemblance to actual persons, living or dead, business establishments, events, or locales are entirely coincidental.

Wahida Clark Presents Publishing
60 Evergreen Place
Suite 904A
East Orange, New Jersey 07018
1(866)-910-6920
www.wclarkpublishing.com

Copyright 2017 © by Zaid Zah'id
All rights reserved. This book, or parts thereof, may not be reproduced in any form without permission.

Library of Congress Cataloging-In-Publication Data:

ISBN 13-digit 978-1944992-54-5 (paperback)
ISBN 13-digit 978-1944992569 (ebook)
ISBN 13-digit: 978-1944992552 (Hardback)
LCCN: 2017904233

1. Crime 2. Drug Trafficking- 3. African Americans-Fiction-
4. Urban Fiction- 5. Mafia- 6. Chicago-

Cover design and layout by Nuance Art, LLC
Book design by NuanceArt@aCreativeNuance.com
Edited by Linda Wilson

Printed in USA

ACKNOWLEDGMENTS

Thank you to my family and friends who believed in me. Thank you to Kayenne for mentoring me. This is dedicated to all the hustlers on these ghetto streets. The Black Senate is a fictional tale about a man on a quest to reclaim all that he's lost.

Zaid Za'hid

I

PENITENTIARY CHANCES

CHAPTER ONE

Dressed in all black, Malachi, YaYa, and Jerusalem sat around a chestnut brown table loading and checking their automatic weapons. The crew had graduated from just young hustlers to controlling their own turf. If it came down to it, they killed for their respect with no hesitation. They quickly got a reputation and a name for themselves. Some even called them the BBB—Bad Black Brothas.

Inside the rundown apartment, one of the most notorious projects in Chicago, they passed the blunt around as Tupac's song, "Get Money" played in the background. Jerusalem recited on beat, ". . . today I make a killing . . ." He stopped rapping so they could go over their plan to rob First National Bank.

If they pulled off the heist, they would have enough money to increase their drug supply and expand their organization. This would eliminate some of their competitors. The old heads in the drug game were not showing Jerusalem and his crew any love. They hated to see the young soldiers moving up so rapidly, and they wouldn't let Jerusalem score from them. When they did let Jerusalem score, they almost doubled the prices on the product, making it hard for him to profit. So Jerusalem came up with a plan. With an inside connection, he, along with his crew, planned to hold up one of the largest banks in the city. If he possessed more money, he could bypass the old heads and one day get close enough to kill them all. This was the day they were to put their plan in action.

Jerusalem turned toward Malachi and said, "Remember, your job is to hold off the guard, but without killing him."

Malachi, with dreads that barely sat on his shoulders, responded, "If anyone flinches, I'm shooting. I'm not hesitating to plug their ass."

"Just don't get trigger happy, 'cause I know you have a hair trigger finger. If it's not necessary to commit a murder in this robbery, then don't do it. Our whole mission is to go in, get this money, and come out. We got two minutes to do this from the time we enter the bank," Jerusalem said.

"Where Pinky's yellow ass at?" YaYa asked.

"You know she's always late. That bitch will be late for her own funeral because her stupid ass would be trying to put her own make-up on," Malachi said.

They all laughed but got quiet when they heard the secret knock—two taps and a pause then one tap and a pause and three taps. Malachi jumped up and opened the door. "Bitch, where you been?"

"You think stealing a SUV is easy," Pinky, the streetwise and curvaceous eighteen year old said while rolling her neck with lots of attitude. "Jerusalem told me specifically to get a dark SUV. Motherfucker, I had my girl drive me all over Chimney Hills this morning before I found one." Her role in the heist was only to be the get-a-way driver.

Jerusalem eyed the 5-feet 5-inches tall, big, emerald eyed beauty in the tight fitting jeans she loved to wear to show off her body. Her heart-shaped head was filled with long, dark curly hair drawn up into a ponytail.

"You're looking beautiful, ma," he said. "What you have on is perfect? 'Cause you're supposed to look like an ordinary patron, a beautiful woman behind the wheel. When we enter the car, we don't want you to do no speeding. Drive the speed limit, because we're going to duck down where it looks like you're the only one in the SUV.

"YaYa, your role is to make sure that all the customers and workers in the bank are under control. Whatever you do, don't let a motherfucka get to their cell phone."

"I got you," YaYa responded.

While talking, they loaded their guns, ski masks, and gloves into one duffel bag.

Jerusalem asked Pinky, "You strapped already?"

Her full-sized, pink lips moved as she replied, "Yes, I keep my man with me." She patted her small waistline to indicate the weapon was securely hidden. With the curves she carried, every hustler in the neighborhood attempted to get their hands on Pinky. Men drooled over her every time they saw her thick hips and ass like Serena Williams.

They exited the project doors.

An hour later, after casing the area one last time, Pinky pulled the SUV in front of the bank. Jerusalem looked around the area. "Go," he said.

Malachi, pulling the black Spider-Man mask over his head, was the first to exit the SUV. He held the AK-47 assault rifle out as he entered the bank doors. YaYa followed suit, holding a .357 Smith and Wesson with extra bullets around his waist. When he walked, his shirt swayed, revealing the weapon. Jerusalem patted his pocket, confirming he had four extra clips in each one. He tightened his Spider-Man mask down under his chin and extended his .45 automatic weapon as he entered the bank last.

"Everybody get the fuck down!" Malachi yelled. "Don't nobody fucking move!"

It looked as if the security guard was contemplating a move. Malachi immediately put the gun to the white security guard's head and said, "Motherfucka, don't even flinch. If you do, I won't hesitate to put a bullet in your fuckin' head."

YaYa yelled out, "Down on the floor, now! Keep your hands visible where I can see them." He waved the gun near the customers to show he meant business. Some of the customers wailed, but they all obeyed.

Jerusalem jumped over the bank counter with the duffle bag. "You three, on the floor. Now!"

The three women crowded together and whimpered. One sounded like she was hyperventilating as they bent down and got on the floor. Jerusalem ignored them and pointed the gun at the bank manager. "You too."

Only one cashier remained standing, and she was the one Jerusalem knew.

"A minute and forty-five seconds!" YaYa yelled near the frightened customers.

Jerusalem turned his attention to the cashier and pointed the gun to the side of her head and said, "Bitch, you know what to do. Take me to the money."

Instead of Jerusalem taking her to the cashiers' drawers, he led her to an open safe that held over 200 thousand crisp hundreds and twenties. "This is what I'm talking about," he said as he held one gun on the cashier and used the other hand to load the money.

YaYa shouted, "Sixty seconds!"

Jerusalem forced the cashier to the floor and stuffed as much money as he could into the bag.

"Forty-five seconds!" YaYa yelled, looking at his watch.

Jerusalem pointed the gun at the cashiers and the bank manager. "Get up." He directed them to walk around the counter. "Down. Now!" He demanded them to lie on the floor with the rest of the bank patrons.

Malachi walked the unarmed guard to the same location. "On the floor, motherfucka!"

"Fifteen seconds!" YaYa said.

Jerusalem passed the duffle bag to YaYa, who rushed out of the bank first and hopped into the SUV. He was unaware of the off duty undercover officer who happened to be in the area. The officer was entering the restaurant next door but stopped when he saw YaYa exit the bank.

Malachi exited next and climbed in the back of the SUV. They both kneeled down in the backseat.

Jerusalem, with his eyes still on the people on the floor, held his weapon in their direction, while backing up toward the door.

Pinky kept the SUV running, and was first to notice the plain-clothes officer. When he reached for his gun, she saw the sunlight reflect off the metal badge on his belt. "There go a motherfuckin' cop!" she yelled.

As Jerusalem backed up out the bank, the cop yelled,

"Freeze, motherfucka, and slowly put down your weapon!"

Jerusalem turned and faced the cop with his weapon drawn. "No, you drop your weapon."

"Drop your fuckin' weapon now!" the cop demanded.

"No, you drop your weapon!" Jerusalem replied calmly.

Pinky roared the engine to signal to Jerusalem that it was time to move out. Both the officer and Jerusalem turned their head toward the SUV. Malachi was in the backseat with the AK47 pointed at the off duty cop. Jerusalem eyed Pinky. Pinky looked at Jerusalem.

"Go!" Jerusalem said.

Pinky hesitated as sirens wailed in the distance. Water filled Pinky's eyes. She didn't want to leave him, but Jerusalem yelled out, "Bitch, did you hear what I said? Go!"

Thinking Malachi was ready to fire at any second, YaYa pulled down Malachi's arm and said, "We got the money. No need for that. Jerusalem can take care of himself."

Malachi bit down on his bottom lip and reasoned with himself as YaYa told Pinky, "Drive, baby girl!"

Pinky smashed on the gas, dodging the bullets the officer fired toward the SUV. She sped off into oncoming traffic.

Jerusalem, using himself as a sacrifice to save his crew, set off running. A foot chase got underway. He dodged in and out between cars and turned a corner, hoping it would lead to an escape route to freedom. Two police cars sped out of nowhere and blocked his way. He turned and the plain-clothes officer was still coming fast behind him. He slipped in a shop and ran through the store knocking down items. Customers in the store screamed as he ran toward the back of the store looking for an exit door.

Pushing the door open, he ran down the alley away from the main street, while taking off his mask with one hand. He jumped over the wall as his heart beat out of control. Jerusalem hoped he'd lost the cops pursuing him. The moment he looked up, a group of officers were pointing their guns directly at him. He bent down and placed his weapon on the ground just in case a trigger happy cop was in their midst. Defeated, he lifted both hands in the air as the officers ordered him to the ground.

One of the officers rushed over to him and yelled, "Put your hands behind your back! You're under arrest!"

Tired and exhausted, Jerusalem did as ordered. The officer said, "You have the right to remain silent," as he picked Jerusalem up from the ground.

Jerusalem held his head back and closed his eyes as the officer continued to read him the Miranda rights.

The sound of the lock clicking brought Jerusalem back into present day—eight years after the bank heist.

Being in solitary confinement was a mental battle that Jerusalem Williams was determined to win. Dressed in just his boxers, he lay on the hard concrete floor of the jail cell with his hands locked behind his head staring up at the ceiling. t here.

CHAPTER TWO

Because Kaleef feared Allah, he felt responsible for the poison he sold to other prisoners and the violence that occurred these last several months. He cringed. Without anyone on the outside looking out for him, he felt he had no choice.

Kaleef was the main distributor of narcotics in the Roosevelt Federal Penitentiary, and he controlled other illegal activities within the penal system. Due to his power and illegal millions, there had been many attempts on his life. Fifty percent of the prison guards were on his payroll. In the penitentiary, it was hard to tell who was the convict and who was leading the free life. Even the warden was getting his share of the money passing hands. Kaleef was the leader of the most notorious, vicious, and murderous organization in the Midwest Federal penitentiary, the Black Warriors.

He glanced up at his second in command, Jerusalem, who was still sleeping and snoring on the top bunk. Kaleef knew the moment he met Jerusalem eight years ago, that the then eighteen year old was a special breed and had come from a royal bloodline. Kaleef was a master at recognizing a young warrior. Jerusalem had entered one of the most vicious federal penitentiaries in America, but he walked in with confidence and showed no fear in his eyes.

Jerusalem, dark-skinned with piercing slanted brown eyes, entered his new cell without saying a word. He immediately began to make up his bunk. Kaleef wondered what the eighteen-year-old young man did to land him in the federal pen. It was a sign of disrespect to ask, so they both remained silent as young Jerusalem finished straightening up his bunk. Jerusalem jumped up on the top bunk, lay down, and stared at the ceiling in silence. Kaleef immediately recognized this as a sign of strength and knew this from his experience of being in the system. Entering these prison walls too friendly was prey for the wolves, because to the dogs, it was a sign of weakness. Formal introductions were not needed.

The clinking of the jail cell bars opening brought Kaleef back to the present and reminded him that it was time for breakfast.

Jerusalem woke up and said, "Assalamu Alaikum."

Kaleef responded, "Wa Alaikum Assalam. Let's get ready for chow. Got some important business I want to discuss with you."

A few minutes later, Kaleef's bodyguard, Malik, walked up to the cell. Malik had been Kaleef's bodyguard for the last ten years. He loved Kaleef and wouldn't think twice about giving his life for Kaleef. Now that a war was going on behind the prison walls, Malik stood closer to Kaleef more than ever. Standing in the doorway of the cell, he asked, "Y'all ready to head to chow?"

"You know who we waiting on," Kaleef responded. "Jerusalem is slow as a snail when it comes to getting up this early in the morning."

"Kaleef, you've been getting up before sunrise for twenty years," Jerusalem said. "Damn, when do you have time to sleep? You stay up 'til the middle of the night reading and then turn around and get up with the chickens."

"When you have a mission to complete, young king, you don't sleep, you rest. One day you're going to be given a mission and you'll understand."

Jerusalem said, "Malik, why you standing up there looking at me with that stupid ass look? As if you love to hear Kaleef school me. You find that amusing?"

Malik responded, "Somebody needs to school your little young ass."

"Nigga, don't make me get up in your shit this early in the morning," Jerusalem said as he continued to get dressed.

Kaleef interjected, "Check this out, Jerusalem. How many times must I tell you that, *that* word is not appropriate when speaking to your brothers? We're kings and warriors. We come from a tribe well respected . . . high intelligent black men and women. A real king teaches family how to act with royalty. You have to get off that mentality, Jerusalem. One day your time is going to come, and you're going to have to take on leadership. You think you're going to be able to get your people to follow you by calling them niggas and bitches? You got to raise them up so when they look at themselves, they will be proud to be part of this Black Nation."

Malik said, "Kaleef, you want me to put him in a death lock."

"Try it, big man, if you want to." Jerusalem held up his fists and stood as if he was ready to box. "You know how I get down. You have seen me in action before. You know I'm a fuckin' warrior."

Jerusalem and Malik got into a playful boxing match. Although the two talked shit to one another all the time, they really had love for one another. They were as close as brothers. Malik knew that although he was 5-feet 10-inches and weighed 235 pounds of pure muscle, Jerusalem was a warrior and would be a very good opponent. It wouldn't be easy to defeat Jerusalem. Jerusalem was taller at 6-feet 1-inch, and his 200 pound frame was cut and muscular. Malik possessed strength, but clearly, Jerusalem possessed power and speed.

"Y'all stop that horse playing and let's roll out," Kaleef said.

The three of them walked down the tier, and at least fifty Black Warriors stood waiting on Kaleef, their leader, and Jerusalem, his second in command, his general. This was their normal protocol as they all walked together to the chow hall.

As Kaleef and his soldiers entered the chow hall, Kaleef bumped into a short and chubby Latino. Jose, the leader over the prison's most notorious Latin gang, was Kaleef's arch enemy. Both stopped on opposite ends of the door way and a staring match got underway as their soldiers lined up behind them. One of Jose's men walked forward and attempted to block the open space beside them.

Jerusalem stepped up and stood right next to Kaleef. "Y'all motherfuckers bow down to Black royalty and let real kings and rulers enter this motherfucker."

"We run this motherfucker," Jose responded. "Y'all niggas are getting too big for y'all jail suits. There's going to come a time when a person's going to have to shrink y'all back to size."

"Shrink who down to size? You wetback piece of shit," Jerusalem shouted. "You motherfuckas are still operating because we allow y'all to still operate. You need to kiss Kaleef's right hand and thank him for letting y'all still eat. 'Cause motherfuckas, if it was up to me, I wouldn't give you dirty motherfuckers a crumb."

Jose's voice cracked as he laughed. His long, black ponytail shifted as he moved his head. "You dumb nigga. You can't give me shit. I take what I want if I choose to take something. Believe me, it wouldn't be crumbs."

Kaleef, without flinching, said, "Jose, you know like I know that this ain't the time nor place for this. Step to the side. Let me and my men go and enjoy our breakfast."

"I choose the time and the place. Who are you, Kaleef? You think you can give orders to me? You think you that motherfucking powerful? Walking around here as if you're King fuckin' Tut or somebody. Like this prison is your kingdom. So no, motherfucka, you step to the side and let me and my crew pass."

A baldheaded Latino with a body and face full of tattoos moved forward. Carlos was Jose's right hand man. He stopped and stood directly in front of Jerusalem, invading his space. They were standing so close they could feel each other's breath. Jerusalem stared down into his eyes and whispered, "What, motherfucka? You ready to die?"

One of the guards who had been watching from the sidelines the entire time said, "Let's break this little meeting up. If you're eating, go get in the chow line. If you're not, get the fuck out of my chow hall."

As Kaleef and his men walked through the door, Jose's men had no recourse but to move and stand aside. When Jerusalem walked past, Carlos said, "We will meet again, my friend. You can bet your life on that."

CHAPTER THREE

The tension in the yard was so tense you could feel it in the air. Every general of every organization seemed to be on alert. Almost every foot soldier stood near their homemade weapons. Kaleef began his five mile run, while his Black Warriors keep a close watch. Jerusalem, Malik, and the other soldiers worked out on the weight benches to ease some of the tension.

Thirty minutes later, Kaleef completed his run. Dripping with sweat, he walked up to Jerusalem, who was still pumping iron. Breathing heavily and trying to control his breathing, Kaleef said, "Jerusalem, come take a walk with me."

Jerusalem completed his rep, draped his towel around his head, and walked on the side of Kaleef as they walked through the yard.

The armed guards stood on the tower holding twelve gauge shotguns. The spacious yard separated the races of the prisoners with an invisible line. If you were not part of that particular race, you weren't supposed to cross that invisible line uninvited.

Most of the Mexicans stood or sat near the outdoor boxing rings directly across from where the Blacks congregated. Jose and some of his Latin brothers were hitting on the punching bags and jumping rope. Some of the white prisoners were in their small designated area sitting on benches and shooting the breeze.

The neutral zone of the yard was the only place where anybody could come and go as they pleased. Besides it being a neutral zone, what the other prisoners called weaklings, snitches, punks, pedophiles, rapists and outcasts, also occupied it.

"What's going on?" Kaleef asked.

"We need to make a move on these esés before they make a move on us," Jerusalem replied. "You know it's just a matter of time before they feel like they're powerful enough to come up against us again."

"Yeah, I know. However, I'm trying to avoid another war. Because it's bad on our business when blood is shed. The guards are going to crack down on us, and we're not going to be able to make moves like we normally make. However, I know Jose is not going to want peace right now 'cause he doesn't have anything to lose; especially now that I control all the drug activity that goes in and out of here."

"Yeah, 'cause it's big business. A lot of money changing hands. A lot of money to be made."

Jerusalem and Kaleef each took a seat on a bench near the track away from everybody, but in plain view of all that was going on in the yard.

Kaleef leaned over and put his hands on his chin. "I got something very important to talk to you about. I've always known that when I came here, I wouldn't be leaving a free man. When I leave here, it's going to be as a dead man because I'm doing natural life."

Jerusalem continued to look around the yard as he listened to Kaleef.

"See, this society is ready to see warriors like you and me die before we fulfill our destiny. I was once the most notorious drug lord in Illinois history. I made hundred millions of dollars through drug trade. Twenty years. Since I've been incarcerated, a lot of my family has passed away. All I have left now is Khadijah, my twenty-four-year-old daughter and Raheem, my one-year-old grandson. Khadijah doesn't want anything to do with me because of my past life. But she's still my daughter and I love her and my grandson very much. Jerusalem, I still have fifty million that the Feds didn't get."

"Fifty million!" Jerusalem said.

"Yes, fifty million. That's not including the money I've made since being here. Most of that money was spent on making sure our organization and their families were taken care of. I realize you have less than a year left." Kaleef smiled. "I know you have the capabilities to continue where I left off. Because the mission doesn't stop . . . the baton is passed to the next person to lead the position. Jerusalem, I want you to have that money and continue where I left off by building us a Black nation. Since America won't let us build our own home for our people, we're going to build us a nation for our people—by any means necessary."

Jerusalem was no longer looking around the yard. He stared at Kaleef to make sure he didn't miss any words.

Kaleef said, "If it's our fate to complete this mission, let it be. If it's our fate to die as we try to complete this mission, let it be. But we can't be afraid to walk through these flames knowing who we are and what we're here for."

"How am I supposed to do that?" Jerusalem tapped his foot. "All I know is these streets. I learned a lot from you since I've been here. You've been like a father to me, but now you talking like you not sure if you going to be around much longer. I can't understand where all of this is coming from. Why you decide to mention all this to me now?"

Kaleef dropped his hand from his chin. "I got faith in you, Jerusalem. You'll figure it out, young king, when the time comes. Khadijah still lives in the house that I bought her mama. I hid the money in the walls of the basement. I need you to get that money and continue to build the Black Senate."

"With you guiding me every step of the way, I can't fail and I won't fail," Jerusalem responded, not fully grasping the huge responsibility he had taken on.

"I have faith in you, Jerusalem. You're one of the chosen ones. It's time for you to recognize your capabilities and start to feel your bloodline. You are a born king, Jerusalem. Your destiny is to rule. It's your turn to go out and build your kingdom. I love you like my son."

"And I love you like my father," Jerusalem replied.

They embraced.

Sounds of prisoners yelling echoed from the other side of the yard. That's when they noticed the Mexican Mafia attacking Kaleef's organization of Black Warriors. No words needed to be said. They rushed toward the commotion. From a distance, all they could see was the Mexican Mafia with shanks and other homemade weapons involved in combat with the Black Warriors.

Since they were already expecting another war at any given moment, Kaleef's organization was prepared with homemade weapons and shanks of their own. When they noticed Mexican Mafia soldiers charging them, Kaleef's army attacked, and when they collided, it was like two trains crashing.

Malik was being tripled teamed. He could handle two of the guys with no problem, but the third one posed a problem. Jerusalem noticed one of their enemies' inches away from shanking Malik. He kicked the guy, catching him off guard. The shank dropped from his hand, giving Malik the opening to bum rush him. Malik swung a vicious blow to his face with his iron fist. Jerusalem reached under his jacket and retrieved the shank he had taped to his side and shanked the guy who originally had intentions on killing Malik.

Jerusalem now stood face to face with Carlos, Jose's right hand man.

"Are you ready to die now, motherfutha?" Carlos asked as he swung at Jerusalem with his shank.

Jerusalem backed back and said, "Oh, you're going to have to come better than that. 'Cause you're fucking with a born warrior."

"I'm Carlos Sanchez, motherfucka!" This time Carlos swung upward, aiming at Jerusalem's stomach.

Jerusalem tilted his body, giving him enough time to catch Carlos with his shank in his lower side. He drove the shank in with full force as he whispered in his ear, "So we meet again. Now die, motherfucka!" Jerusalem twisted the shank as the man squealed like a little pig. He yanked the shank out as the dude fell to the ground. He bent down and wiped the shank across his mouth, making Carlos taste his own blood as he choked and died. Jerusalem continued on attack mode in the battle of the Mexicans against the Blacks.

Kaleef, being a born warrior, was destroying some of Jose's soldiers upon immediate contact with just the power of his hands. One of Jose's men tried to shank him in the stomach. Kaleef jumped back, grabbed the man's wrist that held the shank, and with his right hand, hit him in the throat, making direct contact with his windpipe.

The alarm sounded, alerting the guards to the riot. The alarm sounding didn't stop either camp from going after one another. Instead, the fights got more intense as some soldiers fell to the ground.

No one ever noticed Jose. His eyes remained glued on Kaleef as he crept like an alley cat through the commotion. Kaleef put down another one of Jose's soldiers with a knee to the abdominal. For Kaleef's age, he kept his body in tip-top shape for war at all times just like he trained his soldiers.

This day fate intervened. Jose grabbed Kaleef around the neck with his left arm, catching him off guard. Jose bent Kaleef's neck back, and with a direct hit to the lower part of his throat, hit one of his main arteries with the shank. Blood gushed out like a water fountain as Kaleef's body hit the ground with a loud thud. Jose sped off into the crowded commotion.

Jerusalem heard one of Kaleef's soldiers yell out. He spotted Kaleef's body and ran as quick as his body would take him to where Kaleef now lay. He kneeled on both knees calling out to Kaleef.

At the same time, the guards, with their black riot gear, scattered across the yard and shot gas bombs to clear the riot. Several guards yelled, "Everybody, face down now!"

Knowing the routine, some of the prisoners were lying face down before the guards commanded them. Malik, ignoring the initial command, ran near Jerusalem. Without asking, he took the shank from Jerusalem and placed it in a hidden grave with other discarded shanks. Malik used his hands and attempted to cover it up before the guards came in their direction.

Jerusalem got on the ground as instructed. He lay face down near Kaleef, who turned his head, and they looked directly into each other eyes. Kaleef's chest rose and fell as he gasped for air. Blood spurted out of his mouth and some splattered into Jerusalem's face.

"Hold on, Kaleef. Please don't die. Don't die on me! Fight, king!" Jerusalem said.

Kaleef attempted to talk, but more blood spurted out of his mouth, leaving him speechless. His eyes said what his mouth couldn't as he and Jerusalem stared at one another.

Jerusalem knew this would be the last time he would see his leader, his teacher, his closest friend, and the only father figure that he ever knew alive. His eyes watered as he watched Kaleef transition from this world to the next.

His thoughts ran rampant as he looked at Kaleef's lifeless body lying next to him. Jerusalem had lost many close friends, but losing Kaleef was like losing his father. The pain he felt inside was almost unbearable. Feeling like a part of him was taken, he effortlessly followed the commands of the guards.

CHAPTER FOUR

Jerusalem lay motionless on the bunk inside a dark hole of the cell. He was placed there after the riot on the yard. Being in solitary confinement gave him time to deal with the loss of Kaleef without others being around. The guard yelling from the other side of the steel door caused Jerusalem to tense up. The guard was Black on the outside, but he had no regards to race. He treated Black inmates more like dogs than part of the human race.

"Young blood, your leader's gone now. What you going to do now? No more fight left in you, is there?"

Jerusalem remained silent.

"You ain't got nothing to say?"

"Your conversation doesn't interest me," Jerusalem responded.

"Oh, you think you're more than me?" the guard asked.

Jerusalem sat up and looked the guard directly in the eyes. "It is what it is."

"I can make your life here in the hole harder than what it is."

The guard leaned back with a wicked grin on his face.

"I'm a soldier. I'm built for this type of shit. Motherfucka, nothing you do can break me."

"Kaleef got your Black ass well programmed."

Jerusalem wanted to wipe the smirk off the guard's face but knew that it would not only get him more time in the hole but also extend his stay. He didn't want to do anything to jeopardize his release date, so he clenched his fists and tried to tune out the words coming out of the guard's mouth.

"You have to deal with me for the next six months you got in this rat hole, or until we get this drug war under control. I wish we could have nailed your ass to the cross for the murder of Carlos. I'm pretty sure his death was at your hands."

Jerusalem remained strong in his stance and didn't blink.

The guard said, "You better not even piss too loud, or I'm going to make sure you never leave this motherfucka." The guard paused, laughed and said, "Now, you have a nice time in my little roach motel."

Spending his life in a cage wasn't what Jerusalem wanted, but it was a chance he had to take for Kaleef's sake. He couldn't let Kaleef's killer go unpunished.

Jerusalem thought back to when he entered his assigned cell after being convicted for armed bank robbery. He would have gotten less time if he snitched on his crew, but Jerusalem was no snitch. Brought up on a street code of ethics, he would give his life before he broke the street code.

As soon as he entered through the bars, Jerusalem noticed his cellmate, an older Black male with hanging dreadlocks sitting on the end of his bunk reading a book. Kaleef looked up at him and they caught eye contact. No words exchanged between the two cellmates at this point.

Kaleef moved to a small desk, took his seat and went back to reading his book. Jerusalem made up his bunk and thought, *I hope I don't have to fuck this dreadlock motherfucka up, and I hope he ain't no fucking faggot. 'Cause one of us going to have to go. I die and kill for mine. I hope he ain't the type of motherfucka that talk a lot and ask a thousand damn questions 'cause I'm going to check his ass off top and let him know I ain't taking no shit. I run shit.*

Jerusalem finished making up his bed and hopped on the top bunk. He stared at the ceiling thinking about the ten years of time he received. He would be spending the next eight and a half years behind these bars. He would do it with ease knowing about all the money that Malachi, YaYa, and Pinky got away with. It was well over two hundred thousand. One thing he knew about his crew, it was death before dishonor. They would stay loyal and make his stay behind these prison walls as smooth as possible.

The next few days, Jerusalem and Kaleef went without saying hardly a word to one another. Only speaking and saying cordial words such as "excuse me" to show each other the proper respect. On the third day, Jerusalem noticed how the Blacks and some of the guards showed Kaleef supreme respect. From their actions, Jerusalem concluded that Kaleef held a lot of pull in between the prison walls.

Jerusalem began to be acquainted with some of the younger soldiers around his age. He became close friends with one of Kaleef's young warriors, Raychone, also known as Ruthless. Ruthless was tall and slender and reminded Jerusalem of the rapper Snoop Dogg with four long plaits lying on his shoulder.

The twenty-one year old schooled Jerusalem about the jail system as they stood on the yard.

Ruthless smoked on a hump, taking a long drag off his cigarette and blowing a cloud of smoke out of his nose. "Us Black Warriors stick together up in this camp. We like family. But it's rules that we live by. And we break those rules for no one. This place ain't no motherfucking joke, my nigga. Man, don't you know I'd done seen at least six motherfuckas get it since the two years I been here? Shit, I got fifteen more to go. I'm only twenty-one, but I'm glad that we got a leader like Kaleef here. That's a good motherfucka."

Jerusalem squinted and said, "You talking about my cellie. The black motherfucka with all the facial hair and those long dreads."

"Yeah, nigga, what other Kaleef you think I'm talking about?"

"My cellie Kaleef?" Jerusalem repeated in disbelief.

"Nigga, Kaleef your cellie? Nigga, how you pull that off? You tell me you in the cell with King Kaleef."

"Yeah." Jerusalem shrugged.

"Kaleef is the most notorious drug dealer in fucking all America. He runs this fucking place. He's the head of the Black Senate and the leader of the Black Warriors. That motherfucker got more money than Jay Z, Russell Simmons, and Puff Daddy, or P Diddy or whatever his fucking name, put together. And jail ain't stopped that nigga. 'Cause that nigga making more money in jail than he did on the streets."

Jerusalem took his hand and rubbed it across his face to clear his eyes and thoughts. Ruthless noticed the confusion in Jerusalem's eyes. Ruthless said, "Nigga, you didn't say nothing or do nothing disrespectful, did you? That nigga Kaleef can have your ass killed in a fuckin' heartbeat."

Jerusalem responded calmly, "Naw man. We have hardly said two words to one another. All he does is sit around the cell and read. I bet you he got a thousand fucking books under his bunk. Ain't that much reading in the world."

"Knowledge is the key, my nigga. Ain't nothing worse than a dumb ass nigga that ain't ever picked up a book, and the only thing he ever picked up was a gun. Kaleef teaches us that we must educate ourselves no matter what we do. Because knowledge is something that can never be stripped from us. Man, you sitting in the cell with a fucking mastermind and a genius and you ain't taking advantage of that shit. I thought you was smarter than that." Ruthless blew out some more smoke.

"Man, I'm not a friendly motherfucka. I just don't meet a nigga and begin to tell 'em my whole life story. I never said anything to him, and I didn't give a fuck if he ever said anything to me. I came here to do my time. I know how to do time by my fuckin' self."

"Man, this is one place that you can never make it by yourself. This is the motherfucking federal penitentiary. Shit is segregated. Don't you see all the Mexicans standing right over there? That's the Mexican Mafia. Don't you see the Cubans over there? Part of the Cuban Cartel. Don't you see the whites over there, that's the Three Elevens. You see those few African motherfuckas over there; those are the motherfucking Nigerians and Jamaicans. Some of the leaders of the heroin trade. Man, shit get real serious around this camp. And no telling when a fucking war will jump off. Shit, we Black Warriors. We run this motherfucka. And we'll die and kill before we are dethroned."

After Ruthless and Jerusalem finished their conversation, Jerusalem headed back toward the compound to take a piss. Lost in his thoughts about the conversation that just transpired with Ruthless, Jerusalem crossed an invisible line he shouldn't have crossed.

All the Mexicans stared at Jerusalem, and before he could get to the end of their section, Carlos approached him. "Hey, homes. What the fuck you think you doing? You on our fucking turf. You fucking crossed the boundary lines. What the fuck, you stupid esé?"

Jerusalem stopped, stared, and looked at an imaginary line that wasn't there. "My bad." He frowned and looked Carlos directly in the eyes. "I've only been here a few days. Still learning my way around."

"You need us to fuckin' help you, esé? How about I stick my foot up your ass and help your ass back to your side of the yard. You fuckin' bendajo."

Jerusalem knew a little Spanish, and Carlos was straight up disrespecting him. "Motherfucka, didn't I tell you my bad? I meant no disrespect, but motherfucka if you want to take it there, we can." Jerusalem's nostrils flared. "You ain't dealing with nothing soft over here, you understand?"

Jerusalem noticed Carlos' facial expression change to a calmer state. Carlos appeared to be looking past him. Jerusalem looked back and noticed Kaleef and some of the other Black Warriors standing and ready for battle if necessary with Malik standing by his side.

Kaleef looked directly at Carlos. "Jerusalem, is there a problem? You okay?" he asked.

Jerusalem turned his focus back on Carlos, who responded,

"Kaleef, this one of your soldiers? If it is, he violating, homes. By crossing on our side. You know that's against the law. You know that's a violation."

Kaleef responded, "I understand that. But he's only been here a few days, and plus he's a very good friend of mine, so let's act like this never happened. I'm going to make sure it'll never happen again. I'm sure if you want to go chest to chest with this young warrior, he don't mind. But anything other than a one on one, gonna cause all hell to break loose."

Carlos said, "Well, homes, just don't let it fucking happen again. I'm going to give him a fucking pass this time. But next time, we going to make it rain blood."

Kaleef gave a slight smile. In a commanding voice, Kaleef said to Jerusalem, "Come on with me, young warrior. Let me have a word with you."

Jerusalem put in work over the next few years and quickly moved up in rank in Kaleef's organization, just as Kaleef knew he would. With Jerusalem's training and natural skills, he became Kaleef's second in command. Some didn't like that, but they never let Kaleef hear their murmurings. Jerusalem had proven he could hold his own, so no one would dare voice their concerns without suffering some repercussions.

CHAPTER FIVE

The trustee slid Jerusalem's last meal of the day through a slot in the steel door. The man whispered, "I got something for you. I know you don't have much to do here, so I brought you something to read. I was able to go in your cell and get some of Kaleef's books and literature that he wrote. I thought you might like to have it. You know your cell is safe because everyone knows not to go near that cell without losing their life. The guards left all of Kaleef's belongings. I guess for you to do what you want to do with it, since it was you and Kaleef's home. If you need anything else, I'm working this tier now. So just holla at me. I got you. Stay strong, young warrior."

For the past three and half weeks, Jerusalem started to adapt to his new environment in solitary confinement. Jerusalem was on a twenty-three hours a day lock down. During the hour outside of his cell, he was only able to stretch his legs, then shower and back to the hole he went. He started to do extreme workout regiments. His daily routine included a combination of pushups, crunches, and squats for hours at a time. He was only able to tell what time it was based on when they brought him a meal. Jerusalem slowly walked from the steel door and sat on his homemade bed on the floor. He placed his meal next to him. Now, not having an appetite, he began to look through Kaleef's literature. Jerusalem read the literature and it's almost as if he could hear Kaleef's voice speaking to him.

For that's what you are in the earth—Kings—being defined as a processor of power or objects that are worshipped. There is only one God —one "True" God. Allah, the God.

There is no other on the face of this planet like us the Black race. That is why we excel in all we do. Our main problem here on this North American continent is that we as a whole will not work together. Once we were freed, we were just a bunch of free folks. Given new names, new concept of God, new food, new language resulting in a new mindset—"Dead."

The brain is like a computer. It stores information to be retrieved when needed. The computer also learns how to process, sort, file, etc. The key is how to trigger the synapses and fire those neurons. Simply—read, read, and read.

Knowledge is truly power, but the application thereof is most effective for goodness.

Do not allow the illusions to intimidate or make a fool out of you. They are just a test of our sincerity, faith, and devotion.

The more you are tested spiritually, the better connected you are. Do not be surprised at the illusions that your eyes will witness. We must welcome our tests. All will come to pass in time—on time.

Seek knowledge from the cradle to the grave . . .

We have received our orders to do for self. Train our youth and become a nation within a nation.

Study these facts, among the essence and become a master, a king, a son of light. Riches shall be reaped by numbers untold. No one will truly help us but us. Us as slaves, the Black man known for our greatness, but some shake their head at us; wondering what's taking us so long to rise back in position.

The European has done his thing to us and moved on, still reaping the benefits as we are stressing mentally and spiritually. Look what the Caucasians has done to us. The founding fathers of the earth . . . they wanted to re-create here what was discovered in Africa.

Allah is the true source, but your intentions must be pure. Those Caucasians that make mockery and hide behind their source of light are hypocrites. Trying to play Caesars, kings, queens, czars, pharaohs, presidents. We are the true Black kings in the earth with no kingdom to rule.

- This system founded on trickeration for no more than to control the masses—those who are sleep—mentally dead—are being led by the powers that's be. This is being and has been done scientifically. Having this type of power in the wrong hands can be very corrupting. The upper government is plotting to kill a king.

The light of truth. The sun, Allah's creation shines from above downward on his creation. That which is produced is the true essence of that which is shined upon—darkness, its original composition and make-up, everything in our creators cosmic design has original pattern; including our individual purpose on this plane of existence. We must keep traveling and seeking truth. Always duplicated but will never be authenticated. We are Kings, so we must take our thrones.

For the next five months, Jerusalem focused more than he had since he arrived at the penitentiary. He began to read day and night, only getting an hour or two of rest. It's as if he was taking on another formation. He even began to get up at sunrise every morning. More disciplined than before, he prayed as he'd seen Kaleef do every morning. The more he read, the more he heard Kaleef speak to him. He figured out that Kaleef still lived because he had Kaleef's words and words never die.

Jerusalem was more than ready when he finally heard the keys to the steel door open. This was the day he would be released back into general population. The guard opened the door and stared at Jerusalem for a moment. He noticed something different about him. Jerusalem had put on a little more muscle, but he had cuts as if someone had drawn him with a pencil. From the six months of being in the hole, not being able to shave, Jerusalem had grown a full beard and his hair was uncut. Jerusalem knew he definitely needed a grooming session.

The guard wanted to say something to Jerusalem, but he noticed the gleam in his eyes. Jerusalem's aura was so powerful that the guard had no recourse but to show him respect. He finally got the words out of his mouth and asked, "You ready to go to your cell, Mr. Williams? I know you're about ready to shower and clean up. Six months is a long time in the hole. I've seen some men stay in here for years."

Jerusalem didn't say anything; he just picked up his reading materials and followed the guard. He heard different inmates calling out his name as he walked back to his original cell that had been his home for the previous eight and half years. Like they were crowning him the new king.

CHAPTER SIX

Jerusalem was only three weeks away from being a free man, but killing Jose was something he had to do. As he sat in what was once Kaleef's bunk, he knew he was taking a risk on this particular day. His mind would never be free if he didn't avenge Kaleef's death by his own hands. It was easy for him to get someone with a longer stay to do this job, but this was personal. Malik and the other generals of the Black Senate argued with Jerusalem over this matter. They tried to convince him to let one of the warriors who specialized in handling this type of business put in the work, but Jerusalem wasn't trying to hear it.

He stood his stance. Once they realized they couldn't convince Jerusalem not to do this job, they started to put their plan in action. First, they had to get the guards who were on their payroll to all work the same evening shift. They were in control of the cameras and planned to ignore Jerusalem sneaking out of the kitchen door.

Jerusalem pretended to be one of the trustees assigned to

unloading a truck carrying produce. He, Malik, Sahid and Amir, all members of the Black Senate, unloaded the produce onto a large cart. One of the boxes they loaded didn't carry any frozen food. In fact, it was empty.

Malik looked at Jerusalem and whispered, "Man, you sure you don't want me to do this?"

"I'm positive," Jerusalem said without hesitation.

The empty box was big enough for Jerusalem to climb in. The guard on duty turned his head and pretended as if he didn't know what was going on.

Jerusalem positioned his body in the box with his knees folded toward his chest. Malik closed the top of the box, making sure to leave room for air. Sahid strategically placed the other produce boxes on top of the box holding Jerusalem. The three members of the Black Senate finished unloading the truck and filling the carts. They each pushed a cart. The box with Jerusalem sat on the cart that Malik was pushing.

When they entered the kitchen, the first person Malik noticed was Jose. Six other members of the Mexican Mafia and several members of the Three Elevens were also nearby. The Mexican Mafia and the Three Elevens ran the kitchen. The Black Senate ran the laundry room and were eighty-five percent of the trustees. With Black Senate members in those positions and the guards and some of the Black Senate members bringing in illegal drugs through visits, Kaleef was able to run his drug ring within the prison walls.

Jose hated Kaleef and his organization with a passion. Due to Kaleef and the Black Senate's rise to power, Jose's organization was losing its pull. The only thing they had to hold on to was their respect. Now that Kaleef was out of the picture,

Jose was ready to put the Mexican Mafia back in power.

Malik and Jose's eyes locked as he passed by pushing the cart. Jose blew him a kiss of death and gave him an evil smile. Malik eyed him for a couple more seconds without blinking. Sahid opened the freezer, and they began to unload the produce into the freezer with Jerusalem still hidden in the box.

They stocked the freezer with the produce and carefully discarded the boxes while making sure not to stack any more boxes on Jerusalem. They wanted to make sure he had an easy exit out of the box when he was ready. Malik, Sahid, and Amir finished their job and left the kitchen, pushing the empty carts. Malik looked back and took one last look at Jose, who was standing over the stove stirring the beans for last chow.

Jose joked, "I make the best beans of all Mexico. There's nothing like my chili beans. This shit is finger lickin' good. Did you see those fuckin' niggas lick their fingers after eating my chili beans like they just finished eating some fuckin' fried chicken?"

The other Mexican Mafia members broke out into laughter. Jose said, "Rico, I know you full of that sess, esé, that's why you laughing so fuckin' hard. That shit ain't that fuckin' funny, homes. You better keep an eye on that fuckin' cornbread. Don't let it burn up. Y'all lazy bastards get back to fuckin' work 'cause I ain't staying in the kitchen all night. I got business I got to handle. I run this fuckin' prison now. Before it's all said and done, them black, ashy niggas going to be eating crumbs off the bottom of my feet. 'Cause I'm going to make it where the Black Senate is going to be begging me to let them eat. Then I'm going to crush their asses like a fucking beer can where none of them exist. I'm tearing down their whole organization. Worse thing I hate more than a nigga is a nigga with power and think he run shit."

Jose continued to cook. "Hey, Rico," Jose called out. "Come here, let me talk to you, homes. You still got some of that sess, homes."

The short and stocky Rico nodded because he was too high to speak. He just wore a silly smile on his round face. Jose said, "Give me a joint, homes. And wipe that stupid ass smirk off your face. 'Fore I slap it off. Silly ass dude."

Rico slipped Jose a joint.

Jose eased it into his pocket and said, "Go to the freezer and bring me another box of ground beef. And hurry up. Don't fuckin' be all day. I want you to watch these beans while I go take me a break so I can get high. I want to feel like you. Minus that stupid ass smirk."

***

Jerusalem hid behind boxes in the freezer. The door opened, his heart began to pound. Even though it was below thirty-two degrees in the freezer, his palms still perspired. He kneeled even lower, to avoid being seen by anyone. He wished that it were his intended victim entering the freezer but it wasn't.

"Where's the fuckin' ground beef? I don't see that shit nowhere," he heard someone mumble as he

stepped closer and closer to Jerusalem.

Jerusalem hoped the guy didn't notice his hidden location, so he wouldn't have to kill this motherfucka. He gripped a special made nine-inch shank just in case he had to kill. If the guy walked a couple more inches closer in his direction, Jerusalem would have no choice. He was seconds away from rising and

41

charging Rico, when Rico noticed the ground beef to his left.

"Shit, there it is," Rico said as he picked up the box of ground beef. "This shit is heavy, or I'm just high as hell."

Rico exited the freezer.

Jerusalem sighed with relief. He only wanted Jose. He didn't want to kill anyone else unless he had to.

***

Rico took the ground beef to Jose. "Here you go, homes," he said placing the box of ground beef on the counter.

"Put that ground beef in the water in the big tub so it can thaw out. Watch my beans. Don't let 'em burn. You know I take pride in my chili beans. I'm going to go take me a break and smoke this joint. I'll be back in five minutes. I'm going to the freezer, so I can feel like an Eskimo when I get high," Jose said. "I think we might be related. 'Cause I sure want to fuck me one of those Eskimo bitches."

Jose walked off and headed toward the freezer.

He entered the freezer and took a seat on one of the boxes with his back turned to Jerusalem. Jose placed the joint in his mouth and struck a match to light it.

***

Already, Jerusalem started to tremble. He didn't know if it was from nervousness or the cold freezer. His bottom lip shivered. He had been in the freezer going on an hour now. His body was really starting to feel it. He felt like he was turning into an icicle. As soon as he closed his eyes for a second to try to strengthen his brain, he heard the door open and there he was—Jose. The man who killed his leader—his father.

Jerusalem focused in on Jose like a lion focused on his prey. He eased up slowly behind Jose, who was in another world and didn't notice that death was knocking on his back door. Jerusalem raised the knife, aiming it at the side of Jose's neck.

Suddenly, he brought it down because he wanted Jose to look him in his eyes and know who ended his life. "Turn around, motherfucka," Jerusalem said.

Jose jumped, startled. "What the fuck? What the fuck you doing up in here?"

"What you think, motherfucka?" Jerusalem responded. "Come to kiss you good-bye."

Jose, not wanting to show any fear, laughed. "Kiss me good-bye. Shit, I got life, motherfucka. This is my home until I die."

"You said the magic word," Jerusalem replied. "Until you die. 'Cause this is the day that you greet death."

"You think it's going to be that easy. Won't you make this thing even and give me one of those things you have in your hands?" Jose said.

"I brought one just for you." Jerusalem went in his waistline, pulled out another shank, and threw it to Jose. "Let's play with fate. Let's see whose destiny is to die or live."

Jose, surprised by Jerusalem's actions, took the first swing, aiming for Jerusalem's stomach. Jerusalem leaped backward, and Jose missed hitting his stomach by inches. Jose continued on the attack and tried to gut Jerusalem again in the midsection, but he blocked it with his freehand knocking Jose's arm downward and caught Jose in his left shoulder.

Adrenaline pumping, Jose caught on to the top of the shank and pulled it out, but Jerusalem still had control of his weapon.

Jose let out a slight moan. Jose charged Jerusalem at full speed. Jerusalem bent down, grabbed Jose by the waist, and lifted him up in the air. Jose raised the shank high above Jerusalem's head, looking down and seeing that he had a straight aim at his upper back. Jose shifted and began to come down with his weapon. Jerusalem did a reverse body slam and slammed Jose on the frozen produce, knocking the shank from Jose's hand. Jerusalem punched him in the face several times, dazing him and drawing blood from his mouth and nose. For some strange reason, he stopped and stood while letting Jose regain his senses.

Jose stood up and noticed that he was empty handed. Jerusalem's foot stood on top of the shank, and Jose felt cornered with no weapon or no exit. The only exit was to get past Jerusalem. He noticed the look in Jerusalem's eyes. Something very peculiar and something very sacred was behind his stance.

It was as if Jose saw death approaching him. He began to beg for mercy. "Come on, Jerusalem. Don't do this, esé. You and the Black Senate, y'all can have this. This prison. I'm out of the drug game. I just want to live in peace now."

"Now you want peace, motherfucka. Now you want peace. After you killed Kaleef. After he was trying to avoid the bullshit you was bringing. Now you want peace. After you snuck up behind him like a fuckin' coward and stabbed him while he wasn't looking. You didn't give him a fuckin' fair chance. You lowdown piece of shit. I gave you a chance that you didn't deserve. Because I'm nothing like you. You could never be anything like me. I'm a fuckin' King. Royalty. Bow down. And kneel and kiss my fuckin' feet."

"All right, Jerusalem. I'll bow down." He started getting down on his knees.

"Bow down then, motherfucka, and kiss my feet." Jerusalem stepped forward once.

"Just let me live, Jerusalem. Just don't kill me."

"Bow down and kiss my feet and I'll think about it."

Jose, at his weakest point of his life, with no way out, kneeled on the floor and kissed Jerusalem's left foot, then right foot as Jerusalem stood over him feeling the power of having Jose's life in the palm of his hands.

"Now, look at me, motherfucka," Jerusalem said as he stared down at him.

Without another word, he took the nine-inch shank and brought it straight down in Jose's left eye. He extracted the shank and Jose fell backward, holding his eye. Before he could let out a scream, Jerusalem covered his mouth with his left hand and took the shank, this time hitting him in the neck. Taking the shank out, he stabbed him right in the heart, and ended Jose's life.

Breathing heavily, Jerusalem kneeled over Jose's dead body. He stood up, took off the bloody long sleeve shirt and gloves and wrapped the shank up in the clothing. He looked for the box with the small mark that Malik had left for him to place the items in once he completed his mission. He located it and placed the items within it. The box would later be disposed of. He took the clear tape he had with him and sealed the box up as if it had never been open.

Jerusalem eased to the exit door, cracked it, and listened for any close voices. He only heard voices from a distance. He stuck his head out of the freezer and slid the door wide enough for his body to slip through. Then he began his way through the kitchen, making sure any other members of the Mexican Mafia didn't notice him. As he neared his destination, he heard two Spanish voices coming in his direction. He ducked into a nearby storage room where the cleaning materials were stored.

Two Mexican Mafia members passed, unaware that their leader's killer was inches away hiding in the closet. They were not aware that their leader's dead body lay as stiff as frozen beef in the freezer as they walked on by him. Jerusalem left the storage room, not worrying about the cameras, because the guards had that under control.

Jerusalem continued on his journey and entered the hallway and met the guard who'd been waiting for two hours on his exit from the kitchen side door. "Did you get that motherfucka?" he asked.

In response, Jerusalem looked him in the eyes. Without saying a word, the guard knew that he completed the mission.

"Come and walk with me," the guard said, pretending to be transporting Jerusalem to the law library, where Malik, Sahid, and Amir were waiting.

II

ROAD TO FREEDOM

CHAPTER SEVEN

"Take care of yourself, Mr. Williams. It's a crazy world out there. Don't get caught up in the rapture," the female officer said as she passed Jerusalem his property.

Jerusalem smiled. "Thank you. I'll die before I let them cage me up again. I'm a Black king. I'm made to be free."

He turned and walked through the doors of freedom on this sunny spring morning. Closing his eyes, he breathed in his first breath of freedom. He opened his eyes and continued walking toward the gates. When the guard opened the prison gates, he saw YaYa sitting in a black late model Jaguar with chrome rims.

YaYa turned and noticed his best friend, who was more like his brother, walking. He excitedly opened the door and jumped out of the car. "What's up, fam'?"

They gave each other a brotherly hug. YaYa, light brown complexion with oval black eyes, was 5-feet 11-inches, a few inches shorter than Jerusalem. At one hundred and seventy-five pounds, he had wide shoulders and wore his hair in a low cut fade.

"What's up, YaYa?" Jerusalem responded and stepped back. "You looking good, fam'. Look at you. Looking like Nino Brown. That's an Armani suit. Got to be tailor made. Black on black looks good on you. Black representing the kings that unite the brothers as one."

"Look at you. You all ripped." YaYa said. "You must have been pumping iron the whole eight and half years you been here."

"I've been doing a little something something."

"A little something. Nigga, you make LL want to put his shirt on."

"Come on. Let's get the fuck out of here."

It was a twelve hour drive from Roosevelt Federal Penetiary back to Chicago. Jerusalem and YaYa got a chance to do a lot of catching up. Jerusalem explained to YaYa some of the things that went on behind the prison walls and about Kaleef and the fifty million dollars that he had buried in the walls of his daughter's basement.

The sun was just beginning to go down when they hit the outskirts of Chicago. YaYa said, "We got to get you fresh, fam'. We put away your cut of the robbery, and plus we got your percentage put away from the business we've been running."

"How's that business?" Jerusalem asked. "Who running these streets now?"

YaYa answered, "Those old heads still got shit locked down. They are not sharing their connect. Bank Roll, he breaded up. That cat got the west, the north, and the south side on lock. But you know we getting our share. I mean, we might be pulling in close to a half million a month. That's not no chump change if you really look at it. Malachi got the projects on lock. That's where most of our profits are coming from. We've been waiting for you to come home, Jerusalem. Things haven't been the same without you. It's been a long eight and half years. Now that you here, I know things are about to change."

Jerusalem said, "A lot of things are about to change. I've been given the blueprint and I got a major plan. We are kings, YaYa. Time for us to build our kingdom and anything fall on top of us, shall be mounted to dust. Anything fall beneath us, shall be crushed. It's the Black Senate's time to rule."

YaYa and Jerusalem hit the galleria and went on a shopping spree. Bags of designer clothes and shoes filled the backseat and trunk of the Jaguar.

They headed to the presidential suite at the Omni Hotel in downtown Chicago that YaYa had already reserved for Jerusalem's homecoming. YaYa pulled up in front of the hotel. He generously tipped the valet fifty dollars. The bellhop helped Jerusalem and YaYa bring in the bags. They got on the elevator. YaYa used the special key that he'd had on a key chain to access the presidential suite on the top floor.

YaYa unlocked the door and entered the suite first. Jerusalem walked in behind him and placed the bags in the living room as YaYa turned and tipped the bellhop fifty dollars.

The plush white carpet felt like cotton as they walked through the suite. The marble bar in the living room and the marble counter attached to the kitchen were trimmed in gold.

Jerusalem said, "This is definitely fit for a king."

"Only the best," YaYa responded. "All four of us would have been in those prison gates if you wouldn't have held off that undercover cop. You did that real heroic shit. You made it where we were able to make a clean getaway. I don't know how I could ever pay you back for the eight and half years that you did, fam'."

"What's meant to happen, happened. I guess you can't run from fate. Everything happens for a reason. I'm stronger now, wiser now, and plus I know where fifty million cold, hard, tax free drug money is at."

"Fifty million. Fifty million. Fifty million. I just can't stop saying it." YaYa's smile widened.

"Do you know how you going to go by getting to the fifty million?" he asked Jerusalem.

"Yeah, I got a plan. But we got plenty of time for that. We have other business we have to handle first. Look at this room."

Jerusalem ran in the bedroom and dived on top of the king-sized bed. "Man, do you know how long it's been since I lay in a bed?" Jerusalem said. "This feels like heaven on earth to me. I can lay here for days and not move."

YaYa walked in the bedroom, stood in the doorway, and smiled at his blood brother. He was happy to have his better half with him again.

Jerusalem grabbed the pillows and squeezed them almost like he was squeezing a woman, taking in the scent. "Damn, it feels so good to hold something this soft."

"Do y'all want to be alone? Seems like you about to make love. I know you haven't had any in some years, but I never thought you wanted to make love to a pillow. You that desperate, nigga?" YaYa asked.

Both men laughed.

YaYa said, "Get dressed. I know you're ready to see the city."

Jerusalem entered the luxurious bathroom. He walked by the gold toilets and went straight to the sunken Jacuzzi. The vanity area in the bathroom displayed several different soaps, bubble bath and colognes in various scents. Jerusalem chose a masculine scent and added the bubble bath to the Jacuzzi. The invigorating aroma filled the air. Jerusalem felt like he was in a form of heaven when his body encountered the hot water gushing across his skin. He leaned his head back, closed his eyes, and felt the tension uplift itself from his muscles.

It feels good to be free, he thought.

While waiting on Jerusalem to bathe and get dressed, YaYa decided to take advantage of the fully stocked bar. He filled his glass with ice and poured Dom Perignon over it. He sat on top of one of the barstools and nursed his drink as his mind thought back to when he and Jerusalem first met.

"He's a nerd. I bet he can't fight," Henry, one of the neighborhood bullies shouted, as he and two of his friends walked up behind YaYa one day after school.

"Man, he's always holding a book," another one of the boys said.

Someone came from behind and snatched the book that YaYa had been reading from under his arms, causing him to stop and look at the group of young boys. He watched them as they tossed his book from person to person. "Will you give me my book back, please?" YaYa politely asked.

Henry, acting as the ringleader, took YaYa's book and threw it on the ground. "What now, schoolboy?"

YaYa walked up to Henry. His action surprised Henry and the others. YaYa bent down to pick up the book. Henry kicked it toward one of his friends. YaYa said, "My daddy gave me that book. Give it back. He said there's knowledge in that book."

"You ain't got no daddy," Henry said. "Your daddy's a crack head and your mama be sucking your crack headed daddy dick."

His eyes glazed over with anger as YaYa threw down his backpack and clenched his fist.

"What you going to do, school boy? You don't like me talking about your raggedy ass mama? Nigga, you don't want no part of me. I'll beat your weak ass up and down these streets. Do something, punk. Do something if you think you're bad."

Henry was a few inches taller and several pounds heavier, but YaYa didn't show any fear when he swung. His punch didn't land anywhere as Henry weaved out of the way andstarted laughing. "Y'all see this? That little nigga swung on me. I'm really finna fuck his ass up now."

Even though Henry had a reputation of being a bully and was known for his fighting skills, YaYa felt like he had gone too far to turn around now. He swung again, this time making contact with his right cheek. Henry stumbled back from the impact. He swung back at YaYa and a full-fledged fight was underway.

Every punch that YaYa threw connected accurately. Henry could never get his bearings, and from the onlookers, it was obvious that YaYa was winning the fight against one of the neighborhood bullies.

His two friends jumped in the fight, knocking YaYa off balance. Now the two boys were holding YaYa, allowing Henry to get a punch into his stomach. "You've fucked up now, motherfucka. Hold his ass still."

Henry threw another blow, causing YaYa's head to turn. "Nigga, say I'm your daddy."

"Your dumbass will never be my daddy. Fuck you!" YaYa responded,

"Say it, nigga!" Henry caught YaYa with another blazing right hook.

"I ain't saying shit! Y'all would have to kill me before y'all make me say anything."

As Henry was about to throw another punch, Jerusalem, who had been standing with some of the other neighborhood kids on the sidelines, socked Henry. The blow knocked Henry to the ground. Jerusalem then turned and socked one of Henry's friends that held YaYa. YaYa punched the other boy while Jerusalem started welding on Henry before he had a chance to get back up. This knocked Henry back to the ground a second time. This time, Jerusalem kicked Henry in the guts.

"Motherfucka, pick on me! You always fucking with somebody smaller than you. Pick on somebody your size. With your punk ass," Jerusalem said.

Henry was unable to respond because Jerusalem had kicked all the wind out of his body. YaYa continued to hold his own with the other boy. At the end of the fight, Jerusalem and YaYa were the only two standing. Henry and his friends were no match for the duo. They took off running in retreat.

Some of the kids in the crowd yelled, "Did y'all see that? Henry and his friends got their asses whooped."

As the crowded kids slowly dispersed, Jerusalem bent down, picked up YaYa's book and handed it to him. "Man, you got a lot of heart."

"Thanks. Why you stick yourself out there for me like that?" YaYa asked.

"I don't know. It just seemed like you needed some help. I don't like Henry and those punk ass niggas anyway. They always fucking with the new kids. You live in the projects?"

"Yes. My parents moved here about a month ago."

"Man, it's a jungle out here. You got to be quick to fight for your respect in order to survive. Where you from?" the young ten-year-old Jerusalem asked.

"I'm from Louisiana," YaYa said as they started to walk toward their project building.

"Y'all country boys sho' is tough. You definitely can take an ass whooping."

"It was three on one. How could I win?"

"Why your stupid ass just didn't run?"

"Then I would have to run from them niggas every day for the rest of my life."

"You's a little soldier, huh?" Jerusalem stared at him.

YaYa smiled, spitting blood from his mouth. "Thanks, man. Thanks for everything. What I got to do to pay you back?"

Jerusalem grabbed one of the books. "Teach me how to read some of these books you got. And I'll teach you how to survive on these streets."

That's how their friendship started.

The two young boys became tighter than tennis shoes and shoelaces. When you saw one, you saw the other. They were inseparable. YaYa slowly adapted to the project way of life with the help of his newfound friend, Jerusalem.

The sound of the door interrupted YaYa's trip down memory lane.

Now fully dressed, Jerusalem exited the bedroom, causing YaYa to look in his direction. "You clean up well."

"Yeah, it's a lot different than those jailhouse suits." Jerusalem smiled.

Jerusalem turned and admired himself in the mirror. His crooked smile made him resemble Tupac Shakur, with a unique shaped and baldhead. He had thick eyebrows with slanted beast-like eyes. His wide shoulders made his black Armani button down dress shirt fit well. With black matching slacks and black gators, Jerusalem was satisfied with the reflection staring back at him. His hand automatically went up to his freshly trimmed moustache over his full set of lips. He turned to the side and admired his goatee. The diamonds in his diamond cut Rolex and two-carat platinum squared pinky ring sparkled.

"What you drinking on?" Jerusalem asked as he walked to the bar.

"This that Dom P. Would you like to have a drink with an old friend?" YaYa responded as he refilled his own glass.

"Certainly. Why not?"

YaYa poured him a drink. "I got a very special surprise for you."

"Special surprise? You got some strippers about to jump out the closet or something?"

"Naw, later for that. I got something a lot better."

"Better than a piece of ass after eight and half years? What could be better than that?"

YaYa walked to the closet located by the living room door and pulled out two duffle bags. Jerusalem, slowly sipping on his glass of Dom Perignon, stared with curiosity.

YaYa placed the duffle bag on the coffee table and unzipped

it. He reached his hand inside and pulled out two brand new pearl handle nine millimeter automatic weapons.

"Them bitches nice," Jerusalem said. "But they ain't nicer than two females. You got to come better than that."

"Slow your horses, fam'," YaYa responded, pulling out ten thousand stacks at a time and neatly lining them up on the coffee table. "This is your share of the bank robbery and your share from the business we've been running. It's three point five million. I figured it would get you off to a great start."

Jerusalem walked over to YaYa. "You right. This is better than a closet full of strippers. MOB."

"That's right, money over bitches," YaYa said.He reached in the other bag and passed Jerusalem a shoulder strap that held two gun holsters. Jerusalem placed the holster across his shoulder and adjusted the strap so it would fit him comfortably. He picked the guns up one by one, loading each gun by putting one into the chamber before placing the weapons in his holster.

Jerusalem gave YaYa a firm handshake and pulled him closer to embrace him. "Black Senate for life." While in prison, Jerusalem had shared with YaYa some of the knowledge he'd learned from Kaleef. YaYa had passed on some of the information to Malachi and the rest of their crew.

"Black Senate until our casket drops." YaYa said.

Jerusalem added, "Triple L—love, life, and loyalty."

"You ready to roll out?" YaYa asked.

"Yeah, let me grab my leather coat. Put that money back in the duffle bag for me. And then we out."

"Where we headed first?" YaYa asked.

"To the projects. Where else we going to find Malachi?"

"Yes. That dreadlock-wearing fool love the projects. All that money that nigga making and he won't leave. When that nigga die, we going have to bury that nigga in the projects. Cause if we don't, that nigga going to rise from the dead and carry his casket and rebury his damn self in the heart of the projects."

"That's a project nigga for real," Jerusalem said,grabbing his coat.

Seconds later, he and YaYa exited the penthouse suite. Some of the people they met on the way down to the lobby looked at Jerusalem as if he didn't belong there.

"Boo." Jerusalem said to one couple on the elevator.

YaYa laughed.

The couple rushed off the elevator as soon as the doors opened, holding on to each other for dear life.

"We better go before security comes to see who the two big bad black guys are,' YaYa said.

"Fuck 'em. I got every right to be here just like them." Jerusalem hopped off the elevator. He placed the designer shades on his eyes and followed YaYa out the hotel, ignoring the stares from some of the patrons in the lobby.

CHAPTER EIGHT

YaYa hit I-90 and went through the Hubbard Cave tunnel. Jerusalem glared out the window and at the streetlights as YaYa drove slowly through his hood. Some things had changed, but much stayed the same. The drunks and the homeless still hung out in front of the local liquor store trying to bum change. The prostitutes patrolled the corners looking for a john as their pimps parked nearby in their Cadillac or Lincoln, monitoring their moneymakers.

YaYa pulled up to one of the far back buildings of the project. Jerusalem said, "That got to be Malachi's black Maserati."

"One of many," YaYa responded as he pulled on the side of the black Maserati.

"Malachi's always been flashy," Jerusalem said.

"Everybody knows not to mess with nothing that belongs to Malachi, or else they as good as dead."

Jerusalem and YaYa stepped out the black Jaguar looking like two bonafide black gangsters. They walked toward the building entrance. Jerusalem looked around and noticed a few Black Warriors standing post.

"What's up, YaYa?" one of the young boys asked.

"What's good?" YaYa responded. "Every day you wake up breathing is good."

"You right about that, my nigga," the young boy replied.

The young boy looked in Jerusalem's direction. "Who is this cat you with?"

"You'll find out soon enough. Is the elevator ready?" YaYa said.

"Yeah." The elevator was only for YaYa and Malachi's use. Everyone else had to take the stairs.

One of the young warriors sitting on the steps stood and pressed the button for the elevator doors. Seconds later, they stepped off the elevator on the top floor where they met two more of Malachi's warriors guarding the floor.

"What's up, YaYa?" the 350 pound Black man asked.

YaYa gave him a firm handshake. "Nothing much. It's a good day 'cause my man is home."

"This Jerusalem? Damn! Nigga, you done changed. I barely recognize you."

"What's up, Tiny? Long time. See you ain't getting any smaller."

"Yeah, huh," Tiny repeated, rubbing his stomach. "Women's love a big man these days, and I love them when they call me big poppa."

"Everybody ain't able," YaYa commented as they walked toward Malachi's door.

They could hear DMX's song, "Where My Dogs At" blasting in the background.

YaYa knocked on the door.

A female voice asked, "Who that?"

"It's YaYa. Open the door."

A tall, slender, model-type female opened the door dressed in a silver sequined mini dress with five-inch platform heels with diamond hoops dangling from her ears and diamonds dripping from her neck and wrist. A diamond ring was on almost every finger.

"Hey, baby." The ebony beauty kissed YaYa on the cheek.

"Sabrina, this is my brother, Jerusalem."

She looked at Jerusalem and became instantly attracted. Women melted at the sight of the dimples on each side of his cheeks every time he smiled, revealing his big, perfect white teeth.

"Hi, handsome." Sabrina's words seemed to roll off her tongue.

"Hi, beautiful," Jerusalem responded.

"Handsome and charming, how could a girl lose?" Sabrina said.

Move your ass out the way, girl," YaYa said. "Let us at least get through the door before you start throwing your panties."

"Whatever, nigga!" Sabrina responded as she eyed Jerusalem and walked to the back of the penthouse project apartment.

Jerusalem and YaYa entered through the door that led to the living room. Jerusalem yelled out, "Malachi! Where you at?"

Malachi, wearing a black wife beater T-shirt, with black designer jeans and gold Timberland boots, entered the spacious living room. He had renovated three apartments, knocked down the walls, and turned it into one big condo with plush, dark burgundy carpet and expensive furniture, statues and paintings. "Is that my nigga?" said Malachi as he entered the room, followed by two huge Rottweilers by his side.

Malachi looked like a young Bob Marley. His dreads hung down to his lower chest. Tattoos covered Malachi's entire body up to his neck with a crescent moon and star in between his eyebrows that stood out. With his golden complexion, his artwork showed vividly on his body. Every marking told a story.

"Is that my nigga?" Malachi repeated.

"Go home, Capone," he ordered the male Rottweiler. "Home, Mae West." Both dogs followed Malachi's orders and retreated into a back room.

He walked up and embraced Jerusalem. "Good to have you home again, people."

"Good to be home," Jerusalem responded.

"Look at you," Malachi said. "You sure done matured. I see the difference in your eyes."

"I see you still ruling these projects," Jerusalem said.

"Call me King Malachi, the ruler."

"You got that right."

Malachi said, "I've been waiting on you niggas for hours. What took y'all so long?"

"We had a lot of catching up to do," Jerusalem responded.

"Y'all been doing all that catching up without me. I thought this was BBB."

All of them said in unison, "The three Bad Black Brothas." They embraced.

"Nigga, what you done did to the apartment?" Jerusalem asked. "It's like you had a penthouse flown in and placed it on top of the projects."

"Naw nigga. I just turned three apartments into one. You know how a king do it."

"I see. I've never seen nothing like this in my life. You have a hell of an imagination. 'Cause I never would have thought of this. I would have rather just moved into a penthouse. Nigga, you done remodeled the whole top floor of the projects."

"Almost, huh?" Malachi replied.

YaYa interjected, "Malachi is definitely a hood legend. Never been one before him, and I don't think there will ever be one after him. He's definitely one of a kind."

"That's the most intelligent thing you done ever said, Einstein," Malachi said.

Jerusalem said, "Look at you. Look like you bathed in diamonds."

"You like?" Malachi said. Wrapped around his right wrist was a platinum diamond bracelet. On his left wrist was a diamond Rolex watch. Three diamond chains hung from his neck, each one longer than the next with the longest and thickest one hanging down to his waist with a big diamond encrusted medallion on the end. Two-carat earrings were in each ear. When Malachi smiled, there were four platinum diamonds, one on each of his front four teeth.

Malachi rubbed his neatly trimmed beard, and Jerusalem got a good look at the rings adorning almost each one of his fingers. The ring that stood out the most was the custom-made diamond ring that sat on his left pointing finger. It was a three-tier diamond ring with each tier smaller than the next surrounding one huge diamond. Two other diamond rings were on the same hand, one on his ring finger and one on his pinky. On his other hand, a diamond sparkled on his middle finger and a diamond wedding band fit securely on his thumb.

"I see you got GQ'd out the game," Malachi responded.

"Nothing GQ about me. I'm gangsta," Jerusalem replied, opening his leather coat and flashing two 9-millimeters sitting in the holsters on each side of him.

"You ain't the only one gangsta, nigga." Malachi reached around his back and pulled his hands forward, holding two nine-millimeter automatic weapons also. "I stay ready for war."

YaYa said, "What? Y'all having a showdown at the OK corral? What y'all trying to see? Whose guns are the biggest? We all know it ain't about whose guns the biggest. It's whose heart's the biggest. Come on, let's show Jerusalem a tour of your project castle."

"I got a hell of a night planned for my man. Come on, let's go where the party at."

It felt good to Jerusalem to be back in the free world but his mission in life now was different than what it was before he went to prison. He hoped YaYa and Malachi were ready for the changes. He was a man on a mission and would accomplish it with or without his friends support.

CHAPTER NINE

Jerusalem felt on top of the world. He was free. He wanted to scream that at the top of his lungs. He'd imagined being with his friends and now it was a reality. He followed Malachi and YaYa and checked out each room as they headed closer to the music. First, they entered the kitchen that looked like it came straight out of a scene from *MTV Cribs* with stainless steel counters, a huge stainless steel refrigerator and double decker stove. Black marble tiles covered the floor. Jerusalem could see his reflection on the floor as they walked through the wide hallway.

The walls displayed autographed pictures of Malachi with Black celebrities and athletes that he had collected over the years. Jerusalem glanced to his left and saw an open door that displayed a bedroom with an African safari theme with a wooden high-posted bed by the wall. He increased his pace to keep up with his friends.

The music got louder and louder as they went through what must have been a den. The dark brown leather sectional sat right in front of a theater-sized television that was currently playing music videos.

Malachi opened the door and in unison people shouted, "Welcome home, Jerusalem!"

Jerusalem smiled and entered the room packed with some of his old friends and acquaintances as well as new faces. One of the first old friends he recognized was his girl, Pinky. Pinky was the first to run up to Jerusalem. She wrapped her arms around his neck and pulled him into a tight embrace. "I missed you so much," she whispered in his ear. Tears of happiness flowed down her cheek.

"I missed you too, baby girl."

Pinky released her grip from around his neck. "Look at you. Look at what almost nine years in prison has done for you. Look like you ready for a runway show. Tyson Beckford will feel the competition."

Jerusalem smiled. "Look how you've grown over the years. Looking like one of them red bones I see on a rap video."

"Them bitches ain't got nothing on me," Pinky responded. "That shit is fake. This is all real." She turned and the black mini sequined dress she wore displayed her perfect curves.

Although she was still as short as Jerusalem remembered, the black patent leather platform heels made her look taller. The long, pink diamond necklace flashed its brilliance around her neck. Pinky's platinum blonde straight hair dangled to her shoulders. With perfect manicured hot pink nails, Pinky grabbed Jerusalem's hand and led Jerusalem further into the crowded room.

On the way to the bar, Jerusalem stopped and received many handshakes and hugs. The bartender that Malachi hired asked,

"What you drinking?"

Jerusalem said, "Ladies first. Pinky?"

"Give me a Grey Goose on ice," Pinky responded.

"I'll have the same," Jerusalem said.

He and Pinky turned and faced the crowd. Jerusalem asked, "So what's been going on?"

"Living. Enjoying life." She smiled, looking him directly in the eyes.

"I can see that." He looked down at her pink diamond rings on her fingers and pink diamond bracelets that glistened.

Pinky said, "I know you haven't been having too much fun where you've been. I want to thank you, Jerusalem. It took a lot of courage to do what you did on that day. 'Cause none of us would have been enjoying life. We all put your money to the side to make sure you was good when you came home. I love you for everything you've ever done for me." She kissed him on the lips.

Her kiss caught Jerusalem a little off guard. He pulled back and said, "I'm home now, so what's done is done. It's time for all of us to enjoy life. For tonight, that's exactly what I plan on doing."

The bartender handed them both their drinks. Malachi, with his hands draped around two women on each side of him, walked up to where they stood. "Hey, man, I was wondering where you were. I want you to meet Tiffany, and you've already met Sabrina."

Pinky looked Tiffany and Sabrina up and down. She then turned her attention toward Jerusalem and kissed him on the cheek. "Have fun. We'll talk tomorrow."

Jerusalem responded, "Yes, we have a lot to discuss."

Pinky walked away. Tiffany and Sabrina left Malachi's side and walked over to Jerusalem and draped their hands on his chest and shoulder. Jerusalem looked up and saw Pinky roll her eyes before she turned and walked to another side of the room.

Malachi grabbed a bottle of Dom Perignon from the bar and said, "Y'all show my man a good time."

"Ladies, let me talk to my man here for a minute. Y'all go ahead and order a drink and I'll be with y'all in a minute."

Jerusalem and Malachi stepped away. Jerusalem said, "I was told that Bankroll still got the market cornered and not really opening the doors for any outsiders."

"Yeah, that old motherfucker got it where he forcing everybody to buy from him at his prices. For some reason, he ain't showing us no love. The product is half way decent, but the prices are ridiculous. I'm sick of that motherfucker," Malachi responded.

"It's a new day and a new breed. It's time for a change." Jerusalem drank from his glass.

Malachi brought the bottle of Dom P up to his mouth. He then said, "Me and my warriors are ready. I got all my soldiers in order. What's your plan, Jerusalem?"

"To build a legacy. To build an empire. To build our own Black nation of Black senates," Jerusalem said, "and you play a very big part of this."

"I'm with you Jerusalem. Triple L."

"I got something else I want to tell you before I take Tiffany and Sabrina to heaven."

"And what's that, lover boy?"

"I know where fifty million in drug money is at."

"Fifty million! Motherfucker, who we got to kill?"

"We don't have to kill no one. It was given to me to help build our empire from Kaleef, my teacher, father, and friend."

"Yeah, I heard of Kaleef. That motherfucka's a legend on these streets. Wasn't he doing life or something?"

"Yes, he was doing life. He's dead now. Before he died, he told me where fifty million is at. It's in the walls of his daughter's house."

Malachi, now holding the bottle to his side, said, "Have you figured out how we're supposed to get fifty million out of this lady's house? Pretty sure she's not going to allow strangers in and just start tearing her house up."

"Yeah, I'm coming up with a plan, but before we do that, it's time to get rid of Bankroll and all them old heads. 'Cause eventually, it's going to be a problem. So let's just eliminate a problem before it gets started."

"That's no problem. We've been waiting for years to kill those old dirty bastards."

"Now's the time." Jerusalem looked in the direction of the bar. "I'm about to go enjoy the rest of my night. I see my guests are getting impatient."

Jerusalem walked to the bar and stood in between Tiffany and Sabrina. He said to the bartender, "Hand me a bottle of Dom P." The bartender did as requested.

"Y'all ladies ready?" Jerusalem asked.

Sabrina responded, "I was ready when I first saw you."

"Y'all more familiar with this resident than I am right now. So lead the way."

They headed out of the party room. While walking, Jerusalem made eye contact with Pinky sitting on the arm of one of the leather chairs next to an unfamiliar male. YaYa was sitting near and appeared to be busy in conversation with some female.

Tiffany grabbed Jerusalem's hand and led him into one of the guest bedrooms. Candles flickered as the two women started to undress each other. Jerusalem stood and watched as Sabrina and Tiffany kissed each other. Fully naked, they both lay across the black satin sheets in the king-sized bed. Sabrina took one of Tiffany's nipples in her mouth and Tiffany moaned in pleasure. Jerusalem could feel his dick getting hard as he watched both women perform oral sex on one another in a sixty-nine position.

After they both climaxed several times, Tiffany looked up at Jerusalem, who was now naked, holding his hard dick in his hand. "Would you like to join us?" she asked.

Sabrina looked at Jerusalem's long, hard dick and said, "Wow. Can't wait to ride that."

Jerusalem walked to the bed and joined in. Both women took turns pleasuring him orally. Jerusalem fucked Tiffany while Sabrina sucked on her breasts. Tiffany screamed in ecstasy, "You're so deep in me."

Tiffany's body shook in pleasure. Sabrina and Tiffany switched places. Jerusalem lay on his back as Sabrina climbed on top of his dick and rode his ten inches as they both came to a climax. They repeated their fuck session several more times before both women were out cold, sleeping like babies. Jerusalem lay back and thought about his plans for the old heads.

CHAPTER TEN

Thanks to a tip Malachi received the night before, Jerusalem was able to expedite his plans. Malachi, Jerusalem, YaYa and Tiny sat in a black Lincoln SUV down the street from where the old heads were scheduled to meet. They watched as the old heads entered the building of their headquarters. Four black luxury cars pulled up and lined up behind each other one by one. The drivers got out of the cars and opened up the passenger door. They watched the old heads exit along with their own personal bodyguards.

All four of the old heads, including Bankroll, strolled into the building. All except two bodyguards followed their bosses. The two remaining guards posted outside at the front door.

YaYa called Pinky on her cell phone and said, "It's time."

"One," Pinky responded and hung up.

Ten minutes later, Pinky strolled around the corner walking like a Persian cat wearing a short, yellow mini dress that stopped right below her ass cheeks. The guards were shooting the breeze with one another. The heavyset guard on the left hand side was first to notice Pinky. He tapped the taller of the two and said, "You see that?"

"Hell yeah! Even Stevie Wonder can see the curves on that bitch."

Pinky walked closer and flashed a million dollar smile. Both bodyguards watched in silence as she passed them by.

Malachi said to Jerusalem, "They must be some fucking faggots. They not biting."

Jerusalem said, "Just be patient. Let Pinky do her thing."

Pinky dropped her cosmetic bag and the contents if it fell on the ground next to the sidewalk. She stopped and bent over. The mini dress crept up, giving the bodyguards a clear view of her round butt cheeks.

The heavyset bodyguard said, "Oh shit! She ain't wearing any panties."

He slowly jogged over to help Pinky pick up the items. The guard said, "Let me help you with that, ma."

"Thank you," Pinky replied in a sultry, sexy voice.

Pinky rubbed against him. Her sweet perfume lingered in the air. Her cleavage exposed her full breasts and held the bodyguard captive as he stared at her beauty. There wasn't a man on earth who could resist Pinky when she turned on her charm.

"What's your name, gorgeous?" the bodyguard asked as they stood.

"They call me Kandie because I love to be licked." She zipped the cosmetic bag and continued to say, "You're such a gentleman. Is there any way I can repay you for your courtesy?" Pinky licked her full, luscious pink lips.

He had never been that close to a gorgeous woman such as

Pinky. The idea of having her to himself caused him to stutter. "Wh-wh-at do you mean?"

"What do you think I mean?" Pinky replied. "I haven't had my pussy satisfied in days. A big, strong handsome man like you seems like he can get the job done. Are you up for it?"

The other bodyguard looked at Pinky and his cohort and wondered what they were saying. He couldn't keep his eyes off Pinky's butt. The heavyset guard looked back at the other bodyguard and proceeded to say to Pinky, "I'm working now. Maybe we can hook up later."

Pinky walked closer to him, grabbed his dick, looked into his eyes, and said in a soft voice, "You're going to pass up a golden opportunity like this. I have a sexual appetite that needs to be filled. Plus, I'm headed to Atlanta later on tonight."

"What do you do for a living?" he replied.

"I'm an exotic dancer. Plus I'm a freak on the side, and I've been looking for some good dick since I've been here in Chicago," she replied. "Would you like to taste my candy?"

A sly grin crossed his face. "Hell yeah!"

"Is there any place we can go?"

The bodyguard thought for a few seconds. "Yeah, but hold on for a minute."

He walked back up to the front of the building near the other bodyguard. "Man, this bitch is a freak."

The other man replied, "She ain't just a freak; she's a fine fucking freak. What she standing there for?"

"Man, I need you to cover me while I go handle this business with her."

"Shit nigga. Just take her in the women's restroom right on the inside of the door. Ain't no women in there."

"Hell yeah. Just stand post until I finish. I'm gonna make it quick."

The other guard replied, "What about me, nigga? I want to tap that voluptuous ass just as well as you do."

"She's a freak, my man. She'll probably do both of us. Let me do me, and I'll talk to her about it."

"Bet."

He signaled Pinky to come to him.

Jerusalem and the crew watched from a distance as Pinky worked her magic. The bodyguard said, "This is my partner."

Pinky stated. "I'm Kandie." She licked her lips.

"My friend might want to have some words with you after we finish."

Pinky replied, "Today must be my lucky day. I thought I was going to leave Chicago disappointed."

The heavyset bodyguard grabbed Pinky by the hand. Pinky turned and winked at the other bodyguard, as she was led into the building. She scanned the area and didn't see any other occupants as she followed him into the women's bathroom. Once inside, she sat on the sink and slowly raised her dress, exposing her shaved pussy.

The bodyguard said, "You don't waste no time, huh ma?"

Pinky replied, "What's there left to talk about? Besides, too much talking spoils the moment. Come and taste my candy, baby."

The bodyguard quickly placed his face in between Pinky's legs. Pinky replied, "Let me reach in my purse and get a condom. Just don't stop licking me, baby." She moaned, "That feels so fucking good."

While he was giving her head, Pinky pulled out her pink

pearl handled .380 with a silencer, placed it to his head, and pulled the trigger with one shot to the head ending his life. As the bullet exited the back of his head, blood splattered as his body hit the bathroom floor. Pinky hopped off the bathroom sink and pulled down her dress. "Damn, you give bomb ass head. Too bad this is business and not pleasure. You could have come in handy."

Pinky carefully avoided stepping in the blood. She cleaned herself up and rushed out of the bathroom, careful that no one else was in the surrounding area as she went back to the door where the other guard was still holding post. "Your friend can't handle all this sweet pussy by himself. You want to come and help him."

Pinky turned toward the women's bathroom. The bodyguard forgot he had a job to do and followed her, leaving the front door fully exposed. Jerusalem and the rest of the men saw this as an opportunity to set their plans in full action mode as they exited the SUV. Pinky stood behind the bathroom door as the bodyguard entered. He said, "What the fuck?"

Before he could get another statement out, Pinky held out her gun and said, "Boss bitches run the world, motherfucka" and pulled the trigger, ending his life. Pinky exited the building as Jerusalem and the rest of the Black Senate entered.

***

Bankroll, a spitting image of the R & B singer Ronald Isley, sat at the head of the table and the three other old heads sat around the oval shaped mahogany table discussing street business. Each old head had one bodyguard standing behind their seat.

Bankroll, holding his golden cane with a snake on the end, said, "Business is better than ever. We can't release the chokehold off our competition. We going to squeeze them until not a drop of liquid can drip from their bodies. These young motherfuckas these days have forgotten the rules. They have no respect for us. And we built this shit."

One of the old heads mentioned, "Word on the street is Jerusalem's home. You know that motherfucka's going to cause us problems."

"How is he going to cause us problems when he no longer exists? That motherfucka's already dead and he don't even know it. And after him, I can't wait to do that flashy motherfucker, Malachi. That nigga's doing too much. He doesn't have any respect for no one," Bankroll responded.

"How you plan to do that?" another one of the old heads asked. "When he got those young warriors around him twenty-four seven? Them young niggas not going to let a fly get close to Malachi."

"I already got that under control," Bankroll responded as he took a puff from his Cuban cigar. "I then sold one of them young niggas in his army a dream. And Wet Bird is ready to react at the proper time."

Neither the old heads nor their bodyguards had time to react when Jerusalem, Malachi, Tiny, and YaYa entered the meeting room with their guns drawn. Jerusalem said, "Long time, no see, Bankroll."

Bankroll smiled and took another puff from his cigar. He blew smoke out of his nostrils.

"Did you miss me?" Jerusalem asked.

"I don't think I can say that I did. What the fuck you doing here, Jerusalem? And where the fuck is Big Fred and Ice?" Bankroll replied.

"You can say that they are sleeping on the job," Jerusalem responded.

"If it's not a permanent sleep, it will be when I finish with them," Bankroll said.

"Bankroll, why wasn't I invited to the meeting?" Jerusalem held his weapon steady. "You know that I'm a businessman, don't you? And you knew that I was home. Why wasn't I given an invitation?"

"Well, Jerusalem, I didn't know you conducted business with the gray heads. Besides, I don't think your young ass know how to conduct proper business anyway because you came here uninvited. That shows me you haven't matured because you entered my humble abode without knocking."

"You want me to step back out and knock?" Jerusalem asked.

"That won't be necessary. Just tell me what this is about."

"This is about your disposal. This is a new set of gangstas. Under a new breed. Time for you old heads to retire."

"Motherfucker, you think I'm going to retire because you said so. I was running these streets when you was in pampers, nigga. Still crying behind your mama. And you have the audacity to walk up in my place of business and tell me what I should do. Nigga, you's a motherfucking joke."

Jerusalem slowly walked up to Bankroll and snatched the cane from his hand. "This is exactly what you are, motherfucka. A snake. You crawl on your belly so no one can see you. You hide under the surface and blend in with the dirt. Your tongue is split in two. You mix truth with lies and cause confusion. It's you old motherfuckas that separate the old from the young. It's 'cause you have some type of self-hate . . . where we could never unify. You hate the way that we walk. You old motherfuckas hate the way we wear our clothes. You hate the way that we talk. You even hate the type of music we listen to. But y'all the same motherfuckas helped birth us. How can you dislike something that you created? It's time for y'all way of thinking. Y'all way of doing things and your way of business to end."

Bankroll replied, "Let's try to work this out. Maybe we can now do business. I see you've grown and gotten a little wiser."

Jerusalem looked him in the eyes and responded, "No, motherfucka. I recognize you from the moment that I saw your ass. I knew from the beginning you were an old dirty bastard. Your time has expired."

Jerusalem raised the 9-millimeter automatic with the silencer to Bankroll's head and released two shots. Bankroll's body hit the table, bounced and fell to the floor. Jerusalem pointed the gun at Bankroll's lifeless body and shot seven more times.

Bankroll's bodyguards reached for their weapons. Jerusalem aimed and shot the bodyguards with three shots, killing them instantly.

The scene turned into gunfire as the bodyguards for the old heads did their best to protect their bosses. Malachi, YaYa, and Tiny opened fire killing the bodyguards. One of the old heads Malachi had beef with stared at him, so without saying a word, Malachi retrieved the freshly sharpened machete and with his right hand drew it back and with one swift swing cut the old head's neck off. His head rolled around on the table. The other two old heads stared in disbelief as Tiny and YaYa ended their life with two bullets to the head.

Malachi, with death in his eyes, chopped off Bankroll's head and the other two leaders. He placed the heads in a plastic bag that Tiny held. Tiny grasped the top of the plastic bag, and they all headed out the same way they came in with Jerusalem walking behind them.

For the next sixty days, people in Chicago lived in fear, as dead bodies dropped as if it were a war zone. Jerusalem and his men tried not to leave any of the old heads' soldiers alive. Malachi led the blood bath. The heads of Bankroll and the other top men hung from street poles in each one of their territories. Letting everyone know that the Black Senate was taking over.

CHAPTER ELEVEN

"Shit," she cursed as she accidentally bumped her toe, after having just put her last load in the washer and dryer. The light in the utility room had flickered on and off and then stayed off. She felt along the wall and walked out of the room until she could see some form of daylight when she reached the kitchen. She picked up the kitchen phone and dialed the number to the electric company written on a notepad on the wall.

"A call's coming through from her house," YaYa said, tapping on the keyboards of his laptop and redirecting her phone call to Pinky's number. YaYa used his computer skills and one of his connections who worked at the phone company to gain access to Khadijah's phone line.

Pinky answered, "Northern Electric, how may I help you?"

YaYa and Jerusalem were both impressed with how professional Pinky sounded.

"My names Khadijah Washington and I live in Chimney Hills at 423 Elm Grove. My electric's off and I paid my electric bill last week so I don't know why it's not working."

"Ma'am, can you hold on for a second while I check to see if there's trouble in your area?" Pinky said, as she put her on mute.

"She's good," YaYa said, as he and Jerusalem listened in on the call from the laptop. YaYa turned to Jerusalem and asked, "Man, how did you end up finding out where she lived?"

Jerusalem responded, "When I was in prison, after Kaleef was killed, I was going through his belongings and I found a letter she wrote. Matter of fact, it was the only letter she ever wrote. Telling him how she wanted nothing to do with him and blaming him for the reason her mother was murdered. Of course, it had the address on the envelope. If I wouldn't have found the letter, it would have been hard for me to find Khadijah; because Kaleef was killed before he had the chance to fill me in on the rest of the information."

YaYa responded, "He told you it was in the walls of the basement, so now all we have to do is get entrance into the house."

They went back to listening to Pinky and Khadijah's conversation.

Pinky said in a professional tone, "Ma'am, we're not showing that there are any problems in your area."

"There's a problem because I'm telling you my electric's not working," Khadijah responded in a frustrated tone.

"Ma'am, calm down. I'm here to help you."

"When can you send someone out because I just bought groceries and I can't afford for my food to spoil."

"Let me see if we have anyone in the area." There was a long pause and then Pinky came back on the line and said, "This is your lucky day. We have some technicians already dispatched to your area. I will get in contact with them and have someone come check out your situation. Will you be there? They may need to come inside, and we need to make sure someone is there to let them in."

"I'm not going anywhere."

"Good. We'll send someone out as soon as we can."

Their call disconnected. Pinky called Jerusalem on his cell phone. He hit the speaker button so YaYa could hear too. "I did my part. Now it's on you," Pinky said.

Jerusalem chuckled. "Baby girl, I got this."

"If y'all need anything else, you know where to find me."

"Man, let's go ahead and get this over with," YaYa said. "Let me do most of the talking."

"I'm just along for the ride," Jerusalem responded.

Twenty minutes later, they pulled up in a Northern Electric company van. They both were wearing Northern Electric uniforms with tool belts around their waists as if they were seriously there to work on her electric.

YaYa rang the doorbell. They stood and waited. Khadijah, dressed in a pair of blue jeans and a Chicago State University T-shirt, answered the door. Her hair, pulled back in a ponytail, complimented her slanted hazel eyes. Jerusalem could immediately see her resemblance to Kaleef.

"Ms. we're from Northern Electric and we're here to see about fixing your electrical problem."

"I'm so glad you came."

She opened the door and allowed YaYa and Jerusalem to enter.

YaYa picked up his clipboard and pretended to be reading a service order. "According to the service order, your electric is completely out. Is that correct?"

"Yes. It went out while I was washing clothes."

Jerusalem stood on the sidelines and allowed YaYa to talk to Khadijah. His mind was on the fifty million dollars down in the basement. YaYa said, "We'll be outside checking to see if there are any problems out there. We may need to get to your main electric source. It should be somewhere inside the house."

"According to our records, it's located in the basement." Jerusalem pretended to be looking at a diagram.

"The basement. I haven't been down there in months. I don't have any candles or flashlights, plus I'm somewhat scared of the dark. That's why I really need my electric fixed today if y'all can."

YaYa attempted to calm her. "Ma'am, don't worry. We're going to do everything within our power to get you up and working in no time. Just trust me."

Khadijah seemed to be fixated on every word that came out of YaYa's mouth. *Good,* Jerusalem thought. *He can keep her distracted while I figure out how to extract the money from the basement walls.*

"Just give us a little time outside, and we'll let you know if we need to get to the basement," YaYa said.

Jerusalem followed YaYa outside. They pretended to be working on the electric. YaYa caught Khadijah peeking out the curtain at them. "Man, since you're trying to get your mack on. I need you to keep her occupied when we go back in and tell her we need to do some work in the basement."

"She is a beautiful woman," YaYa said.

"This is business. Get pussy on your own time."

"Khadijah's not the type of woman I would just want some pussy from. She seems special. There's something different about her. I can tell."

"Man, you must be smoking on that love drug. Focus." Jerusalem looked at his watch. "It's time to get back to business."

YaYa closed the outside circuit board. "We've been out here long enough pretending to be checking out an electric problem that doesn't exist."

"Then get your flirt on and get me to that basement," Jerusalem responded, as they walked back toward the house.

Khadijah met them at the door. "The electric's still not on," she stated.

"I know, ma'am. We think the problem's coming from the main one. I'm going to send my man here downstairs to check it out."

Jerusalem removed the big factory size flashlight from his tool belt and turned it on. "This should be enough light. Now, if I'm not back in thirty minutes, come look for me. The boogeyman might have me."

Khadijah cringed.

Jerusalem laughed.

"Ignore him," YaYa said. "He thinks that he's a comedian with those corny ass jokes."

Jerusalem left YaYa and Khadijah in the kitchen as he turned the light on and headed down the dark stairways to the basement. He removed a second flashlight and placed it in a stationery position as he placed his ear against the wall and tapped. He tapped until he found an area that wasn't hollow. "Jackpot!" he said aloud and marked the spot.

He knew the money had to be there. Now all he needed was the right equipment. He eased his way back up the stairs and saw that YaYa and Khadijah were in deep conversation. "I hate to interrupt, but I've found the problem. We can get your electric back working temporarily, but we will need to come back and rewire downstairs. I see some bad wiring that may be a fire hazard."

Khadijah held her head down. "How much is that going to cost me?"

YaYa picked up his pad and pretended to be reviewing her account. "Fortunately, for you, you have the inside wiring, so all it's going to cost you is your time and maybe a date with me."

She blushed. "I have to work tomorrow but I get off at three. Can you come back at three?"

"Ma'am, we get off at five and this type of job is going to take at least four hours."

"If you want this done, you may have to take off work," YaYa said.

Hesitant at first, she finally said,

"Okay, why don't I do this? I can come back and let you guys in on my lunch break. It's not like I have anything of value you can steal; besides, I know where you work at." Khadijah smiled.

Jerusalem and YaYa faked a smile too. If only she knew.

CHAPTER TWELVE

Wet Bird and three members of Malachi's warriors sat in one of the project apartments that Malachi used as a safe house. They were seated, smoking blunts and counting money through a money machine. D-Dog said to Wet Bird, "Pass the motherfuckin' blunt, nigga."

He took one long puff before handing it to D-Dog. Wet Bird said, "Like I was saying, nigga. That bitch was a freak. Man, I must have fucked her in every hole she had on her body. Then she let me jack off in her face. Nigga, I should be a porno star."

Cash said, "Nigga, all the motherfuckin' flicks you be watching, you should have it down pat. Don't you know that shit is a disease? You need help. You got an illness."

The other members laughed. Mice said, "Yeah, nigga. I heard from one of them bitches you used to fuck that you like her to stick her finger in your ass. How freaky is that?"

Wet Bird responded, "Who the fuck told you that? That bitch's lying. Ain't nothing been up my ass."

Mice responded, "Yeah. Bitches don't lie about shit like that.

Did you let one of them faggots turn you out that you were fucking on when you was locked up? Were y'all flip-flopping?"

Wet Bird's face turned red. "Nigga, why you coming at me like that? Like I'm some sort of punk or something."

Mice kept his cool. "Nigga, I'm just saying. When shit doesn't go right . . . when you stop giving those bitches money and spending time with them, they expose you."

"Man, you going to believe some bitch over me? We supposed to be boys. Ain't nothing sweet about me. Been keeping this shit gangsta. From birth."

Mice repeated, "Oh, you have." Mice took the blunt that D-Dog handed him.

Cash said, "Fuck all that, man. Let's count this money, man; before Malachi come and think we just in here bullshitting around."

Wet Bird gave Mice a killer stare. Mice eyed him back with a light smile, blowing the weed smoke in his direction. Malachi entered the apartment with Capone by his side. One hand was on Capone's leash and the other hand held his machete. Tiny walked behind him.

"What y'all niggas in here doing?" Malachi asked.

"Counting money from today," Wet Bird responded. "We almost finished."

Malachi glared at Wet Bird with fire in his eyes. Wet Bird noticed Malachi's stare and began to get nervous. His hands shook as he put the twenty dollar bills in the money machine.

"Pass me one of those blunts," Malachi said.

D-Dog passed Malachi the freshly rolled purple cush blunt. Malachi placed the blunt into his mouth and pulled a lighter from his pocket and lit it. He never took his eyes off Wet Bird.

Sweat beads formed on Wet Bird's forehead.

"Y'all wrap this shit up," Malachi said.

"Is something bothering you, boss?" Wet Bird asked.

"Yeah, motherfucker. Yeah, something is bothering me."

"Is there something you need me to do? You need me to take care of anything for you? If anything's bothering you, it bothers me. You know I won't hesitate to kill a motherfucka for you."

"Oh, you won't?" Malachi asked. "Not even yourself?"

Fear appeared in Wet Bird's eyes. "What do you mean by that, Malachi?"

"Because your unloyal ass is what's bothering me."

"Unloyal? I've been loyal to you from day one."

"Motherfucka, you going to sit in my fucking face and lie to me. Like I'm stupid. Nigga, I know you been plotting against me with that nigga Bankroll."

"Where you get that from? That's some jealous nigga trying to come between us. They want my position."

"Naw, motherfucka. It's you who want my position. You let that slimy ass nigga Bankroll sell you a pipe dream. Nigga, you could never be me. Nigga, you could never be King Malachi. It's only one of me, and after me, there will be no other. You don't have the mind or the nuts to take my throne. Are you crazy? Or are you just a stupid motherfucka?"

Wet Bird knew that he was caught in a deadly situation. There was no way he could talk his way out of it. D-Dog, Cash, and Mice stood up and surrounded Wet Bird. He glanced around, noticing the look of vengeance on all their faces.

Malachi walked up to him and slapped him. His mouth bled. The hit was so hard; it knocked him out of the chair and the money machine fell on the floor. Twenty dollar bills scattered on the floor near him. Capone barked viciously. Malachi placed the machete to Wet Bird's neck. "Nigga, get naked. Take off all of your motherfucking clothes, or do you want Capone to help you?"

"No, Malachi, please."

Malachi released his leash and commanded Capone in Swahili, "Damu," which meant blood. The command caused the seventy-five pound German Rottweiler to attack Wet Bird. Capone ripped the clothes and flesh from Wet Bird's body. Wet Bird screamed but there was no one there to hear his calls for help.

"Get him off of me, Malachi!" Wet Bird screamed out in agony as Capone continued to rip into his body.

Malachi used the Swahili command for stop and said, "Koma, Capone."

Capone returned to Malachi's side with blood dripping from the side of his mouth. He was still barking and showing his vicious teeth. "Lay!" Malachi commanded. Capone obeyed but never took his eyes off the whimpering Wet Bird.

Malachi walked over and stood over Wet Bird's bloody body, picking him up by the back of his neck and leading him to the table. Malachi said, "Place your hands on the table."

"Please, Malachi."

"Place your motherfucking hand on the table before I cut your head off."

Wet Bird did as instructed. Malachi lined Wet Bird's fingers up neatly as Wet Bird moaned in pain. Malachi said, "You want to bite the hand that feed you? Nigga, you'll never be able to feed your motherfucking self." Malachi came down with the machete, chopping off all four of his fingers on his right hand.

Blood splattered all over the table.

Wet Bird screamed out in agony, "Aweeeeee. Please don't do this."

"Don't do what, motherfucka? What you and Bankroll had planned for me. Don't do that! Did you think you would ever get close to me to kill me? Nicky Barnes ain't got shit on me. I'm the real untouchable, motherfucka. Nigga, give me your other hand."

Wet Bird paused.

"Give me his other motherfuckin' hand," Malachi instructed Tiny.

Tiny walked over, jerked his hand, and placed it on the table.

Wet Bird begged, "Please ... please ... please Malachi, don't do this."

Malachi raised his hand up and chopped off the other four fingers with the machete. "Motherfucker, now you'll never be able to feed yourself. Since you want to bite the hand that feeds you. Now you'll be forced to be fed by someone else."

Wet Bird fell to his knees with his body curled up in pain. Blood was dripping everywhere.

"Motherfucka, it's too late to fall to your knees and pray now. Nigga, I'm god to you right now. Your life's in my hand," Malachi said. "I decide whether you live or die. You disloyal motherfucka. Nigga, that Mercedes that you driving out there, I helped buy that motherfucka. Your mother and your sisters is eating cause of me. Nigga, I raised you from the gutter. Nigga, this how you repay me. That platinum chain around your neck, you wouldn't have if it weren't for me. Matter of fact, give me that motherfucka."

Malachi snatched the platinum chain from around his neck.

The clasp broke as Malachi raised the machete, and with one swift powerful swing he beheaded Wet Bird, whose head rolled across the floor.

"Damu!" he told Capone, who attacked the head, biting out his eyes, nose, and ears.

D-Dog, Cash and Mice looked at the scene in disbelief. None of them had ever witnessed the ruthless rage of Malachi. They had always heard about it, but to experience it was very different. They knew beyond any doubt that they would never ever cross Malachi.

"Capone!" Malachi yelled.

Capone walked back to Malachi, who took the platinum chain he snatched off Wet Bird's neck and tied it around Capone's neck. He placed the leash back on Capone's collar. He looked at Tiny and then at the rest of his warriors. "Clean up this fuckin' mess. Dump his ass in the dumpster with the rest of the trash."

CHAPTER THIRTEEN

Jerusalem and YaYa put the equipment in the back of the Northern Electric van. "I really hope this is all the equipment we need," Jerusalem said as he hopped in the front seat on the passenger side.

YaYa started the van up. "I hope so too. We got four hours to get the money."

Khadijah stood in the door. She'd been waiting on them to arrive. "I made y'all some turkey sandwiches, and there's bottled water in the refrigerator if y'all want something to drink," she informed them as they entered.

"Miss, that was very nice of you," YaYa said.

"I got ten minutes to get back to work. If you have to leave before I get back, please just lock the front door." Khadijah kept her eyes glued to YaYa. It was as if Jerusalem wasn't in the room.

YaYa said, "Will do." He reached into his pocket and handed her a personalized card with his contact information. "If you have any more problems, here's my direct number."

Khadijah said, "I do have a ceiling fan I need put up in my son's bedroom. It might need to be re-wired though."

"I got you covered. Call me."

Jerusalem cleared his throat. "Now that you two are through making other plans, we need to get busy and do what we came here to do."

"Give me a minute," YaYa said,

He walked Khadijah to her Nissan Maxima and held her door open for her. Khadijah smiled and thanked YaYa. She waved at him as she pulled off and headed back to work. When Khadijah was out of eye distance, Jerusalem and YaYa went back to the van and carried in bag after bag to the basement. YaYa hit a switch on the outside circuit breaker, which turned the electric back on. With the basement fully lit, they each put on goggles to protect their eyes. YaYa handed Jerusalem one of the drills, while he held on to the other.

"This is where I think it is," Jerusalem said, as he stood near the wall in the place where he thought the money would be.

"We only need to go in a few inches and should be able to pull out some of the plaster," YaYa stated.

Jerusalem turned the drill on and it made a hole in the wall. Dust flew as he and YaYa both used their drills. "I think I see something," YaYa said, turning off the drill. "Hand me that flashlight."

Turning off his drill, Jerusalem picked up the flashlight nearby and handed it to YaYa. YaYa turned it on and pointed the flashlight in the hole. "Bingo!" he said, as his eyes came across a couple stacks of money wrapped in plastic lining the inside of the wall.

"We need to tear down these walls," Jerusalem said.

"I'll have some of my boys come put the plaster back up later. But time is of the essence," YaYa said.

Jerusalem and YaYa each picked up a sledge hammer and beat the walls as the plaster fell down around them. By the time they finished, the basement was a mess, but they had easy access to the money that Kaleef had hidden. Jerusalem and YaYa removed their goggles. Each unzipped the black duffle bags they brought with them and filled them with the stacks of hundred dollar bills that totaled fifty million dollars. Jerusalem said, as they stacked the money, "YaYa, this is it. This is all we need to take the Black Senate to the next level."

YaYa went outside and backed the van up closer to the front porch. He opened the back of the van. With the van doors wide open, Jerusalem handed him bag after bag while he placed them inside.

Jerusalem glanced at his watch. "She'll be back in about two hours."

"That's enough time for my boys to clean up and get the 'wall back up." YaYa assured him and handed Jerusalem the keys to the van. "I'll leave with the crew. You go ahead and do what you need to do with this money."

Jerusalem eased behind the driver's seat and thanked Kaleef silently as he pulled away from Khadijah's house with the fifty million dollars stowed away in the back of the van. A police siren wailed behind him. He looked in his rearview mirror and saw a police car behind him with the lights flashing.

"Fuck!" Jerusalem yelled out, glancing at the speedometer.

He didn't realize he had been speeding, yet he pulled over to the side of the road. Jerusalem made sure his weapon was nearby but out of eyesight from the approaching officer.

"Officer, is there a problem?" Jerusalem asked as he rolled down his window.

"Yes, I need to see your license and registration."

Jerusalem handed him the information as requested. The officer glanced at the information. "Is someone having electric problems over here?"

"We had to do some re-wiring at a house that's being remodeled," Jerusalem responded.

"They have you working alone?"

"Yeah. If I needed help, I can always call for another person. Right now, I have it under control."

"You must know your shit. I got some electric work I need done at one of my rental houses. You got a card?"

Jerusalem patted his pockets as if he was looking for one of his business cards. "Naw, officer, I'm out. But give me your card and I'll call you and see what I can do for you."

"You just cut me a nice deal, and I'll cut you some slack on this ticket. This time I'll let you get away with a warning."

"All right, officer. That sounds like a deal to me."

The officer handed Jerusalem a business card. "Just slow it down a little bit. The next officer might not be as understanding as I am."

Jerusalem watched from his rearview mirror as the officer got back into his police car. He felt relieved that he didn't have to off the officer. The officer waved at him as he re-entered traffic. Jerusalem waved back, unable to imagine being stopped and searched, then having to explain how millions were in his possession. As he headed to YaYa's house, he knew he'd have to kill the next unlucky cop who stopped him.

CHAPTER FOURTEEN

As Malachi requested, the soldiers showed up in the City of God in packs. The name was known to all in the area because God had to be with you in order to survive living there. All wore black. Some had black bandanas tied to their heads. Some had black bandanas hanging from their pockets. Some had black bandanas tied around their necks. They didn't have to worry about outsiders or the police, because no one ventured that deep within the projects unless they lived there.

It looked like a Young Jeezy concert was about to be held as they socialized and gave each other their signature handshake. Tiny pulled up in a customized Black Hummer with Tupac's song "Hail Mary" bumping out of the sound system. Tiny exited first. He walked around and opened the front door for Malachi, who exited the front passenger side wearing black gym shoes, a black sweat suit with a black wife beater under it. A black bandana held his dreads in a ponytail. Everyone noticed the platinum diamond chain hanging from his neck that reached his navel. A diamond and gold jaguar medallion dangled from the chain, representing the number one killer in the jungle. Two black diamonds represented the jaguar's eyes.

Tiny opened the back door and YaYa exited. A black bandana dangled from his left back pocket. He too wore all black, a T-shirt, jeans, and boots. He also wore a platinum diamond chain with a diamond and gold eagle medallion, which represented the spiritual bird.

Jerusalem exited from the same side as YaYa, wearing a black sweatshirt, jeans, and boots. A bandana was tied around his head like Tupac once wore. An all diamond chain hung from his neck with a huge lion's head that appeared to be roaring. Four huge diamonds sparkled from the fangs of the lion's mouth as well as the black diamonds that served as its eyes. The lion represented leader, one with courage and one that's fearless.

The warriors all moved out of the way as if the sea were parting. All eyes were on the four men who walked toward them. Jerusalem walked in front. Malachi, YaYa, and Tiny walked behind him toward the front of the warriors, who ranged in age from early teens to the mid-thirties.

Malachi ordered the warriors to form a single file line. The warriors raised their right arms and touched each other's shoulders with their right hand in order to form a perfect line. Once done, they all dropped their right hands.

The Black Warriors faced the east, and Jerusalem walked to the front. Malachi, YaYa, and Tiny placed themselves behind Jerusalem. They bent their elbows and brought their hands up at an angle. With the palm of their hands facing up and with each hand their pinky fingers touched the other hand. Their fingers touched one another without leaving an open gap. They bowed their heads as Jerusalem led them in prayer in Arabic.

"In the name of Allah, the most generous, the most merciful. All praises be to Allah, the cherisher and the sustainer of the universe. The generous and most merciful Lord of the day of judgment. Thee do we worship and thou aid we seek. Oh Allah, show us the straightway. The way of those who have earned thou grace and those whose portions are not wrath and who goes not astray. Amen."

Everyone repeated after Jerusalem, "Amen."

Jerusalem took his place to the back of his warriors.

YaYa stepped up and prayed in Arabic. "Allah, the one and only. The absolute. He begets not, nor is he begotten and none is like him. Amen."

Everyone repeated, "Amen."

YaYa walked to the back of the warriors and stood next to Jerusalem. Malachi stepped up and prayed in Swahili. "Allah, punish us not. If we forget or fall in error and lay not upon us a burden like that which you laid on those before us. Put not upon us a burden greater than we have strength to bear. Pardon us, grant us forgiveness, and have mercy upon us. For you're our patron, supporter, protector and helper. And give us victory over our enemies. Amen."

"Amen," Everyone repeated.

Malachi took his place beside Jerusalem and YaYa and screamed out to his warriors, "About face!"

All the warriors faced Jerusalem, Malachi, and YaYa. Jerusalem said, "May peace and blessings be upon you."

They responded in unison, "May peace and blessings be upon you also."

Jerusalem looked at the crowd of soldiers and said, "It's a new day. It's a new breed. We are that new breed. We are gangstas under a new law. We are all born gangstas because we are willing to jeopardize our bodies for what we believe in. We are the Black Senate. Anything that falls on top of us shall be turned to dust. Anything beneath us shall be crushed. We're living a life that we love. We're living the code of the streets. Triple L—Love, Life, and Loyalty."

"Our right arm represents love." Jerusalem held up his right arm. "We reach out to shake our brothers' hand in love." He held up his left arm.

"Our left arm represents loyalty. 'Cause when we hug our brother with our left arm, we're locked in loyalty."

"Our heads represent life–to transform into something productive in our community. We unify to build our own nation here in the ghetto. Because these devils won't allow us to form our government with them, so we'll form our own government here inside of America.

"It's death before dishonor. As long as we honor one another, nothing can stop us. My Black Warriors, together we're stronger than a thousand bulldozers. And God, He holds us. Now let us walk this path, and whoever walks in the opposite direction, let them feel our wrath. We're unified as one. Let nothing separate us. Let nothing discourage us. Let's remember our ancestors that came before us. Remember the blood, sweat, and tears of our ancestors and what they went through.

"But this is a new breed . . . the seeds of American slaves."

Every warrior screamed out, "Ahhhh."

Jerusalem called for Tiny, who walked up to him. "I want to christen you General of the Black Warriors. The second in command under Malachi," he said.

Baby Stone, a six year old, walked up with a black box in his hand. Jerusalem took the box from Baby Stone, opened it, and placed the medallion around Tiny's neck. "The gray black gorilla represents your characteristics of strength and power. I hope Allah blesses you to be this way until the day you die," he said.

Jerusalem turned and faced the crowd. "This is the beginning of a legacy. The Black Senate and y'all play a very important part. My black warriors under a new breed. Let's build our kingdom. The kingdom that is made for kings."

They shouted in unison, "Black Senate. Black Senate. Black Senate."

Many people were sitting in their window ledges watching the christening of the Black Senate take place. Soldiers, all dressed in black, could be seen as far as the eye could see. Young and old watched in silence and amazement as Jerusalem led a new breed of warriors into a new era. Everyone within eyeshot recognized that what they witnessed was something special and people would be talking about this day for years to come. Even the birds began to chirp as if they recognized Jerusalem was saying something powerful.

"Follow me and I will feed you and your family," Jerusalem said. "I will enforce my laws. No socializing with the enemy. No public intoxication. No disrespecting the elders."

Jerusalem, with his hand at his side and in military style paced back and forth as he spoke. "Protect our women and kids. No fighting one another in public 'cause they will view us as nothing but hoodlums. No killing one another unless it's been ordered by someone in command. No gambling without money being placed upfront. We must bathe at least once a day. We must dress presentable at all times. Your clothes must be washed and cleaned and wrinkle free. We must read two books a year."

Jerusalem made sure he made eye contact with as many of his soldiers as he could while talking. "We must rid our kingdom of all child molesters, women beaters, and rapists. These are my laws, and I will stand on them without budging. Now you're looking at the three kings of kings." Jerusalem looked in Malachi and YaYa's direction. "I will christen and place those worthy in higher positions. We're all brought here to rule, so let's be rulers. The Black Senate and the Black Warriors, from the cradle to the grave."

Baby Stone returned with three more boxes. He handed one to Malachi, Jerusalem, and YaYa. Malachi called out D-Dog's name and placed a medallion of a crescent moon and star around his neck and placed a matching ring on his right ring finger.

YaYa called out Mice's name and placed a medallion of a crescent moon and star around his neck with a matching ring on his right ring finger.

Jerusalem called up Cash and placed the same type of medallion and ring on him. "You three are lieutenants. Y'all report to me, Malachi, and YaYa directly. Y'all each will be given a project building and a project apartment that's already been furnished. Each will be given seven men of your choosing to be under your command. The Black Senate has been born."

With Malachi, YaYa, and Tiny close behind him, Jerusalem turned and walked back to the Black Hummer, confident The Black Senate would have a prosperous future, as long as no one rebelled and got out of order.

CHAPTER FIFTEEN

Seven months later . . .

The leaves from the trees were changing colors as the October breeze filled the air. Jerusalem, dressed in a black Armani suit, approached the front door of one of the apartments in the project. He held a bouquet of roses as he made his way to the seventh floor. Memories of him being a little boy flooded his mind.

A six-year-old Jerusalem walked out of his small bedroom into the hallway of the raggedy and roach infested apartment. He called out, "Mama, Mama." He was afraid to yell too loud just in case she was there and he didn't want to provoke her anger.

Her bedroom door was ajar. He walked to the door and peeked inside to see if she was in the bed, but the unmade bed was empty. There was no sign of his mother anywhere. Jerusalem was afraid to open the front door because the last time he did, she beat him and then lectured him about not going outside because she didn't want the people to be all up in her business.

He waited in the apartment by himself for several days without his mother returning. Hungry, Jerusalem walked into the dirty kitchen filled with dirty dishes in the sink. A rat ran across the kitchen counter startling him, but didn't make him afraid because he was used to sharing his space with rats.

Jerusalem opened the door of the refrigerator to empty shelves. The only thing the shelves bear was an empty jar of mayonnaise and molded bread. He took the bread and scrapped the mayonnaise out the jar. After eating, he was still hungry but not as much as before.

Pushing a chair near the sink, he climbed on top of it and turned the faucet on and water ran into a dirty glass. He drank the water to fulfill his thirst.

He heard the jiggling of keys and his mother coming through the front door. Anna Marie, thin and puffy eyed, with arms scarred with needle tracks. Her frail looking face was once a dark, black beauty queen before she fell victim to heroin. She yelled, "Jerusalem, what the fuck you doing?"

Jerusalem jumped out the chair and ended up dropping the glass and breaking it. She walked fully into the kitchen area. "Look what the fuck you done did."

"I was just getting some water, Mama." Jerusalem responded in a low voice.

"Get the broom and get this shit up."

As he picked up the glass, he cut his hand and blood dripped on the floor. She stood by him and said, "Look at what your stupid ass has done. Go to the bathroom and turn on the cold water and put your hand under the faucet."

Jerusalem ran to the bathroom and did as ordered.

She walked up behind him and yelled, "Look at what your dumb ass is doing. You're dripping blood all over my fucking floor! You's a dumb motherfucka. What is your ass doing up at this time of the night anyway?"

Jerusalem's little hand started to tremble as he tried to stop the bleeding. Tears rolled from Jerusalem's eyes as he listened to his mom rant on and on.

"I hate your little black ass. I wish I hadn't had you. You ain't shit, like your daddy wasn't shit and you ain't gone never be shit. You want something to cry about? Bring your ass here."

"I'm not crying, Mama," Jerusalem said.

"You going to sit in my fuckin' face and lie! What you call that running from your eyes?"

"My eyes just hurting, Mama." Jerusalem did his best to hold back the tears.

She walked up to Jerusalem. "You going to still sit and lie in my fucking face and tell me that your eyes is hurting and that's why you crying. You expect me to believe some bullshit like that?"

She slapped Jerusalem so hard he fell to the floor.

"I'm sorry, Mama. I'm not going to cry no more."

"Now, you admit you was crying. I'm a teach you about lying to me." She walked away and returned holding a leather strap.

Jerusalem knew what was about to happen. It had happened many times before. He stared straight ahead as Anna Marie swung the leather strap in his direction. It made instant contact, stinging his little legs. He knew if he moved a lot, it would prolong the abuse, so he took the pain and tried not to shed any tears. He couldn't hold back the water that flowed from his eyes.

It wasn't the physical pain that hurt him the most; it was the inner pain knowing that his mother didn't love him. Knowing that the unconditional love he had for Anna Marie was not reciprocated. He tried everything within his power to please his mother, but nothing was ever good enough. At six years old, young Jerusalem felt like life was hopeless.

Anna Marie ordered Jerusalem to get a wet cloth and to clean up the blood droppings as she followed him and continued to verbally and physically abuse him.

The following day, Jerusalem sat in the middle of the floor watching a hazy television. He could barely make out what was on the screen, but he could hear his favorite cartoon voices coming from the little speakers. His eyes darted up toward the door when he heard a knock. Anna Marie rushed from the bedroom to the front door. A tall, dark-skinned man wearing wrinkled slacks and run over alligator shoes with a matching wrinkled dressed shirt with a godfather hat tilted with a feather on the tip, walked in.

"Hi, Daddy," Anna Marie said with a smile on her face.

"Hi, baby girl. I got something major I want to discuss with you," Melvin said.

"Do you got something for me, baby?" She eased her body close to his.

"Damn, bitch. Can you give me time enough to take off my fucking hat?" He pushed past her as he walked further into the apartment.

Melvin ignored Jerusalem as he plopped down on the couch. He reached in his pocket and pulled out foil paper and a syringe. Anna Marie ran to the kitchen and got a spoon. She placed the heroin in the spoon and then placed the cigarette lighter underneath the spoon to melt down the heroin.

He took the syringe and inserted the heroin in the needle. Both freebased the heroin as if Jerusalem wasn't there. Jerusalem watched as they both nodded, experiencing the effect of the heroin. Minutes later, Melvin grabbed Anna Marie by the hand, led her to the bedroom, and closed the door.

Tired, Jerusalem got up, lay down on the worn out sofa, and fell asleep. In the middle of the night, Anna Marie awakened Jerusalem. "Jerusalem, get up and get dressed."

Melvin stood and stared at Jerusalem. With sleepy eyes, Jerusalem obeyed his mom. He saw some suitcases. When he entered his room, he noticed a plastic bag that contained the few items of clothes he owned.

Jerusalem looked in the drawer and noticed that they were all empty. He walked back to the trash bag and retrieved his blue jeans, socks, and sweatshirt to put on.

Anna Marie said, "You ready? Grab your coat."

She grabbed the trash bags and one of the suitcases. Melvin picked up the larger suitcase. All three exited the apartment. The wind chill that night was below zero causing Jerusalem's little body to shake as Melvin unlocked the door of his old beat up Cadillac.

"Get in the back, little nigga," Melvin said as he held the door open.

Jerusalem jumped in without daring to say a word.

Anna Marie slid in the front passenger seat as she held her coat tight around her frail body.

Jerusalem looked out the window as Melvin drove away from the only home he had known. He noticed Melvin looking at him in the rearview mirror. He shifted uncomfortably in the backseat.

Anna Marie yelled to Melvin. "Stop. This is it."

Melvin pulled over to the shoulder. Jerusalem looked at the homeless women, men, and kids under the bridge. Some were living in cardboard houses; some surrounded a burning trash barrel trying to keep warm from the blazing fire. Anna Marie exited the front door and opened the back door. Melvin popped the trunk, retrieved Jerusalem's trash bag of clothes, and passed it to Anna Marie.

She kneeled down to speak to Jerusalem. "Jerusalem, this is your new home."

Jerusalem repeated to Anna Marie in a shivering voice, "My new home?"

"Yes, Jerusalem."

"Are you coming with me?" he asked.

"No. You are going to be fine. You can't go with mommy. Melvin said you would just be in the way. I will come back and get you one day. Now take this five dollars. This is enough to get you something to eat with until I return."

Tears rolled down Jerusalem's eyes. "Don't leave me, Mommy. I don't like it here."

"Jerusalem, you'll be just fine. Now stop all that crying. Straighten up your face. Now, I told you I was coming back to get you. Go find you a nice warm spot up there with those nice people." She pointed in the opposite direction from where they stood.

Jerusalem pled one more time. "Mommy, please don't leave me."

Anna Marie ignored him. "Jerusalem, do what I told you. I don't have time to baby you right now."

Melvin walked back to the car. "Come on, Anna Marie. Bring your ass on. We already behind schedule. That little nigga going to be all right."

Anna Marie bent down and kissed Jerusalem on the cheek as she wiped the tears from her eyes from the guilt. She knew that she had no plans of ever seeing Jerusalem again. Jerusalem stared at his mom as he watched her get back into the car with Melvin. Anna Marie stared back at Jerusalem as the car pulled away. Jerusalem ran after the car and yelled out, "Don't leave me, Mama. I'm a be good. I'm not going to cry no more. I won't cry no more. I promise."

His words were unheard as Melvin drove away out of eyesight. His birth mother left him to fend for himself at the young tender age of six years old. It was hard for him to find a spot underneath the bridge because none of the other families would accept him, until he found his own little space that wasn't occupied.

Anna Marie cared more about her next high and pleasing Melvin more than she cared about raising her son. He wondered if other little boys had to endure the things he did. Back then, he would cry himself to sleep at night, but soon the tears dried up and turned his heart cold.

At six years old, Jerusalem adapted quickly to the homeless life. He learned to hustle for nickels and dimes by standing in front of stores begging for money from strangers. He stole out of various markets and fruit stands. Sometimes he would even sleep in an abandoned building or eat from the trashcans from the back of restaurants where they threw away their extra food.

Quickly he learned how to defend himself. Some of the food and other items that he would scramble across, the other homeless people would try to take it or steal from him. One old homeless man that they called Harry was the only one who didn't steal from him. Harry taught Jerusalem the ropes. He taught him about life but his foster mom taught him about compassion.

Jerusalem remembered the day he met his foster mom. He had been on the streets for a year. He was a brassy seven year old. Sherry Sims worked at one of the markets he would frequently visit and steal from. She would catch him stealing, but would never turn him in to the store owner. Instead, she would pay for the items that he stole.

Seeing Sherry Sims was the bright spot of Jerusalem's week. Sometimes Jerusalem would have money to buy some small items, but she would never charge him; instead, she would give him five or ten dollars during those times. One day he attempted to steal something and her store manager caught him. If she hadn't stepped in, he would have been sent to juvenile for sure.

After pleading with the store manager and agreeing to pay for the items, Jerusalem and Sherry's bond tightened. "Where's your mom?" Sherry asked him on that day. She noticed his clothes were unkempt and that he wasn't being taken care of properly.

"I don't have one," Jerusalem responded.

"Where are you staying? I get off in a few minutes so I can drop you off."

"I stay in different places."

Sherry read in between the lines and knew she could not let the cute little boy continue to fend for himself. She was a widow and she and her husband never had any kids. "Wait right here. I would love for you to eat dinner with me tonight."

The thought of a hot fresh meal was enough to make Jerusalem wait. Less than fifteen minutes later, Sherry clocked out and Jerusalem followed her to her old small two-door car. He hopped in the front and watched as the area that had become his home disappeared and she drove into an area known as the projects.

"Now, it's not much, but its home," she said as he followed her up the walkway into the projects. They took the stairs to the seventh floor because the elevator wasn't working. Jerusalem followed her inside the apartment.

Sherry said, "Wait right here and I'll be right back. I need to go ask my neighbor something."

Before leaving, she turned the television on a station playing cartoons. Jerusalem sat and watched the clear screen. Less than fifteen minutes later, she returned carrying some clothing. She said, "Why don't I go run you some bath water and then you can change into these clothes I got for you."

Jerusalem was amazed at the generosity of the woman who had become his guardian angel. While he bathed, Sherry cooked them a nice dinner. Being able to soak in the tub after living on the streets for a little over a year, felt heavenly to his seven-year-old body.

Sherry knocked on the door. "There's a brand new toothbrush that's never been opened. Look in the cabinet and it's yours to use."

Jerusalem took his time getting dressed. Although he knew the items weren't brand new, the underclothes and jeans and T-shirt felt brand new on his body. He opened the door holding his old dirty clothes.

Sherry said, "Let me get you a bag to put that in. Sit down at the table. Dinner will be ready shortly."

She asked, "What is your name?"

"My name is Jerusalem."

"That's it?"

"My name is Jerusalem Rasheed Williams."

"That's a beautiful name for a beautiful young boy."

Sherry poured him a glass of lemonade and handed it to him. Jerusalem drank the first glass quickly and she refilled it.

She sat across from Jerusalem. "Jerusalem, I want you to come and stay with me. It's such a big world out there for such a little boy. It can get dangerous at times. I know you've seen many things over the years after your mother left you, or even before your mother left you. It doesn't mean your mother didn't love you. Maybe she just fell victim to some type of addiction, and it makes mothers act a certain way, or do things they wouldn't normally do—under normal circumstances. I want you to stay here with me for a couple of weeks and after then, I have a friend that works for social services and you might have to stay there for a little while, until I go through the proper procedure to be able to keep you. I promise you that everything will work out fine. You just have to trust me. I want to help you."

Jerusalem just nodded and responded, "Okay."

They ate dinner and the next three weeks was like heaven to Jerusalem. She provided a safe place and a home cooked meal every day. Sherry even bought him brand new tennis shoes and clothes. She was the most generous, sweetest, nicest person he had ever known in his short life.

The opening of the front door snapped Jerusalem back into the present day.

Sherry stood on the other end of the door staring at Jerusalem in surprise. Tears filled her eyes as she reached her arms out to him, and he hugged her while holding the roses behind her back. Neither of them wanted to break the tight embrace. Tears rolled down her cheeks. "I missed you so much, Jerusalem Rasheed Williams. I knew you were home. What took you so long to come and see me?"

He handed her the bouquet of roses. "Mama Sherry, these are for you?"

"Thank you, baby. Oh, these are beautiful."

Jerusalem walked in the two-bedroom apartment, and it was just as he remembered. He looked at Sherry and said, "Mama Sherry, I came to take you with me."

CHAPTER SIXTEEN

Jerusalem's black stretch limousine pulled up to the security gate. The bodyguard recognized the car. He hit a button and the gate opened. The bodyguard was part of his personal security staff that consisted of seven bodyguards, all members of the Black Senate. They remained on the premises at all times. Their duties varied. Someone was always monitoring the state of the art security system. There were hidden cameras throughout the multiple acre property.

The driver continued and pulled around into the long circular driveway behind the fleet of luxury cars. A huge golden lion statue was on each side of the stairs leading up to the mansion. The black male driver exited the front, went around, and held the door opened as Jerusalem and Sherry exited. The sixty-year-old Sherry stared in amazement and said, "Jerusalem, this is so beautiful. Look at the flowers. How many bedrooms does it have?"

Jerusalem smiled and responded, "I'll let you count them. This is all for you, Mama Sherry."

When they reached the top of the stairs, a black door attendant dressed in a black suit opened the front door. "Greetings, Mr. Williams and also greetings to you, Ms. Sims."

"Thank you," she responded as she entered the two-story mansion.

"My name is James," he said.

"Nice to meet you."

They entered the foyer with a clear view of a spiral golden staircase. Maria was part of a full-time staff that Jerusalem had at his disposal. Maria was the upstairs maid. He had a downstairs maid, a butler, a cook, a gardener, and hired men to take care of his stable of horses. The ten-bedroom mansion also had servant quarters where his live-in help resided.

The rest of the household staff appeared in the foyer and made their introductions. "Hi, my name is Charles, and I'm the chef on staff. I have a three-course meal prepared for you and Mr. Williams this evening, starting off with an appetizer and my special dessert." The mid-fifty-year-old cook was dressed in a black chef's uniform. Charles had cooked in some of the most expensive restaurants around the world.

"Thank you. Nice to meet you," Sherry responded.

Dressed in a black and white knee-length maid uniform, a woman in her late forties said, "My name is Sonya."

Sherry responded, "Nice to meet you."

Another woman dressed like Sonya, who was also in her late forties, greeted Sherry. "Ms. Sims, I'm Maria. Anything you need or want, let me know. Dinner will be ready shortly."

"Thank you, Maria."

After the introductions, Jerusalem said, "Mama Sherry, let me show you to your room."

Jerusalem watched Sherry count the rooms as they passed. He opened the door to her room. "You have your own suite at your disposal."

Tears of joy ran down Sherry's cheeks as she got a clear view of her new room. The queen-sized bed was covered with a pink and white silk comforter and several big fluffy pillows adorned the top.

"Baby, this is beautiful."

"Wait until you see your bathroom," Jerusalem said as he walked to the bathroom door and held it opened.

"A Jacuzzi in the bathroom! I've died and gone to heaven," she said, walking on the white porcelain floor and picking up several items on the golden sink before placing them back down.

"You're a queen, and it's about time you live like one," Jerusalem said.

"Thank you, baby. You don't know how happy you've made me."

Jerusalem led her to the huge walk-in closet. "You should have everything you need, but whenever you get the urge to shop, you have a driver at your disposal."

He moved out of the way so Sherry could see the closet filled with clothes and shoes in all colors and styles. "How did you remember my size?"

"A lucky guess. I know you like eating healthy, so I know your size wouldn't have changed that drastically."

"Lucky for you, you're right. Because these look like some expensive outfits and what would you have done if they were the wrong size?"

"Threw them away and bought you a closet full of more

designer clothes in your correct size."

She went from rack to rack. Sherry had lived in the projects for nearly half of her life. For Jerusalem to be able to provide a comfortable life for Sherry and to see her smile and happy filled Jerusalem's heart with joy. He could never repay her for the love and comfort she provided him ever since she found him homeless on the streets.

"I need to make a few phone calls, and then I'll meet you downstairs for dinner," Jerusalem said.

"If I can find the dining room. This place is so huge, I might get lost," Sherry said.

Jerusalem laughed. "Just yell if you get lost. I'll come and find you."

He left Sherry and walked downstairs to his office, stepping on the black plush carpet that had a golden Black Senate symbol in the middle. He sat in his big black leather chair trimmed in gold behind his ebony wooden desk. The entire office was decorated in black and gold from the bookshelves to the frames of the paintings that hung from the walls. The bookshelves were filled with books by black authors and scholars. *From Niggas to Gods*, *The Willie Lynch Letter*, and *Message to the Black Man* were three books sitting on his desk that he was currently reading.

He picked up the black cordless phone and called YaYa. "Peace and blessings be upon you," Jerusalem said.

"Peace and blessing be upon you also," YaYa responded.

"Did you set up that meeting for me with the Italians?"

"Yes, it's tomorrow night at seven."

"That's a good time."

"You sure you want to meet with them alone?" YaYa asked.

"Yes, I'm sure. I need to make this business deal. Coming with more than myself would make them feel like I'm afraid or something. Italians are wise men. They peek and size weakness. I want them to respect my courage."

"All right. I guess you know what you're doing. We've been making a lot of money these last few months, and I don't think they're happy about that."

"Maybe after tomorrow I can put a smile on Gino's face. He and the Deluchi family should be real happy."

"Is Mama Sherry there yet?" YaYa asked.

"Yes. I just picked her up about an hour ago."

"I know she was happy to see you. 'Cause you know she loves her some Jerusalem."

"I love her just as much. The only real mother I have ever known."

"It gets no sweeter than Mama Sherry. She's like an angel sent from heaven, isn't she?"

"Yes, indeed. She deserves the world. And I plan on giving it to her. If it wasn't for her, I don't know what would have happened to me. She saved my life. I can never thank her enough."

YaYa responded, "I know."

"You and Khadijah are getting pretty serious, huh? I know you've been seeing a lot of her lately."

"Yes, she's one of a kind. I must admit. Even though we haven't been intimate, I think I'm falling in love with her and Raheem. They both have become a big part of my life. But I'm living this lie. She still thinks that I work for the electric company. I'm afraid to tell her I'm part of the Black Senate because of how she feels about her father. That's why I haven't pushed the issue about sleeping with her, because I don't want her to think I lied and played games with her just to get in her panties. I know if I expect this relationship to go any further that I'm going have to tell her soon."

Jerusalem said, "Everything will work itself out. If it's meant to be, then it will happen. Just let nature take its course. When the time is right, you'll have to tell her. That's my man's daughter, and I know you have a beautiful heart, YaYa. You would be good for her if everything works itself out. I will talk to you after the meeting tomorrow. Peace," Jerusalem said right before hanging up the phone.

Someone knocked on the office door. Jerusalem pressed a button under his desk and the door opened. Mama Sherry stood in the center of the doorway. "Oh my goodness! This is a beautiful office. The whole house is unbelievable. Jerusalem, come and show me around."

"You look beautiful, Mama Sherry. Do you like the clothes that I bought you?"

"Yes, Jerusalem. They are gorgeous. It was so hard for me to pick out what I wanted to wear. I eventually decided to pick this beautiful blue floral dress. I feel like Cinderella." She then did a slight spin. Her face glowed, and she looked like she was in her mid-forties, a version of the actress Angela Bassett.

"I got another surprise for you. Close your eyes." Jerusalem opened his desk drawer and pulled out a black velvet jewelry box.

He walked up to her and opened the box. "Now open your eyes."

Jerusalem stood with a wide smile showing his pearly white teeth and dimples. Sherry looked down at his hand and covered her mouth in awe. "Is this for me?"

"Who else would it be for?"

"Oh, Jerusalem! I've never seen anything like this."

"Let me put it on you." Jerusalem took the white pearls out of the box and placed them around her neck.

"I feel like I'm living in a dream. Is this real? Is this day really happening?"

"Yes, Mama. This is all real. Come on mama; let me show you the grounds."

Jerusalem led her to the back of the house. They exited the patio door that led to an Olympic-size swimming pool surrounded by several waterfalls. A tennis court and a nine-hole golf course were on opposite sides of the pool. Behind the tennis court was a full-size basketball court. A guesthouse the size of a middle class family home was also on the premises. Jerusalem helped her up on the golf cart. They rode around and toured the rest of the land. To her, everything was so green and colorful. The magnificent landscaping looked like it could have come out of the pages of *Better Homes and Gardens*.

The black stallions galloped along the fence as he drove them around the ranch area. She looked around in amazement at all of the open space. Jerusalem knew she loved horses, and she had always dreamed about being able to ride a black stallion.

"They are beautiful," Sherry said.

"They are trained to ride. You can ride them anytime you feel like it."

"Will you come and ride with me tomorrow?" she asked.

"Yes, Mama. We can ride before I have to go to this business meeting."

"That would be great."

"Come on. Let's head back home. I'm pretty sure dinner's ready by now," Jerusalem said as he turned the golf cart around and headed back to the mansion.

He led Sherry into the living room and said, "Give me thirty minutes and then we can eat dinner."

Thirty minutes later, Jerusalem entered the living room wearing a black tuxedo with a black bow tie. He held his arm out. Sherry wrapped her hand around it, and they walked into the dining room. In the center of the room was a long dining room table that could sit twenty people. Tonight, there were only two place settings, one for Jerusalem at the front of the table and Sherry on his right hand side.

Maria walked in carrying several appetizers on a silver tray. She placed the food in front of each of them.

"Jerusalem, this is all beautiful. I can't stop saying it enough. I always told you that you were special. That you would be able to achieve anything you wanted to. You were always my prince. I reminded you of that many times. I knew you would have a hard challenge ahead of you. It would be hard for you to rise from the concrete jungle that you were brought up in. But I had confidence in you. You're a very intelligent man. I would never ask you about your business. Just be careful Jerusalem. 'Cause I don't want this . . . if it's going to cause me to lose you. But, I know God has always been with you. Because you made it through a lot of trials and tribulations at an early age. You've been through so much. You deserve anything good that comes to you. I did everything I could to raise you right and to make sure you had everything that you needed and most of everything that you wanted. But I knew raising you in the projects, that the streets would one day grab you . . . because you were thrown into the streets at such an early age. But you made it through the fire, baby. And success looks so good on you. You look like the king that you are. Look at my prince; he's grown up to be a king."

Jerusalem smiled, knowing that he had gotten his mama's approval. Knowing that Mama Sherry was not judging him eased his conscience, and he would be able to carry on this mission. As they finished their appetizers of mozzarella sticks with marinara sauce and small chicken fingers with blue cheese dressing, Charles brought them their three-course meal that consisted of a Caesar salad, Peking duck with rice pilaf, and strawberry short cake. They continued to eat and enjoy their evening together. Mama Sherry laughed and cried with Jerusalem throughout the evening as they reminisced about the good times and the not so good times in the past.

CHAPTER SEVENTEEN

After an early morning horseback ride with Mama Sherry, Jerusalem and she ate lunch and talked a little more. Later on that evening, Jerusalem prepared himself for the meeting with Gino, the head of the Deluchi Family. Jerusalem pulled up in front of the five-star Italian restaurant. Wearing a black vest, shirt, and slacks, he exited the black Bentley coupe and handed the valet his keys.

Jerusalem noticed the sign that said "Closed until 9:00 p.m." on the door. He entered the restaurant. A heavyset Italian man greeted him at the door. "Mr. Jerusalem, Mr. Deluchi is expecting you. But first you have to be patted down."

Once Jerusalem raised his hands, the man frisked him. He then led Jerusalem to a table located at the back of the restaurant. Jerusalem was aware of the mob figures spread throughout the room. They all stared at him as he approached Gino's table.

"Good evening, Mr. Deluchi," Jerusalem said.

"Good evening, Mr. Jerusalem. Join me," Gino responded.

Jerusalem pulled out the seat directly across from Gino, who had dark black hair and was dressed in a custom-made gray Italian suit. The waiter walked up to the table. "Bring us a bottle of wine and two plates of spaghetti and meatballs with garlic bread," Gino said.

"No, I'm fine," Jerusalem said.

"Are you sure? Fredo makes the best spaghetti and meatballs in the family. His sauce is magnificent."

"No disrespect, Mr. Deluchi. I don't have much of an appetite right now.

"Just bring the bottle of wine and bring me a plate of spaghetti."

The heavyset Italian mob boss pulled out a Cuban cigar. He used the cigar clipper, clipped the end of the cigar, and placed it in his mouth. He pulled out a lighter from his pocket and lit the cigar, taking several pulls from the cigar before it was finally lit. He blew smoke from his mouth and leaned back in his chair and looked at Jerusalem. "When I heard that you wanted to meet with me, I was very surprised. I've been hearing a lot of talk in the wind about you and the Black Senate. I heard that you've built one powerful organization. That you're bringing in millions of millions of dollars in your line of work. That's why I'm very surprised to see you sitting across from me. And I'm more surprised to see you here alone."

"Why is that?" Jerusalem asked as he looked Gino directly in his eyes. "Do I have anything to be concerned about?"

Gino said, "A man in your position and with your power and making as much money as you're making, should always be concerned. You have many greedy men that would love to bring your empire to an end. Because there will be more money in their pockets and more territories for them."

"Well, do I look worried?" Jerusalem asked. "I'm not caring about what people are plotting. 'Cause if one lived in fear every day, it wouldn't be living. He would just be waiting to die."

"You right, Jerusalem. I heard you and the Haitian family are doing a lot of business together. How's that business relationship going?"

"That's what I'm here to talk to you about. It's not going well."

"How can I help?" Gino asked. "What seems to be the problem?"

"Mr. Deluchi, the Haitians have decent quality but it's not worth the prices. I'm buying at least a hundred kilos a month from them. They refuse to go down on the prices. They have me paying a hundred thousand on each kilo. I only can step on it once without messing up the quality of the product."

"That's a lot of money trading hands," Gino said. "Those Haitians, they have always been known to do a lot of bad business. They show no mercy to anyone other than their own. That Haitian Black, that son of a bitch, excuse my language, Jerusalem."

"No problem," Jerusalem said.

"He's a greedy, disrespectful bastard. He has no respect for anyone. How could you ever do good business with someone with so much lack of respect and with a heart so full of greed? He will never let you get in a position to buy from his supplier. I hope you weren't thinking that was going to happen with an underhanded lowlife like Haitian Black."

"I respect his ruthlessness," Jerusalem said. "Mercy's for the weak. I'm aware of his greed, but at that time, he was the only one that could handle my orders."

"Jerusalem, why are you just now coming to me?"

"Well, with all due respect, Mr. Deluchi, I knew that when I did come to you, I had to come correct. I know you are a businessman and timing is important. Someone always told me there's a proper time and place for everything."

"I like you, Jerusalem. When my family moved here from Italy forty years ago, when I was about eight years old, I watched my father work hard to provide for us. He taught me about dedication and responsibility and most of all, he taught me about family values. At that point, I dedicated myself to build my own family structure. I realize with a lot of hard work and devotion here in America, you can reach the unreachable. You can achieve your dreams. I started as a son of a butcher to becoming the head of my own family and sitting as chairman over the other five families. Surrounded by loyal friends and honest business partners that I've found over the years. Forty years later, look at me now. I have parking lots all over Chicago, five-star restaurants from here to New York, my own casino in Vegas. I've also made many enemies throughout my years, but I never shitted on no one unless they deserved it.

"You're a very smart and wise young man. Your future in this line of work looks bright. You can last a long time if you stay loyal to the right people and be careful of who toes you step on as you walk up the ladder. Calculate your moves very wisely. I did business personally with one of your kind, he was a very wise man, and we did very good business. I heard he was murdered in the penitentiary. He was a very good friend of mine. Kaleef and I did business together for a very long time."

Jerusalem knew through Kaleef that he was connected with

the mob. Gino, the head of the Deluchi family, was a fair man when it came to doing business with Blacks, but would never let them rise above the Italian mafia. But in Jerusalem's heart, he knew one way or another that he would.

"So Jerusalem, how can I help you?" Gino asked.

The waiter came back to the table with the wine and Gino's plate of food. The waiter filled Gino's glass with red wine. He walked near Jerusalem holding the bottle of wine. Jerusalem held his hand out and said, "No, I'm fine."

"Have a glass of wine with me, Jerusalem," Gino said. "It's Chardonnay 1868 straight from my personal wine cellar."

"With all due respect, Mr. Deluchi."

"Please, call me Gino."

"With all due respect, Gino, I'm not much of a drinker."

"Okay. I can respect that."

Gino tucked the white napkin under his collar around his neck. Jerusalem watched Gino eat from a huge platter of spaghetti and other side dishes. The food was enough to feed three or four people.

In between bites, Gino said, "So how can I help you today, Mr. Jerusalem?"

"With all due respect, Gino, just call me Jerusalem."

Gino nodded. "So how can I help you today, Jerusalem?"

"I'm looking for a supplier that I can depend on at least once a month with better quality and a fair price. I will guarantee to buy the same amount every month on the same date."

Gino took his napkin from around his neck and wiped sauce from his mouth. He looked at Jerusalem. "If I decided to do business with you, could you guarantee to buy two hundred kilos from me once a month at a price?" Gina paused as if calculating a figure in his mind. "Ninety thousand a key. I will guarantee a safe shipment delivered wherever you feel is convenient for you."

Jerusalem did the math in his head and knew that he would be saving two million dollars and a guaranteed safe shipment. Jerusalem stood and reached out his hand to Gino. "A deal."

"You know that Haitian Black is not going to be pleased with this negotiation because we cut him out and he would be losing a lot of money. That would make anyone vengeful."

"Just let me worry about that, Gino," Jerusalem replied. "I thank you for your time, your kind words and your wisdom. I hope you enjoy the rest of the evening."

Deluchi called out to Tony. "Show Jerusalem out." He looked at Jerusalem. "You enjoy the rest of your evening and here's to a lucrative relationship." Gino stood at the table and took Jerusalem's hand to seal the deal and their friendship.

Jerusalem turned and followed Tony toward the entrance door. The valet pulled his car up in front of the restaurant. Jerusalem looked back at the restaurant as he got in the car and saw Tony turn the sign over and it read "Open for Business."

As Jerusalem pulled away, he immediately got on his cell phone with YaYa and said, "All is well."

III

DESTINY

CHAPTER EIGHTEEN

The young and carefree twenty-one-year-old Egypt Niambi Toure stepped off her father's private jet into the cool Chicago air. The knee-length mink coat flew open as she walked down the stairway and revealed an aquamarine beaded embellished frock with an Indian motif. Three huge diamonds adorned her brown four-inch heels.

Onlookers watched the ebony beauty grace Midway airport as if she were a superstar. Many mistook her as the actress Gabrielle Union since they had similar features. She had the style and grace of a model. Walking ahead of her was a man she despised. Etheria Frances was her fiancé. Wearing an Italian suit and barking orders to one of the men that stood nearby, Etheria barely showed Egypt any attention.

Egypt tapped her foot impatiently as she waited for Etheria to finish his rant. She had lived and travelled all over, but Chicago, regardless of the time of year, was still one of her favorite cities in the world. She couldn't wait to be dropped off at her Lakeshore Condo with the view of Lake Michigan.

Etheria stayed in a hotel suite whenever he was in town, which gave Egypt a reprieve from his probing hands. If her father, Geoffrey Toure, King of a southern African country hadn't insisted that Etheria come along with her so he could handle some business for him, she would have made the trip to Chicago alone.

The limousine driver held the door open as she slipped in the back with Etheria sliding in right behind her.

"What's wrong now?" Etheria asked Egypt.

She rolled her eyes and turned her head to look out the window, ignoring him.

Etheria placed his hand on top of her arm. "Don't be like that. Chicago's one of your favorite cities. Why all the frowns?"

She shifted in her seat and turned her head to face him. "If you really must know, the problem, Etheria, is, this is the first time you've actually said more than two words to me. You've been on the phone or your laptop ever since we got on the plane. And it's a fourteen hour flight."

"Egypt, you know the pressure I'm under. Your father has me running this part of the business, and in this line of work, play is not an option."

"Whatever. Just drop me off at my condo, and if you can fit me into your busy schedule, I guess I'll see you before you head back."

Etheria knew not to say anything else to Egypt when she was in that type of mood. If she weren't his boss's daughter, he probably would have let her know who was running their relationship; instead, he bit his tongue. Etheria needed Egypt to be his wife so when Geoffrey died, it would be a sure way in for Etheria to take his place. He smiled as he thought of his future.

He would do whatever he could to hold on to Egypt.

Egypt pulled out her cell phone and sent a quick text message to her best friend, Sherena Johnson, to alert her of her arrival. Egypt met Sherena several years ago when her father brought her to Chicago. She was the daughter of a prominent attorney in the area and they hit it off. They had been friends ever since.

The limousine driver pulled up in front of the Lakeshore condominium. Egypt inhaled the air as the driver and Etheria followed her. "Welcome back, Ms. Toure," the doorman, Bill said.

"Thank you, Bill. It's good to be back," she responded.

"Everything is like you like it," Bill assured her.

"Thank you. Can you have flowers brought up every morning?" she asked as he pressed the button for the elevator.

"Yes, ma'am. A fresh set of flowers will be brought up every morning."

"Thank you, Bill." Egypt retrieved a hundred dollar bill out of her small clutch and handed it to him.

Etheria didn't seem too happy about that transaction. Egypt didn't care. He ran her father's business, not her. She held her key in her hand as the elevator went to the top floor. "You can just put the bags right there." She pointed to a spot in the living room as soon as Etheria and the driver walked in.

"Give me fifteen minutes and I'll be down," Etheria said to the driver.

Egypt walked to the window and pressed a button. It was still daylight, so when the curtains opened she had a clear view of the lake. "I love it here," she said aloud.

Etheria walked up behind her and placed his arms around her

waist. "It is beautiful, but not as beautiful as you are."

"Thanks." Egypt softened her stance a little.

"Let's meet for dinner around eight. I'll have my driver come pick you up."

"Maybe we should eat in," Egypt suggested.

"You're too beautiful for me to keep you hidden. Let's enjoy this beautiful city together."

Egypt would probably get tired of being in so she agreed. "I'll be ready by eight."

"I have some business I need to take care of, so if you need me before then, leave me a message, and I will get back with you as soon as possible."

"Business." Egypt sighed. "Just once I would love it if you would put me before your business."

"I'm working hard so when we get married, you can continue to live the lifestyle you're accustomed to living," Etheria responded.

"Whatever. I guess you better get going. Don't want you late for your business meeting."

Etheria walked away, leaving Egypt looking out the window and feeling neglected.

***

Five minutes later, Etheria slipped in the back of the limousine and made a phone call to Haitian Black. "I'm here. I'll meet you at the spot in two hours."

The limousine driver dropped him off at the hotel and Etheria, with his hired men, got in several luxury cars and headed to the other side of Chicago. Etheria, dressed in a long black leather coat, exited the car right after his bodyguard.

They walked to what appeared to be an abandoned building. Haitian Black, along with his right hand man, stood at the end of the walkway. His long dreads covered part of his face until he used his hand to move them out the way. One of the Haitians on the inside raised the garage door when he saw Etheria and Haitian Black from the surveillance cameras. They entered an elevator and went upstairs where they walked into a well-furnished office.

Two half-naked Haitian females, one light-skinned and one dark-skinned, entered.

"Would you like a drink, mon?" Haitian Black asked Etheria.

"Yes, thank you."

Haitian Black held up two fingers, and then sat at his desk while his bodyguard sat at the bar. Etheria sat opposite him while his bodyguard stood by the door. The light-skinned woman went around the bar.

A dark-skinned woman retrieved their drinks from the female bartender, then walked over and gave the two men their drinks. "Will that be all?" she asked Haitian Black.

"For now," he replied.

She walked back over to the bar and Etheria couldn't take his eyes off her. Haitian Black opened the drawer, removed an already rolled blunt and began to light it and smoke it. Etheria said, "Business has slowed down for you, Haitian Black. What seems to be the problem? For the last few months, we haven't been getting our money on time, and King Geoffrey is not pleased. He sent me here to find out the problem. He's thinking about cutting your order in half."

"Well, mon, I've lost one of my main customers. He once

was buying a hundred kilos a month from me, mon. The bumbaclot won't even return my phone calls. I think he's found another connection and has cut me out."

Etheria said, "How could you lose a customer so valuable? We're giving you the purest heroin in the city. You have to be stepping on it more than you have to and bringing down the quality of our product. I specifically told you, if you stepped on it more than five times, that you'll ruin the quality. The heroin is so pure that you can step on it at least four times and still have the best quality in the city. Greed has been the downfall of many empires. For you to lose one of your number one customers, he had to be dissatisfied. You had to be stepping on it too many times or overcharging him or both."

Haitian Black responded, "No mon, that is not the case here. This Jerusalem has built an empire called the Black Senate. They cornered the market, buying up all of the abandoned buildings and real estate that they can get their hands on, taking over most of the territories around Chicago, and making it hard for me to operate. I'm losing my customers on a daily basis, and the only one that I know could supply them other than myself is Jerusalem and the Black Senate or the Italians. I think Jerusalem has combined with one of the Italian families and that's who's supplying him."

Etheria took one swig of his drink. "This is bad business. Not only for you, but for us too. If you want to keep our partnership, you're going to have to fix this problem, or we will no longer be able to do business with you. And I will have to search for another connection here."

Haitian Black pulled from his blunt and took a sip of his drink. "Give me a couple of weeks, and I will have this problem taken care of."

Etheria looked Haitian Black directly in the eyes. "Yes, you need to do that as quickly as possible because we're both losing money. Who is this Jerusalem character that you mentioned?"

"He is the head of the Black Senate. With him and two other bumbaclots that go by the names of Malachi and YaYa. With Malachi acting as the enforcer and YaYa's the second in command. But I believe that all three share equal positions in their organization. They are calling themselves the Three Kings, and I believe Jerusalem is trying to build his own nation inside of America, calling themselves the Black Senate with an army of Black Warriors. And they have expanded rapidly, but I will tear their empire down."

Etheria placed his drink in front of him. "That's definitely a good idea. 'Cause they are definitely destroying your empire. 'Cause I see what you have built is starting to crumble. I'm starting to have a certain type of respect for this King Jerusalem. His tactics are very wise. Because that's how you destroy an empire, you destroy the economic system. And that seems exactly like what he's doing to you."

Rage spread across Haitian Black's face. His forehead scrunched together as he took another drink. "Give me a couple of weeks and business will be back to normal."

"Okay, two weeks is all you have. After then, if things haven't changed, you'll have to search for a new connection."

"What are your plans for the rest of the evening, mon?" Haitian Black asked.

"I had plans to have dinner with my fiancée, but looking at your beautiful guests, I'm starting to make other plans."

He and Haitian Black smiled at one another. "Take either

one of them or take them both. Just when you finish, return them safely," Haitian Black said.

"That I will do," Etheria replied.

***

Egypt was glad that Etheria cancelled dinner. It gave her the opportunity to meet up with Sherena. As usual, Sherena made a grand entrance into the five-star restaurant late. Egypt stood up from her seat at the table and greeted Sherena with a hug and an air kiss. "I've missed you, bestie," Sherena said as she slipped into the chair at the table.

A waitress walked up to their table. "What would you ladies like to drink?"

Sherena ordered first. "Bring us a bottle of Krug Clos d'Ambonnay 1995. It's not every day I get to hang out with my best friend."

She pulled out her Black Visa card and laid it on the table. She noticed the waitress' eyes widen, probably anticipating a huge tip.

The waitress soon returned to their table. She popped the cork on the expensive bottle of wine and poured each lady a glass.

"Thank you," Sherena and Egypt each said to the waitress.

Once she left the table, Sherena and Egypt took the time to get caught up.

"Egypt, you *must* check out this club before you leave. It's where everybody that's anybody goes," Sherena said.

"You know I'm always looking for a good party."

"Club Royalty is grand, but the atmosphere is so that you can relax and let your hair down."

"So when are you going to take me there, my friend?" Egypt asked.

"This weekend is the best time to go."

"I'm hoping Etheria will be gone by then, so that's perfect."

The waitress came back to their table and took their food order.

"I don't see why you won't tell your father you don't want to marry him."

"I've tried, but what King Geoffrey wants, he gets. Not even his princess can make him change his mind. He feels that Etheria will make a good son-in-law."

"Etheria is a pompous asshole if you ask me. You can do much better."

"Well, regardless, I'm going to have as much fun as I can while I'm here. I'm sure you're going to guarantee that."

The twenty-one-year-old Sherena held up her glass. "Forget Etheria. Let's get this party started."

Egypt tapped Sherena's glass and then downed her drink in one big gulp.

CHAPTER NINETEEN

Malachi fucked Kem Su doggy style feverishly. Kem Su screamed out in pain and pleasure. He never took the time out to take off his diamonds as he pounded Kem Su from the back. His diamond chain with the jaguar medallion swung back and forth.

Kem Su screamed out in Korean, her native language, as Malachi went as deep as he could inside of her dripping wet pussy. She orgasmed like she had never experienced before. Her entire body shivered. Malachi flipped her over on her back, handling her rough like Kem Su loved it. He placed both of her legs on his shoulders. His dreads hung down covering his face, making him look beast-like as he rammed his dick inside of her.

Grabbing both of her wrists, he placed them over her head as he pounded her hard, with a steady pace. It was hard for Kem Su to handle a man well-endowed like Malachi, but she loved every moment. Malachi was like a god in her eyes, and she worshipped him as such. To Malachi she was more than just a piece of pussy, but he wouldn't let her know that. He enjoyed the time they shared.

Malachi looked down in Kem Su's slanted eyes. Her long, dark brown hair spread across the bed. Kem Su's skin tone was darker than most Koreans. It was one of the things Malachi loved about her. He also liked her peach sized breasts. Malachi gently kissed her brown nipples. He then pulled out of her and began to lick her well-shaped body. Kem Su breathed heavily as Malachi licked the walls of her shaved pussy. He felt her legs tighten when he sucked on her pearl tongue.

Kem Su arched her back as she began to cum again and moaned, "Oooh, Malachi" repeatedly. Malachi came up for air and kissed her on her reddish, full-sized lips to let her taste her sweetness.

She reached down and grabbed Malachi's stiff dick to guide him back in her. He stroked her until he started to feel himself on the edge of reaching his climax, and he went as deep as he could possibly reach. Feeling Malachi thrust inside of her, was a signal for Kem Su to spread her legs as wide as she possibly could, enduring the pain and pleasure Malachi's sword was giving her.

Malachi released his entire fountain of love inside of her. They both lay there breathing heavily trying to regain control. Malachi rolled over slowly and headed to the showers.

Kem Su adored Malachi and his tattoo—a jaguar seated on a throne that covered his back with 'King of Killers' written in huge letters spread across his upper back.

She followed him and before he could turn on the shower, she beat him to the draw. "Let me do this for you, baby," she said. "Let me wash you. You are my king. Let me treat you like royalty."

Kem Su took off Malachi's diamonds from his fingers,

placed them on the bathroom sink on top of a white towel, and began to take off his diamond chain from around his neck. Malachi grabbed her hand. "No, this is sacred. Nobody touches this but me."

"Okay, baby. I just wanted to help."

"Malachi took off his diamond piece and placed it on the towel with the rest of the jewelry.

She let Malachi enter the shower first. Then she entered behind him. He let the water run all over his chiseled body as she began to lather and wash him.

"Turn around, baby," she said.

He turned slowly and stared into Kem Su's eyes. She stared back as long as she could before dropping her head. Malachi's fierce stare would intimidate a bear if the beast looked too long. She rubbed her fingers across the tattoo across his stomach that read, "Warlord."

As she washed over the tattoos of bullet holes that covered his entire stomach, she noticed his dick rising again. Her heart pounded with excitement. She planted soft kisses on his chest. Malachi turned her around and she placed her hand against the shower walls as he entered her. He planted small kisses on the back of her neck and made love to her gentler than he had before.

They finished making love and got dressed. Minutes later, they sat on the sofa in Kem Su's huge condo. She sat closely to Malachi as he rolled a blunt. Kem Su said, "Baby, I have everything set up for you tonight."

Malachi replied in his deep baritone voice, "What time?".

"They will meet you at the warehouse on Forty-Third Street

at midnight."

"Were they able to fill my full order?"

"Yes, baby. They were able to get everything you told me to ask for."

She recited the list. "One hundred AK-47 assault rifles, all with extra clips and ammunition. Two hundred nine-millimeters, automatic with extra clips and ammunition. Ten rocket launchers with five extra missiles apiece, a hundred forty-five semi-automatic with extra clips and hollow points, two hundred hand grenades, fifty impenetrable bulletproof vests, and one hundred twelve-gauge Mossberg pumps.

"That sounds about right," Malachi responded.

"I've already paid them half up front," she said. "You'll just have to pay them the other half tonight on the delivery."

Without saying a word, Malachi kissed her gently on the lips to say thank you.

"Baby, how's Club Royalty coming along? I think it's a nice investment. I've been hearing that it's the place to be. That a lot of the celebrities, athletes, movie stars, rappers and singers and the top street hustlers are feeling your club."

Malachi responded, "It's filled to capacity every time the door's open. I'm throwing my man Jerusalem a surprise party this weekend. I want you to come and be my guest."

"I wouldn't miss it for the world. I'm here for you whenever you need me. I would fly across the world, if you need me to. I love you, Malachi, with every inch of me. Every part of my mind, body, and soul belongs to you and you only."

Malachi placed a blunt into his mouth, lit it, and inhaled. He turned and stared at Kem Su. It took all the strength that Kem Su had in her not to turn her head.

Finally Malachi spoke after a few seconds. "You know those are powerful words that you are saying to me."

Kem Su seemed to be in a stupor, as if she couldn't speak. She nodded. Her words finally caught up with her actions. "Yes, and I mean them."

"Do you think you are capable of living up to these words that you just spoke to me?"

"Yes, Malachi."

Malachi stared at her again without saying a word. She knew she couldn't turn away. It was a test to see if she could be trusted.

"You said there's nothing in the world that you wouldn't do for me, right?" he asked.

"There's nothing, baby, that I wouldn't do."

"Would you die for me, if it came down to it?"

"Yes, baby. With no hesitation."

Malachi stared at her without blinking. "Would you kill for me, if I needed you to?"

"Yes, baby. I would murder my own flesh and blood if it came down to it. I'm loyal to you, fully. I'm loyal to every letter of your full name, and I'm devoted to every step that you make. If I could, I would perform heart surgery on myself, take my heart, and place it into your hands because I trust you just that much. Every decision that I make is calculated by the way that you move. I study the way you walk, because I'm behind you every step. I kneel to you to kiss your bare feet because you're truly my king."

Malachi leaned over and kissed her long and hard, moving his tongue in and out of her mouth. She grabbed Malachi's hand and kissed his diamond ring. "Would you like a drink, baby?"

"Yes." Malachi watched as she walked off, admiring her well-shaped bottom. He loved the way she walked. Her black evening gown with a low cut back, stopped at the top of her ass. A diamond necklace sparkled from her neck. His eyes shifted to the diamonds around her wrists and fingers. His eyes trailed down and glimpsed the diamonds that sparkled from her ankle bracelet as she walked in her heels.

"You look beautiful tonight, baby," Malachi said as he stared.

She turned and smiled a million dollar smile. "You are so charming at times. You look very handsome yourself," she said as she began to pour him a glass of imported Cognac.

Very seldom did Malachi suit up, but he felt like this was one of the appropriate occasions. Malachi was a hood nigga, and being in the presence of the elite made him a little uncomfortable. He felt a little out of his element. Even with a tuxedo on, everyone still could see that Malachi was from the deepest part of the streets.

Even though he had condominiums in at least three different states, he knew that the projects would always be his home. Being around the slums of the streets is where Malachi fit in the most. To please Kem Su and to gain other connections, he would unlace his Timberland boots and slip on his dress shoes.

Kem Su was the niece of a Korean mob boss and number one illegal arms dealer in North America, Li Wong. Anything that his only niece desired, she got. Kem Su passed Malachi his drink and placed a kiss upon his cheek right before heading to the restroom to freshen her make-up.

Malachi picked up his cell phone and placed a call to D-dog. "Peace," D-dog answered.

"Peace," Malachi replied. "I need you to get Mice, Cash, and Tiny together and meet me at Forty-Third Street at exactly twelve a.m. Don't be a minute late. And bring me a gun that's already cocked and loaded and my sword. We meet with the Koreans tonight, so drive the van. Peace."

As he hung up the phone, Kem Su walked into the room. Malachi stood and smiled, as the four diamonds on his front teeth glistened.

"Are you ready to begin this evening?"

"Yes," she said as she smiled also.

He finished the rest of his drink and took one last long drag of his blunt before putting it out in the ashtray. "Let's ride, baby." He walked to the door with Kem Su right behind him.

Malachi didn't like to get violent, but some situations required him to do so. He didn't know what he was about to walk into, so he remained guarded.

CHAPTER TWENTY

Khadijah and YaYa sat in the den cuddled up on the couch watching *Friday After Next*. Raheem, Khadijah's son, sat on the floor eating the last of the popcorn. She laughed at the scene of Da-Da and Craig fighting Santa Clause. YaYa glanced at Khadijah admiring her beautiful smile and how perfect she looked in his eyes. Her hazel slanted eyes twinkled as she tried to hold her laughter in.

Her black, naturally curly hair placed in a ponytail made YaYa want to inhale her natural flowery scent. He had grown to love Khadijah but played tug of war with himself because of the secret he held inside. Many times, he wanted to come clean and tell Khadijah about the reality of his life. He hesitated telling her because of the stories she shared with him about her father, Kaleef. She grew to hate Kaleef, despised his lifestyle, and blamed him for her mother's death. Her mom died when she was four years old, and she'd grown up without either of her parents. She had learned to live with the pain of losing her mother to a tragic death and her father to the system and being raised by her mom's only sister.

The only thing she did respect her father for was preparing her for the realities of the world by paying for her college education and having their family house set up for her when she reached adult age. Remembering the pain he saw in her eyes caused YaYa to change his mind about telling her about his lifestyle.

The guilt was slowly eating him up inside. His feelings grew deeper and deeper. The more time he spent with Khadijah, the more he realized that she wasn't only beautiful on the outside, but more beautiful on the inside. He knew Khadijah had grown attached to him also.

Many times Khadijah made sexual advances toward him, but he made different excuses for not sleeping with her. He knew that time was running out, along with his excuses and he didn't want to lose her. It was time for him to find a way to tell her the truth.

Khadijah asked, "You like the way that I smell?"

"Uh huh," YaYa responded.

"So why haven't you told me instead of trying to steal a sniff?"

"Your fragrance just has me speechless."

Khadijah rose up off his chest and smiled. She looked into YaYa's eyes and then a look of seriousness spread across her face. "Baby, I feel so comfortable when I'm in your arms. I feel protected when I'm with you. But sometimes I feel as if you have this wall up. That you're holding something back from me. What is it, YaYa? What are you keeping from me?"

"It's nothing, baby."

"Yes, it is. I know there's something. What? You're

married?"

"No, baby. I've never been married. I told you that. And I don't have any kids."

"Well, what is it? Every time I'm ready to take this relationship to the next level, you find excuses not to make love to me. We've been seeing each other every day over three months, and I've grown attached to you. You're starting to become a part of my life, and I want to be with you every moment and every second of the day."

"Baby, if I didn't feel the same, I wouldn't be here," YaYa responded. "You are the most beautiful and intelligent woman that I've ever met in my life, and I'm trying not to rush things. Sometimes, if you move too fast, you can spoil the romance."

"I don't doubt the fact that you care for me. I know you do. I've been around long enough to be able to tell when a man has deep feelings for a woman. If I figured that you didn't, believe me, my feelings wouldn't be so caught up in you. I understand taking our time, but I know that I want you, and I wouldn't mind spending the rest of my life with you. Can you see that far, YaYa?"

"Yes, Khadijah." YaYa rubbed her smooth and soft face gently.

"Mama, I'm sleepy," the five-year-old Raheem said as he stood rubbing his sleepy eyes.

"You're ready for Mommy to tuck you in?" Khadijah asked.

"Can YaYa come with us?" Raheem asked.

Khadijah looked at YaYa and said, "That's up to him."

"Of course, lil' man," YaYa responded. "I would love to help tuck you in." YaYa lifted Raheem up in his arms.

He followed Khadijah to Raheem's room and placed him

under his Spider-Man covers. Khadijah smiled. She kissed Raheem on the forehead and said, "Goodnight, baby."

"Good night, Mama. Good night, YaYa," Raheem replied.

"Good night, Raheem," YaYa said.

"I love you, Mama," Raheem said.

Khadijah turned and said, "Mama loves you too, Raheem."

They exited his room and walked down the hallway.

"You have a beautiful son," YaYa said.

"Thank you."

"And Raheem also has a beautiful, loving mother." He stopped and faced Khadijah at the end of the hallway.

She looked at him, and with both hands on each side of his muscular jaws said, "You say some of the sweetest things."

YaYa grabbed her waist and pulled her closer. Khadijah initiated the kiss, sliding her tongue in a soft and circular motion in his mouth. YaYa felt himself getting aroused as his hands slid up and down her back, gripping her ass cheeks.

She pulled away from him. "I'm about to go take a shower. You can wait in the living room until I return."

"All right," YaYa said in a deep voice.

He watched Khadijah walk away, admiring her beautiful curves and voluptuous behind. YaYa rubbed both sides of his mouth with his thumb and forefinger and felt the vibration of his cell phone. He retrieved his cell phone out of his pocket.

"Peace," he said, when he answered. He looked down the hallway to make sure Khadijah wasn't nearby.

"Peace," Malachi responded.

YaYa walked to the living room and took a seat on the sofa.

"I met with the Koreans tonight and everything went smoothly," Malachi said.

"That's good. Have you talked to Jerusalem?" YaYa asked.

"Not yet."

"Everything's tucked away safely?"

"Of course. I just finished handling that."

"Is everything set up for Jerusalem's party at your club tomorrow night?"

"Yes, everything's set up. I had some of my men pass out private invitations," Malachi replied.

"'Cause I want to show my man how much we appreciate him. Without him, none of this would be possible. He did a long bid. He deserves to have the best time of his life. And we're going to make sure that it happens. Just make sure you beef up security."

"That I will do. I got everything under control. Right now, I'm on my way to meet with Kem Su."

"How did the dinner party go?"

"It was okay. I got a few cold stares here and there from some of them bougie motherfuckas, but other than that, I had a decent time."

"What did Kem Su have to do? Beat you with some chopsticks to get that tuxedo on your ass?"

"Very funny, motherfucka," Malachi responded.

YaYa laughed. "Getting a suit on you is like trying to get an elephant to hula hoop. Almost impossible."

"You know I'm gutter, nigga. But I know how to get fitted when the time is right. But it's nothing like my Timberlands and sweats. I'm more comfortable walking the concrete jungle than dancing around the yellow brick road with Dorothy."

"I understand that," YaYa responded. "You can take the nigga out the ghetto, but you can't take the ghetto out the nigga."

"You said that right," Malachi said. "Where the fuck you at, anyway?"

"I'm at Khadijah's. We just got through watching movies."

"Look at you with your 'in love' ass. You sure have been spending a lot of time with that broad. I guess you still haven't told her about your real life yet."

"No, not yet. And she's not a broad, she's definitely a queen."

"Excuse me. A queen, huh? Every king needs a queen, don't they?"

"How can you be a king on your throne, if you don't have a queen to run your palace? You need to think about that, while you running out here with these different females every night."

"Nigga, that simple lifestyle ain't for me. Give me a harem of bitches. Give me a different one for each day of the month."

"You wild. Just give me one with the qualities of every woman." YaYa smiled as he thought of Khadijah.

"You've always been a lover boy."

"Say what you want. Khadijah's different."

"I believe that shit, my nigga. Just make that shit right. Peace," Malachi said.

"Peace," YaYa responded, ending the phone call.

He leaned back on the sofa and thought about Khadijah.

About fifteen minutes later, Khadijah walked in wearing purple lingerie and six-inch stilettos. She untied her ponytail and her hair hung past her shoulders. YaYa couldn't take his eyes off her. Khadijah smiled, turned in a circular action. "Do you like?"

"Yes, I like," YaYa responded.

He stood and walked toward Khadijah with lust in his eyes.

He swooped her up in his arms and carried her to her bedroom. Candles flickered and soft music played in the background as they entered the room. YaYa laid her gently on the bed and kissed her passionately. He stood and began to take off his clothes. Khadijah sat in front of him and unbuckled his belt and pants.

YaYa kicked off his shoes And Khadijah planted soft kisses on his chest and began licking his nipples, causing him to get more aroused. She licked his earlobes and whispered, "Make love to me, YaYa."

. YaYa laid her gently on the bed, lifted himself over her, and admired how beautiful she was as the light of the candles hit her from every angle. He kissed her passionately and they made love off and on through the night. Somehow, YaYa had managed to push his guilt to the back of his mind.

CHAPTER TWENTY-ONE

Everybody that was somebody showed up at Club Royalty for the special event. Luxury cars pulled up to the front of the club by the dozens, everything from Rolls Royce to Bentleys, Benzes to Jaguars and a fleet of limousines. Everybody pulled out his or her best and was dressed to impress. The place was filled with A-list celebrities that included singers, rappers, professional football and basketball players were all in attendance.

The red carpet was rolled out. The jewelry worn by guests sparkled more than the flashing cameras. Malachi pulled up to his club in his long, black stretch Mercedes limousine, along with Kem Su and four of her friends. Malachi, dressed in a Gucci original black suit with a gold Gucci shirt that matched his skin color, but with no tie and Gucci leather shoes, stepped out of the limousine first. His diamonds sparkled from his earlobes to his fingertips and his trademark medallion polished and shining brightly adorned his neck.

Kem Su stepped out in a short, gold Prada dress. The color

matched Malachi's shirt. Her Jimmy Choo clear diamond stilettos accented her legs. A Chen Lou custom-made diamond necklace adorned her neck. Her friends also wore black and gold designer dresses.

Tiny, D-dog, Mice and Cash exited the Hummer dressed like rap stars. All were wearing their medallions.

Pinky pulled up in her pink Porsche and exited along with her two friends. Pinky, in her fitted light pink Prada dress and five-inch clear platform shoes and blonde hair, lived for the attention she was getting from the captivated crowd. She was draped in diamonds. The gold and diamond chain with a cheetah medallion stood out the most. It represented swiftness, cleverness, and her dedication to the Black Senate.

Pinky's girlfriends, also dressed in designer dresses, followed her as cameras flashed along the red carpet leading into Club Royalty.

Another black stretched Jaguar limousine pulled up in front of the club. The limousine driver opened the door and YaYa exited first. He was dressed in a Black Kenneth Cole designer suit with a dark purple shirt and black tie and Perry Ellis black leather shoes. His gold and diamond medallion with the eagle spread across his chest could be easily seen. He held his hand out and Khadijah grabbed it as she exited the limousine. Her black sequined Christian Dior dress that stopped right above the knee wearing matching five-carat diamond earrings, bracelet and necklace that YaYa gave her earlier that night.

Jerusalem pulled up in a black Mercedes limousine. Wearing a black Cole Haan suit with the same designer dark purple shirt and tie and a black vest with black Cole Haan leather shoes. His wrists were adorned with a diamond Cartier watch and diamond bracelet. He had a diamond ring on his left pinky finger and his signature medallion of a lion around his neck.

Practically everyone greeted Jerusalem as he made his way through the huge golden doors that led into the club. The red carpet outside led into gold carpet that was spread throughout the club except the huge dance floor. Gold imported chandeliers hung from the ceilings throughout the three-story club. The long bars on each floor were trimmed in gold. The tables were covered with gold tablecloths. Several theater size television screens were located on each floor.

Women seemed to be mesmerized by Jerusalem as he walked by. He received many hugs and kisses on the cheek. Many women would love to get a chance to become Mrs. Williams. Even though he traveled around the world and had taken women on expensive and exotic trips, he'd yet to find his queen. That left a void in his heart and he wondered if he would ever find his soul mate.

The deejay played everything from Hip-Hop to R&B, which satisfied the crowd. Mary J. Blige's song, "My Life" blasted throughout the club as Jerusalem made his way up to the third floor VIP area, where the guard stood at the top of the step.

The guard greeted Jerusalem and opened up the gold cord. When he reached the top floor, everyone yelled, "Surprise! Happy Birthday!"

Malachi walked up to him holding a bottle of Cristal and gave him a brotherly hug. "Happy Birthday, Jerusalem."

Jerusalem smiled and replied, "Thank you."

YaYa did the same thing. Pinky waited until the fellows greeted Jerusalem, and then she walked up to him, gave him a hug, and kissed him on the cheek. She whispered in his ear,

"Happy Birthday, Jerusalem."

"Thank you, ma."

A waitress walked up to them and brought Jerusalem a bottle of Cristal. "Thank you," Jerusalem said.

Tiny, D-Dog, Cash, and Mice greeted him and wished him happy birthday. They all cheered with a glass of Cristal. Jay-Z and Beyoncé walked up to him, shook his hand, and wished him a happy birthday. Beyoncé hugged him and kissed him on the cheek.

Other celebrities gave him birthday congratulations.

Jerusalem and the rest of his guests sat at a long table with a black tablecloth trimmed in gold. Buckets of ice containing Dom Perignon, Cristal, imported Cognac, Grey Goose, and trays of appetizers and small saucers of fruit covered the center of the table.

Malachi stood at the head of the table. "Everybody came together. Even some of your celebrity friends and got you a special gift." He prompted the waitress to bring out the gift.

The waitress held a gold tray covered with gold velvet gift wrap and handed it directly to Jerusalem. Everybody stood and watched him unwrap his present. Jerusalem's mouth dropped in awe. "This is too beautiful. I can't believe this. How did y'all pull this off?"

Malachi responded, "Put it on."

Jerusalem picked up the gold crown with diamonds around it off the golden tray. A lion's face decorated its front. He placed it on his head and tilted it to the right, wearing a big smile.

"Thank you, everybody."

Malachi picked up his bottle of Cristal and said, "Everybody, pour up. Let's toast to my man's birthday."

Malachi raised his bottle. Jerusalem and everybody around the table raised their full glasses. "I'd like to give a toast to my man, King Jerusalem." He looked at Jerusalem and looked back at the guests seated around the table. "This is a special day for all of us. It's good to be sitting here celebrating my man's birthday. Ever since we played on the playground, Jerusalem, you had my back. You've always been that type of guy. To be there when your friends needed you. We done walked through the fire together. You, YaYa, and me— we made it and couldn't have made it without Pinky too. We here now. And the world had better be ready because here comes the Black Senate. Everybody drink up to the new ruler and one of the King of Kings, King Jerusalem."

Everybody took a sip. Jerusalem stood, shook Malachi's hand, and wrapped his other hand around his shoulder.

***

Khadijah sat at the other end of the table, looking at Jerusalem curiously. He was the same repairman with YaYa when her electricity went out. She found it odd that so many famous people showed up for his birthday. The way they greeted him and showed him respect as if he were a celebrity was also odd.

She asked YaYa once before how he was able to afford some of the expensive things that he had bought her. She'd even inquired about the expensive cars he drove and wondered why she had never been invited to his home. He always said that his parents left him a nice trust fund before they died, but it wasn't enough to support him for the rest of his life, so he still had to work. Now things started to seem real strange. YaYa kissed her on the cheek and then sat next to her. "Everything okay, baby?"

"Yes, everything is fine," she responded, throwing the thought out of her mind.

The deejay stopped the music and announced, "I would like to wish my man Jerusalem a happy birthday. He is doing big things. Him and the Black Senate. They feeding the community while a lot of motherfuckers not doing nothing. We love what you doing. It's not a lot of rooted niggas like you. You a special breed, my nigga. You were born to do what you're doing, so keep on doing it. I think I can speak for everyone in this motherfucka. We love you, Jerusalem, and we all support you."

The crowded club clapped, showing their agreement with the deejay. The deejay said, "Hold on. Hold on. Everybody be quiet for a minute. We got a special surprise for you, Jerusalem. We have somebody that wants to sing you a song."

Keyshia Cole walked on the stage and sang, "Happy Birthday" to Jerusalem and then dedicated one of her popular songs to him as she graced the stage. Jerusalem never smiled so much in his life. This was the best birthday party he'd ever had. Jerusalem felt like he was on top of the world.

CHAPTER TWENTY-TWO

Everybody socialized and enjoyed the festivities. Jerusalem talked, laughed, and shared jokes with his friends. He walked to the balcony and looked down at the crowded dance floor. Right before he turned away, his eyes caught sight of the most beautiful woman he had ever seen walking through the front of the club's entranceway.

She walked with style and grace as if she were royalty. The woman was dressed in a black and gold sequined Christian Dior dress that stopped mid-thigh. An opening shaped like a diamond showed her flat stomach, and the diamond belly ring on her belly button sparkled from a distance. The gold and diamond crystal five-inch heels she wore accented her long, ebony legs.. She wore ten carat diamond hoops that stood out because her jet black hair was pulled up in a bun with a few ringlets of hair adorning her face. Her ebony skin was spotless. She wore lip gloss on her brown luscious lips. Her neckline showed off several diamond necklaces of different sizes.

Jerusalem recognized her friend as Chad Johnson's daughter. Chad was a prominent African American attorney. He couldn't remember her name, but knew her face from the events they both attended.

***

Egypt looked around the club in amazement. "Girl, this club is beautiful," she said to Sherena. "I've never seen a place like this in Chicago before."

"I told you, girl. Royalty is the shiznit," Sherena responded,

Sherena looked around. "Do you see all the millionaires in this motherfucker? It's a lot of fine, rich niggas up in here. It's like I've died and gone to millionaire heaven, girl."

Egypt glanced around the club and happened to look up and notice Jerusalem staring at her. Their eyes locked and they both were mesmerized. Sherena was talking, but Egypt didn't hear her because her attention was on the Nubian King who happened to actually be wearing a sparkling gold and diamond crown, on the third floor balcony. She smiled, flashing her pearly white teeth. Jerusalem smiled, rubbing his neatly trimmed goatee.

"Girl, let's go to the bar and get us something to drink," Sherena said.

Egypt didn't respond. Sherena said, "Did you hear me?"

"What you say?" she asked as the trance between her and Jerusalem was broken.

"Girl, let's go to the bar and get our drink on. I'm ready to party."

Egypt looked back up, and the man she admired was no longer in view from the balcony. She followed Sherena to the bar, smitten.

***

YaYa tried to mingle with other members of the Black Senate and still spend time with Khadijah, who was quiet and distant. He could imagine the things running through her head. Maybe bringing her to the club wasn't such a good idea after all.

He walked over and grabbed Khadijah by the hand. "Come on, baby, and dance with me. Let me see what you're working with."

"No. I can't dance."

"What sista can't dance?" YaYa asked. "All that you got back there and you telling me you can't shake it. You sure know how to move that thing in the bedroom."

"YaYa," she whispered. "Be quiet before someone hears you."

"Girl, we're all grown folks up in here. I don't think there's nobody in this club that hasn't done their thing in the bedroom."

"But you don't hear anybody announcing it to the world."

"Baby, can't anybody hear me over the music. This is for your ears and mine only. Come on and dance with me." YaYa started to do a little two step.

Khadijah smiled and hesitated for a moment. She got up and followed YaYa to the dance floor.

She leaned closer to him and whispered, "I know there's more going on than you're telling me. When are you going to come clean with me?"

YaYa played it off and continued to dance.

***

Malachi walked over to Jerusalem feeling tipsy but still kept his composure. He held a half empty bottle of Cristal in his hand and took a drink directly from the bottle. Malachi asked, "Are you enjoying yourself?"

"Yes, indeed. I have never had anyone to go out of their way for me like this before. You, Pinky, and YaYa made this a very special and unforgettable night."

"There's nothing I wouldn't do for you, Jerusalem. You deserve this. It comes with success. You're making it possible for a lot of people and their families to eat. We're just showing our appreciation and our love and dedication."

"And I appreciate that," Jerusalem responded.

"With all of these beautiful women in this club eyeing you and approaching you, why are you standing here alone? I know most of these women in here are dying to give you some birthday pussy."

Jerusalem held his head down for a second and looked back up at Malachi. "I realize that I need more than that. Have you ever thought about meeting that perfect woman? The one God made specifically for you. Having access to any woman in the world doesn't mean anything at all because all you can think about is that one woman."

"Hell naw, nigga!" Malachi chuckled. "I don't know what's going on with you and YaYa, but y'all sure on some lover boy shit. There's not one woman in the world that can satisfy all my needs."

"One day you'll realize what I'm talking about. Maybe one day you'll reach that point in your life."

"When I die, I want at least a thousand bitches crying over my casket and all of them fighting about who I loved the most."

Jerusalem laughed. "I believe you."

Malachi took another swig of his Cristal. "We got some very important business we need to talk about tomorrow, but tonight's not the time to discuss it. I want you to enjoy your night. And we need to meet as soon as possible tomorrow."

R Kelly's latest song played throughout the club. Kem Su walked up behind Malachi and wrapped her arms around his waist. "Come and dance with me, baby."

Jerusalem said, "Go ahead. I'm about to walk downstairs."

Malachi turned and followed Kem Su to the dance floor. Jerusalem removed the gold crown from his head and placed it back in the gold box. He didn't worry about anyone stealing the crown because Black Senate members were posted all around the club.

Jerusalem heard Tiny talking loud from the other end of the VIP area and looked up. Tiny staggered and slurred his speech.

"Yeah, Black Senate for life. Anybody crosses us and I'm a bury their ass," Tiny yelled and people began to stare. "Yeah, motherfucka, see this motherfucking chain around my neck, a silver back motherfucking gorilla. And I will smash any motherfucka that cross Jerusalem!"

Mice attempted to calm Tiny down but failed. "I will die and kill for this shit," Tiny stated. The more he talked, the louder he got.

Cash walked over to Jerusalem. "I guess Tiny done had a little too much to drink. What you want me to do about that?"

"You, D-Dog, and Mice take him home. Y'all make sure he gets home safely."

Cash responded, "All right."

Jerusalem was a little disappointed in the way Tiny was

acting. He watched as Cash, Mice, and D-Dog walked Tiny out of the club. Once they were gone, Jerusalem headed toward the stairways to go to the first floor. As he was walking, Pinky grabbed him by the hand. "Can a girl get at least one dance from the birthday boy?"

Jerusalem kissed her on the cheek. "I'll save you a dance before the night's over with."

Pinky said, "You promise?"

"Yes, I promise."

Pinky watched Jerusalem as he walked away. Jerusalem was the only man that Pinky ever loved, but she never crossed the boundaries because their friendship was more important. She knew Jerusalem was a special man and that any woman would be blessed to have him. She hoped that one day Jerusalem would see her in another way.

***

Egypt stood near the bar watching Sherena on the dance floor.. Guys asked her to dance, but she denied them all. Her eyes glistened as she saw her ebony king approaching and her heart skipped several beats. It was a feeling foreign to her. Her stomach fluttered the closer he got.

Jerusalem walked up to Egypt and immediately extended his hand. She shook his hand as he introduced himself. "Hi, my name is Jerusalem Rasheed Williams."

Egypt replied, "Nice to meet you."

Egypt's right wrist had one gold bracelet and several ten-carat diamond bracelets. Her left wrist had a gold Cartier diamond watch and several diamond bracelets surrounded it. Each one of her fingers except her thumbs were filled with at least twenty carats of diamonds on each hand. Some fingers with priceless rubies and rare sapphires.

"So you're not going to tell me your name?" he asked in his deep godly like voice. Jerusalem noticed her accent and recognized immediately she was from another country

She smiled. "My name is Egypt Niambi Toure."

"That is a very beautiful name for such a beautiful woman. That's also a very beautiful dress you have on."

Egypt blushed, showing her perfect smile. "Thank you."

"Are you enjoying yourself?" Jerusalem asked as he moved a little closer.

"It's okay."

"It's okay? You're here at my party and you're just having an okay time. I got to do something about that."

"Oh, you're the birthday boy? All of this is for you?"

"This is my man's club. They decided to throw me a little get together."

"A little get together? You got more celebrities here than the BET Awards."

Jerusalem laughed showing his dimples. Egypt was mesmerized. To her it seemed like he was sent down from heaven. It's as if God molded this man with his own hands.

"I wouldn't say that," Jerusalem replied, "I appreciate everybody for their love. So since you're just having an okay time, would you like to come to my table with me and let's see if I can change that?"

"I have my girlfriend with me. Can she come?"

"Of course," Jerusalem responded.

Egypt walked to the dance floor and whispered in Sherena's ear. Sherena left the man she was dancing with on the dance floor. He looked disappointed to see her walk way.

"Sherena this is Jerusalem. And Jerusalem, this is my best friend Sherena." Egypt made introductions.

"Nice to meet you," Jerusalem responded, kissing her on the back of her hand.

Sherena smiled flirtatiously and said, "Likewise."

Jerusalem grabbed Egypt by the hand. "Y'all come with me."

Egypt looked back at Sherena, who gave her a look without saying a word. *Girl, he is fine.*

They walked to the VIP section. Pinky was first to notice Jerusalem with Egypt and couldn't help but feel a twinge of jealousy. She could tell the woman with Jerusalem wasn't the average woman. She watched them walk to his table.

"What would you ladies like to drink?" Jerusalem asked while he pulled out a chair for each lady.

"What do you have?" Egypt asked, taking a seat.

"Myself, I've been drinking Cristal."

"That'll be fine."

Jerusalem instructed the waitress to bring three glasses and a fresh bottle of Cristal. He stared at Egypt. He'd never been the one at a loss for words when it came to a woman, but this woman's beauty had him speechless.

Egypt noticed him staring. She looked at him and smiled. "Didn't your mama teach you that it wasn't polite to stare?"

"Yes, she did. But you're the most beautiful woman I've ever met in my life, and I can't help myself."

"A man as handsome as you are. . . I'm pretty sure you've been in the presence of many beautiful women."

"But none have captured my attention like you have."

Egypt couldn't stop herself from blushing. Looking into Jerusalem's slanted brown eyes made her nervous. Being so close to him sent electric waves all through her body. She noticed the big diamond medallion around Jerusalem's neck. "That's a very interesting medallion you have on. Are you a lion?"

"I'm just the king of my jungle," Jerusalem replied.

"Where's the gold and diamond crown I saw you in earlier?" Egypt asked.

"I took it off for now."

"Since you're a king, where's your queen?" Egypt looked around.

He paused, looked her directly in the eyes and said, "I think I just found her."

The deejay played R Kelly's song, "Slow Dance (Hey Mr. DJ)." Jerusalem stood up and said, "My beautiful queen, would you like to dance with a king?"

Sherena pushed Egypt out of her chair. "Yes, she would love to dance."

Jerusalem looked into Egypt's eyes. "I would like her approval."

"Yes, I would love to dance with you."

He grabbed her by the hand and led her to the dance floor. They danced close.

Egypt loved the way Jerusalem moved. The way he slow danced with her made her pussy moist. She inhaled Jerusalem's body scent and found herself in a trance.

Firmly, Jerusalem held Egypt around her waist, and it pleased him that she fit so perfectly in his arms. It felt to him as if they were one. Jerusalem felt her soft hair against his neck. It felt like pure silk to him as he inhaled her expensive perfume. Throughout the night, Jerusalem and Egypt danced, laughed, and enjoyed each other's company. In Jerusalem's mind, he had met his Queen. He knew that he had to have her.

She couldn't fight the way she felt being next to Jerusalem. As the night winded down, neither one of them wanted this night to end.

"As much as I hate for this night to end, it's getting very late and me and my girl have to leave," Egypt said, with regret in her voice.

Jerusalem replied, "I understand. Would you like for me to get my chauffeur to take you home?"

"No, I have a ride."

"Can I see you again?" Jerusalem asked, not really wanting her to leave.

"If it's meant for us to see each other again, we will." Egypt smiled at Jerusalem before exiting the club with Sherena.

Jerusalem stared in her direction, unable to take his eyes off her. He'd never met a woman as perfect as her. He would search the world to locate her again.

Pinky walked up to Jerusalem and asked, "Where's that dance you promised me?"

Jerusalem danced with Pinky but couldn't take his mind off Egypt.

CHAPTER TWENTY-THREE

The following day, Jerusalem, with Malachi in the passenger seat, parked his jet-black Bentley coup in a parking spot on the lot of YaYa's limousine company located on South LaSalle. He and Malachi greeted some of the workers who were members of the Black Senate and headed straight to YaYa's office. The door was open, so they walked directly in. YaYa was on the phone seated behind the glass desk in a black leather chair trimmed in gold.

Jerusalem took a seat across from YaYa as Malachi closed the door and then took a seat in the other available chair. YaYa ended the call and they greeted each other like they customarily do.

Malachi got straight to the point. "I got the weapons a couple of days ago. I've already had Tiny distribute them to our foot soldiers because you know the majors and Haitian Black is not going to sit back and let us make all the money. Word on the street is that it's already prices on our heads."

"Yeah, I kind of figured that. You sure that your information is correct?" Jerusalem leaned forward in his chair.

Malachi responded, "Yeah, this shit is correct. I'm fucking one of those Haitian bitches. She said that she overheard him and his supplier talking about how we taking over territories and cutting them out. And she's pretty sure that Haitian Black is planning to try and wipe all three of us out."

YaYa interjected, "Well, we going to have to move on them before they move on us. We can't just sit around and wait on them to try to kill us."

"Maybe, I can talk with him and work something out where he'll be satisfied and we'll be satisfied," Jerusalem said, "Because we did cut him out of a lot of money when we started doing business with the Italians. Maybe, if we offer him one of our low profitable territories with the potential that he can build it up where it's profitable for him and his organization, maybe we can avoid a war."

"Man, that motherfucka is not going to go for that shit. Fuck him!" Malachi said. "Why should we give him a piece of our territory when we the ones that made that shit."

"Sometimes you benefit more from your enemies, if you can make a friend of them. We'll still have our soldiers working the territory, but we'll just have Haitian Black give it to our workers on consignment," Jerusalem stated. "Therefore, we don't have to spend our money with him, and we'll still be feeding our soldiers. We'll get our percentage; the two percent that's given to our treasurer of the Black Senate from each one of our representatives every month, and Haitian Black will still be able to move his product."

"Well, what if he doesn't go for that? Then what?" YaYa asked.

"Well, if he doesn't go for that, there's nothing left to do but go to war," Jerusalem responded.

"I think it's crazy for us to try to negotiate with that low down motherfucka anyway. I say let's just kill the motherfucka and the rest of them Haitian bastards and lets be done with it," Malachi said.

"Just hold up for a second, Malachi. Sometimes war is not always the answer. Everybody that's in this game wants to make money. I'm sure, when he sees the money that can be made we'll come to some type of agreement," Jerusalem explained. "I went from spending ten million dollars with him a month to not spending a dime with him without giving notice. That'll make anybody a little angry and a little vengeful. We got to understand his state of mind. Now that we have basically taken over all the territories on the northwest and the south and our product is ten times better than his, it's hard for him to eat."

"That's his greedy ass fault," Malachi responded. "We buying all them motherfucking keys from this grimy bastard. He overcharging us, stepping on the products so many times, it leaves us no choice but to break all that shit down and move it throughout the projects. If we sell it whole, we might be able to make five to ten thousand profits off each kilo. Who want to pay 100 to 105 for heroin that's already been stepped on? That's bad business. He knew that he was the only one who could fill our order, so he was using us. So I say fuck him! Let's bury his ass."

YaYa added, "Maybe Jerusalem has a point. The less bloodshed it is, the less heat that we bring upon ourselves. If bodies are being found all over the city, the more the police will crack down on us. We know the Feds are watching. If it wasn't for the political connections that Jerusalem has, they would have tried to take us down."

"Malachi, we got to stay out of these streets as much as possible. This shit is bigger than the streets now. We got a lot of legitimate businesses," Jerusalem said. "We got to do what we got to do to feed our soldiers because we're trying to build a nation. How can we build a nation if we don't have armed forces? We must only go to war when it's totally necessary. We have made our statement.

"I mean, everybody, every organization in Chicago knows that we are strong now. Stronger than ever now, especially with my political connections. But if they see us just running wild, like the old western days, they going to think we're just a bunch of barbarians. If we lose our political connections, we lose all of our power. I have at least thirty percent of the federal judges in my pocket and seventy percent of the police department, including the captain and the chief. The Black Senate has given millions of dollars to the mayoral campaign. I really need to help get this brother elected. That's going to give us a lot more room to build. We'll be able to build more businesses and buy more property if we get Gregory Wilson in office. We'll have more political connections and more judges and police in our pockets—more than the five Italian families put together, and we can't mess this up over no drug war. 'Cause if they feel like they will be connected to any of this, they're going to disappear like a hooker after clipping a trick. And we can't afford to let that happen."

"I understand that, Jerusalem. I see exactly where you're coming from. But if I lose one of my warriors, or if they make an attempt on any one of our lives, I'm going to kill that motherfucka and his whole motherfucking family—from the baby to the grandma," Malachi said.

"Okay," Jerusalem said. "So is everything understood? We don't make a move on the Haitians until I have a talk with Haitian Black."

YaYa chimed in, "We still need to make sure we all stay on point. And make sure we're covering our tracks. 'Cause we don't need any surprises from the Haitians. Well, if this is it, I have to go pick up Khadijah. We made plans for this evening. What y'all got up for today?"

"I'm going to get Jerusalem to drop me off at my club. I have to make sure everything's counted and locked up, and then I'm headed to the projects to meet Pinky. She's dropping off those few last birds we have left."

"Well, I'll meet you in the projects," Jerusalem responded. "I need to have a talk with Tiny. I'll try to talk to Haitian Black first thing in the morning."

"All right, peace," YaYa said.

Jerusalem and Malachi said in unison, "Peace."

After Jerusalem dropped Malachi off at Club Royalty, he headed straight to the projects. He parked his car in front of the building, and all the kids swarmed him wanting to get close. Jerusalem pulled out a pocket full of money and started passing out five, ten, twenties and hundreds according to their age. The older kids got more.

Some of the Black Senate soldiers came to surround Jerusalem to make sure he was protected and that no one was able to snipe him from one of the high buildings. They wouldn't hesitate to die or take a bullet for Jerusalem.

"Have you seen Tiny?" Jerusalem asked one of the soldiers.

"Yes, he's right around the corner waiting for you," the solider responded.

As Jerusalem was walking around the corner, a little seven-year-old dark-skinned boy called out to him. "King Jerusalem, where you been?"

"I've been building a nation, young prince. How you been?"

"Shit, I've been out here trying to get my motherfucking paper up," Baby Stone said.

"Baby Stone, you should be worried about school. I need you to grow up to be a lawyer, a doctor, or a judge. Maybe even president. That's more strength that the Black Senate would have. We can't all be in the streets. We can't all be hustling. We need the Black Senate in those high, powerful positions."

"That shit ain't for me, Jerusalem. I want to be a king. I want to be a ruler just like you."

"How can you rule if you have no brain? You got to get in those books, prince. Why you out here hustling anyway when I told you anything that you need, come to me?"

"Man, I don't want no handouts. I want to earn my money just like the rest of these niggas."

"Look. I'm going to talk to you later. Got some business I have to handle right now. Don't you go too far, because you and I definitely have to have a talk."

"I hear you, man," Baby Stone responded.

"Go somewhere and do what kids do," Jerusalem said.

"All due respect, King Jerusalem, but I'm a motherfucking man." The little boy looked up at Jerusalem and looked him dead in his eyes. Jerusalem could do nothing but respect young Baby Stone's mind. He knew that growing up in this environment, you had to grow up fast. Knowing Baby Stone's circumstances, no father and his mother being hooked on drugs, he knew exactly what the young warrior was going through. Baby Stone reminded him a lot of himself.

Jerusalem spotted Tiny and approached him as Baby Stone walked behind him.

***

Baby Stone slipped away, eased up the steps, and went to the second floor where one of the bodyguards was posted in an empty apartment with nothing but high-powered weapons all over the place. Security was very important, especially with Jerusalem being in close proximity. Baby Stone felt like it was his time to stand post.

Frog heard a knock at the door. He opened the door and saw little Baby Stone standing on the opposite end. "What you want, lil' nigga?"

"Nigga, I came to help you stand post. King Jerusalem is out there."

"Lil' nigga I don't need you to help me."

"But Jerusalem told me to come up here just in case you need me to do anything." Baby Stone lied.

Before Frog could say anything, a short, thick project girl wearing tight shorts and a blouse walked up behind Baby Stone. "Hi, Frog. Keisha said that you wanted me."

"Yeah, come in." He turned and looked at Baby Stone. "Come on in, lil' nigga. I think I might do need you."

***

Jerusalem looked at Tiny, who started to feel somewhat

nervous. "What's going on, Jerusalem? You need to talk with me?"

"Yeah. What was that about last night?"

"Oh, I just had a little too much to drink. Feeling good and I got a little carried away."

"You really brought embarrassment upon yourself and the Black Senate. You really disappointed me with the outburst and the way you carried on. You could hardly walk. You lost all composure. That is not the way we act, especially in public."

"I know Jerusalem. I apologize. I just celebrated a little too hard."

No one noticed the unfamiliar face walking up behind Jerusalem. The Haitian, dressed like a bum, had his eyes zoomed in directly on Jerusalem.

***

Little Baby Stone looked out the window and was the first to spot him. He noticed the Haitian quickly approaching Jerusalem. Frog was locked up in the bedroom having sex with the project chick. Baby Stone knew he had to react quickly, so he grabbed the first weapon in sight, which was a twelve-gauge double barrel shotgun. He rushed out the door, frantically running down the steps as quick as his little body could carry him holding the heavy weapon.

The thought of him not making it in time to save Jerusalem started to run through his mind as tears started to flow from his young eyes. He continued to run down the flights of steps as fast as he could possibly run.

***

"I think I can smell alcohol on your breath now. You been drinking already?" Jerusalem asked Tiny.

Tiny shifted from nervousness. "I had a little to drink."

Jerusalem looked at him with anger in his eyes. "How can you expect these men to follow our laws and you're not living by them? They are going to follow our examples. And this is not a good example, Tiny. I've been hearing a lot of things, but I never said anything to you until I saw it with my own eyes. Tiny, don't let me catch you like this again. Don't let what happened last night ever happen again. You understand me?"

The Haitian got close enough to Jerusalem within firing range to make sure that he didn't miss his target. He knew if he messed up the opportunity to assassinate one of the three kings that he would never get close enough to kill any of them ever again, because Haitian Black would behead him if he failed his mission. It was do or die.

He raised his weapon, having a clear shot of the back of Jerusalem's head. Jerusalem's eyes widened in surprise as he saw Baby Stone exit the building holding the double barrel shotgun. Baby Stone raised it to firing level and aimed directly at the Haitian's face and fired a shot.

The first blast hit the Haitian directly in the face, taking off most of his facial features. Jerusalem turned quickly, drawing his weapon and staring at the Haitian's lifeless body. The powerful kick of the twelve gauge knocked Baby Stone backward to the ground. With tears still flowing from his eyes, Baby Stone recovered and quickly stood up. He held the twelve gauge in his hand and ran over to the dead Haitian that lay on the ground and fired a second shot, caving in his chest and causing Jerusalem to jump a little.

"What the fuck!" Jerusalem yelled.

Tiny walked over to Jerusalem. "Get out of here, man! I'll clean this up."

"You had Baby Stone securing me?"

"No, I had Frog on the second floor. He was supposed to be on guard."

Jerusalem looked at Tiny with fire in his eyes. "Where in the fuck is Frog?"

Baby Stone muscled up enough strength to speak. "He's upstairs fucking this project bitch."

Jerusalem rushed up the steps and burst through Frog's door.

After hearing the gunshots going off, Frog had jumped off the young girl and was just putting on his clothes as Jerusalem burst through the door. Without saying a word, Jerusalem shot Frog right between the eyes. The project girl covered her mouth after seeing Frog's lifeless body on the floor, so no one could hear the screams. Jerusalem stared at her for a second, but then focused back on Frog's body and let off five more shots to his body.

He rushed back downstairs, walked up to Baby Stone, and kneeled down. "You all right?"

"Yeah, I'm all right," Baby Stone responded.

"You saved my life," Jerusalem said.

The little boy just stared directly into Jerusalem's eyes.

"Don't worry, everything's going to be all right. Come with me," Jerusalem said.

Baby Stone followed Jerusalem to his ride and got in the passenger seat of his car. Jerusalem left Tiny with the task of cleaning up the aftermath.

CHAPTER TWENTY-FOUR

Malachi was the last person to leave Club Royalty. He double-checked to make sure everything was secure. He exited the club and turned to lock the doors.

An unfamiliar voice said, "Malachi, where you going, mon? I was just coming to pay you a visit,"

Malachi turned and came face to face with two Haitian men. One had a gun pointed toward him and the other one had one still at his side.

"What the fuck you coming to pay me a visit for?" Malachi looked both men directly in the eyes.

"We have some unfinished business, mon," the taller of the Haitian men said. "It seems you and your boys have forgot about us."

Malachi never took his eyes off his opponents. "Motherfucka, you ain't ever been on my mind. You or that bum ass nigga that sent you. Where that coward motherfucka at? He sent your punk ass to do a man's job."

The Haitian let out a loud laughter. "Malachi, oh Malachi,

you don't bow down to shit, huh mon? Even when you're facing death."

"Nigga, I'm a motherfucking king and I don't bow down to shit!" Malachi responded.

"Motherfucka, we made y'all. And y'all just going to turn y'all back on us like y'all never knew us. You should have known, motherfucka, we were coming."

"Nigga, this ain't no surprise to me. I was coming for y'all asses. I knew that y'all Haitian motherfuckas weren't going to let us walk away in peace. You just beat me to it."

"Yeah, motherfucka. You should have made a move before we did. Now it's too late for all of you. Are you ready to die?"

The other man raised his gun and Malachi smiled, showing the four diamonds on his fangs. "I was born to die, motherfucka. Fuck you, Haitian Black, this punk motherfucka that's with you, and all you motherfucking Haitians. Fuck your kids and all the bitches that birth y'all!"

"Kill this bumbaclot," the Haitian said,

The Haitian let off several rounds to Malachi's chest, causing him to fly back against the door. Malachi lay there in front of the club's door with his eyes slowly closed as his head dropped.

The Haitians made a quick exit to the awaiting black SUV. They bragged to the driver about ending Malachi's life. The driver and the Haitians drove slowly through the parking lot. Unbeknownst to the two Haitians, Malachi was wearing a bulletproof vest underneath his clothes.

After hearing the SUV's engine roaring, Malachi opened his eyes and eased himself up. Immediately, he recovered from the pain of the bullets hitting his vest. He pulled out two automatic weapons from the back of his waistline.

Running through the area, he and ended up in the middle of the street, almost getting hit by an oncoming car. The car swerved and went around him. Malachi stood in the middle of the street right in front of the oncoming SUV and began firing off shots. He hit the driver in the neck, causing him to crash into an oncoming vehicle.

Malachi ran up to the banged up SUV. The Haitian that was the first to shoot Malachi back at the club attempted to exit the passenger seat. Malachi blocked his exit. "Look me in my eyes before I kill you, motherfucka," he said.

"Fuck you, you mother—l"

Before he could even finish his sentence, Malachi shot the Haitian dead in his mouth, knocking out the back of his head. The body slumped and slid out of the SUV. Malachi emptied his clip into his body. He lifted up his other gun and ran over to the driver side of the car where the other Haitian was holding his throat to stop himself from bleeding. He was choking on his own blood.

Pointing the gun straight at the Haitian's head, Malachi fired off two quick shots, leaving the Haitian slumped over sideways on the seat.

Malachi rushed back to the club's parking lot and jumped into his black Maserati, throwing his weapon on the passenger seat before driving off.

***

YaYa felt Khadijah's distant behavior as they drove down North Michigan Avenue in silence. "Baby, since I picked you up, you've been distant from me. Why are you so quiet? What's on your mind?" he asked.

Khadijah glanced out of the window before turning to face him. "YaYa, tell me something."

"What is it?" he asked.

"Do you love me?" Khadijah said.

"Yes, I love you. More than I've ever loved a woman in my entire life."

"Do you really mean it?"

"Yes, baby, I really mean that. Where is this coming from?"

"I feel like there's something that you're not telling me. I feel like you're not being totally honest with me."

"What do you mean?" YaYa asked. " What are you talking about? Do you think I'm seeing someone else or something? If so, you need to know that you're the only woman in my life. I would never jeopardize my relationship with you. I would never jeopardize what we have with any kind of cheap thrill."

"No, it's not that."

"Then what is it, baby?"

"Last night at Jerusalem's party, y'all were partying like y'all were millionaires. Partying with the celebrities. The expensive gift that y'all gave to Jerusalem. Isn't he the same man that was with you when y'all came to fix my electrical problem?"

YaYa's heart raced. He wiped the sweat from his forehead with the back of his hand. Speechless, he glanced out his driver's side window for a second, knowing the time had come for him to tell Khadijah the truth.

Khadijah's eyes watered as she spoke. "YaYa, I deserve the truth. I've loved you from the first moment that I saw you. I felt a little suspicious when you started giving me all of these expensive gifts. You're an electrician, so I knew you couldn't afford those types of things on your salary, but I brushed it off when you told me your parents left you a trust fund. After last night, I think it's more than that. I think it's something that you're not telling me, and I need to know what's really going on. I need to know the truth, YaYa."

YaYa attempted to gather his thoughts. He was afraid that being honest with Khadijah would make her feel like he betrayed her. He didn't want to lose her, but felt like she deserved the truth.

He stopped at the red light and looked at Khadijah. The teary-eyed Khadijah looked back at him. YaYa said, "Let's just go to the house and I will give you the truth and answer all of your questions. I need you to have an open mind. Just give me the benefit of the doubt."

A black SUV pulled up on the side of YaYa. The back window eased down and someone shot into the car. Khadijah screamed. YaYa sped off. He bent down and grabbed the mini size Uzi hidden underneath his seat. Whoever was in the SUV was in full pursuit. The occupants fired off shots, knocking out the back window of his car, putting bullet holes in the trunk.

"Get down, baby!" YaYa yelled, pushing Khadijah down on the floorboard of his Jaguar. He maneuvered through traffic with the Haitians right on his trail. YaYa knew he had to think quickly. If not, his and Khadijah's life would be over. Pressing the pedal of the Jaguar all the way to the floor, giving him a little distance from the Haitians, YaYa turned the wheel hard to the left and pressed down on his brakes. This caused the car to face the opposite direction. He headed toward the SUV, aimed the Uzi out the window, and fired off shots spraying the SUV's front windshield. Bullets hit the driver and the front passenger, causing the driver to swerve and hit a parked car. The SUV flipped over several times and landed upside down. YaYa smashed on his brakes and turned the car around and headed full speed toward the crashed SUV with fire in his eyes. He pulled behind the SUV and jumped out of the Jaguar. Then he opened the backdoor of the upside down vehicle. The Haitian in the backseat saw death right in front of him.

"No, mon. Don't, mon," the Haitian man begged.

YaYa fired off shots, ending the Haitian's life. He then aimed his gun at the other two wounded Haitians and ended their lives.

Khadijah stared in shock as she opened the door and ran in the opposite direction.

YaYa ran after her and caught up to her quickly. He grabbed her by the waist, picking her up as she screamed and kicked.

"Let me go!" she yelled.

"Baby, calm down. Let me get you to safety."

"Let me go!" she continued to scream and shout.

YaYa carried her to his shot up Jaguar and placed her in the passenger seat. She didn't protest as he closed the door and rushed to the driver's side. They pulled off as other cars stopped to check on the overturned SUV.

YaYa drove Khadijah to his house to ensure her safety. He kept his head on a swivel, just in case the Haitians sent another hit team.

CHAPTER TWENTY-FIVE

Haitian Black and a couple of his henchmen pulled up in their black SUV in front of Pink Panties, a well-known, popular gentlemen club owned by Pinky located on West Grand Avenue. Even though it was early in the afternoon, it was still a nice crowd of men of all races and economic status there.

The henchmen and Haitian Black exited the SUV, feeling triumphant as they thought of the demise of the three kings of the Black Senate. Haitian Black entered the club with intentions of putting his final plan in action.

* * *

Upstairs, Pinky, dressed in a black and white pinstriped suit, sat behind her desk. She looked through the two-way glass mirror and watched the patrons of the club. She noticed Haitian Black and his henchmen enter. One of her girls and her protégé, China Doll entered the office and said, "Did you see that dreadlock Wyclef looking motherfucka?"

Pinky stood up and walked to the glass window. "Yes."

"I wonder what the hell he wants," China Doll said.

There was another knock on the door. China Doll opened it. Apple, so named because of her apple bottom, stood on the other side. . Men went crazy when they saw her perfectly made voluptuous ass. "I guess y'all see we have some unwelcomed company."

Pinky faced Apple. "Yes, unwelcomed indeed. I know this is not a social visit. Why don't you two go down there and entertain them and see what they up to."

Apple and China Doll walked downstairs as Pinky watched the man and his entourage.

Haitian Black and his henchmen sat at a booth and watched Luscious dance on stage. One of the skimpy dressed waiters asked, "What would you all like to drink?"

"Three glasses of Hennessy on ice," Haitian Black responded.

"Would y'all like a table dance?" China Doll asked once she and Apple walked up and started flirting with Haitian Black and his henchmen.,

"No," Haitian Black responded.

Apple slid in front of him and said, "Well, would you like any company? Can we join y'all?"

Not once did Haitian Black take his eyes off her apple bottom. "No. I tell you what you can do, bitch. Run and go get your boss and tell her that Haitian Black is down here. I want to talk with her. Take that nice ass upstairs and hurry along," he said.

Apple left and delivered Haitian Black's message to Pinky. "He's here on business, because he didn't even flinch when I threw my ass his way. He wants to speak directly to you."

Pinky walked to her bar in her spacious office and fixed herself a drink. With a drink in her hand, she sashayed down the stairs and headed straight to her uninvited guests.

Haitian Black said, "Hi, rude girl."

"What brings you to my humble establishment?" Pinky asked as she sipped on her drink.

"Maybe I came to see if I could get a personal lap dance from you. You got to be the most gorgeous woman in all of Illinois." He flashed his pearly white teeth.

"I hate to disappoint you, but I don't entertain my clients in that way," Pinky said, staring him straight in the eyes. "I'm pretty sure one of these girls would love to satisfy your fantasy."

Haitian Black laughed. "I don't think they can. I really need a one on one moment with you, but you can ex out the lap dance. I really need to talk some important business with you, but the lap dance was worth a try."

Pinky turned to China Doll and Apple. "Keep these two entertained." She turned to Haitian Black. "Follow me."

Haitian Black followed her to her office. She sat behind her desk and Haitian Black took a seat in the chair across from her. Pinky leaned forward. "Now, what is it you wanted to talk to me about?"

He leaned back and stared at Pinky for a few seconds before responding, "I'd like to get straight to the point. It's over with for the Black Senate. As we speak right now, the three heads of the Black Senate are meeting their fate with death. Malachi is dead. YaYa is dead. Jerusalem is dead."

Pinky's eyes began to water, but not wanting to show any weakness in front of Haitian Black, she held back her tears.

"Did you think that I was going to let them get away with the disrespect they showed me? Without them, the Black Senate will definitely crumble and I will be there to pick up the pieces." Haitian Black continued. "But you, on the other hand, my beautiful princess, I want you to join my organization. I really can use someone as beautiful and ambitious as yourself. I will allow you to sit on my right hand as my queen."

"You low-down motherfucka!" Pinky responded. "I would never join your raggedy-ass organization. I would die before I ever sit on the right hand of your grimy, greedy, low-down ass. I will spend the rest of my life hunting your ass down until me or you are dead. Until one of us no longer breathes the same air."

He laughed. "I figured that would be your first response. But once the pain leaves you and the anger fades away, I think you will have second thoughts about joining. I would hate to have to kill a beautiful specimen like yourself. I think it would be better if we joined forces. It's a lot of money in it for you, *if* you consider my offer. If not, I will come back and kill every nasty bitch up in here and leave you headless before I burn this motherfucking place down."

"Well, you better kill me now, motherfucka." Pinky was steaming mad as she thought about the demise of her friends. "'Cause I'm a Black Senate and I'm a die a Black Senate. I'm only loyal to Kings and you're not a fuckin' king. You're slime. And I would never disgrace myself or Jerusalem, YaYa, and Malachi by joining forces with the likes of you."

"Are you sure this is the decision you want to make? I will give you two weeks to make up your mind. By that time, all the female emotions that you're feeling right now should be gone. Until then, I recommend that you close your establishment until you hear from me. If not, I will have my henchmen watching this place, and every stripper and every Joe that walks in and out this place, I will give order to have them gunned down. This is not only a threat, and more than a promise. This is a fact."

Haitian Black stood up, walked around the desk, and leaned over and tried to kiss Pinky. She jumped back. He said, "I don't want to hurt you, beautiful." Haitian Black grabbed Pinky by the hair, pulling it hard, "But I will." He pushed her head back and shoved his tongue down her mouth. When he pulled away, Pinky spit in his face.

He wiped the spit from his face and then slapped Pinky, knocking her from the chair. Blood seeped at the corner of her mouth. She jumped up. "Motherfucka, you better kill me now."

"You have two weeks. And if you haven't come to your senses by then, I might just take you up on that offer."

Haitian Black left Pinky rubbing her mouth, and a few minutes later, he and his henchman exited Pink Panties and sped off in their SUV.

When China Doll and Apple saw Haitian Black leave, they rushed up the stairs to check on Pinky.

China Doll's mouth flew open. "Pinky, what happened?"

Pinky was steaming hot. Between grieving for her friends and anger from what just took place, her emotions were all over the place. She wouldn't allow herself to believe what Haitian Black said. Picking up the phone, she dialed each one of the Kings numbers. Neither Jerusalem, YaYa, nor Malachi answered. Tears flowed down her face as she came to the realization that they were gone.

"Pinky, what's wrong?" Apple asked.

"They're gone . . . Jerusalem, YaYa, and Malachi are all

dead."

Pinky wiped the tears from her face and looked at Apple and China Doll. "Get dressed. We got to go."

CHAPTER TWENTY-SIX

Khadijah sat on the sofa with tears flowing down her cheeks. Her body shook with fear as she stared at YaYa, while he paced back and forth in the living room. YaYa attempted to reach Malachi and Jerusalem on their cell phones, but neither one of them answered. He left urgent messages. "Haitian Black's men just tried to kill me! Where y'all at? . . . Watch your backs. I'm sure he's coming after y'all next. I'm at the house with Khadijah."

With her head in her hands, Khadijah said, "YaYa, you need to take me home. I need to get away from you."

YaYa stopped pacing for a second and stared at Khadijah. "Baby, I know you're traumatized right now. Just give me a few seconds and I'll explain."

"Some people just tried to kill us, and I just witnessed you kill three people right before my eyes. What's going on, YaYa? What kind of things are you into where you got people after you?"

He walked over and sat down next to Khadijah and reached

for her hand. She snatched her hand away. "Listen, baby, those are some Haitians I know. Guess they put a contract on my partners' head and me. I never meant to put you in danger. I would give my life before I let anything happen to you. I will protect you with my life. You and Raheem. I will make sure that nothing like this ever happens again. That's my word."

"Why do the Haitians have a price on your head, YaYa? Are you some type of drug lord?"

"Something like that."

"What the hell do you mean 'something like that!' Are you a drug dealer? I need the truth from you, YaYa, and I need it right now."

"Jerusalem, Malachi, and I are the three kings of our organization that is called the Black Senate. We do a lot of positive things in the community. We develop jobs and opportunities for people that otherwise wouldn't have any because of their background, lack of education, or where they come from. We offer scholarships to high school students. Instead of having the police to secure our community, we have our own community of black warriors that we control through drug trade."

"So, you are a drug dealer?" Khadijah looked YaYa directly in the eyes.

"I consider myself more than just a drug dealer." He stared back. "With the money we make, we do a lot of positive things."

"But the bottom line, YaYa, is that you are a drug dealer and you kill people. So what was that about when you and Jerusalem pretended to be electricians and came and worked on my electric?"

YaYa took a deep breath and commenced to telling her the

truth. "Well, when Jerusalem was locked up in the federal penitentiary he was a general, the second in command, over this organization ran by a drug lord. He told Jerusalem where he'd hidden fifty million dollars. It was hidden in the basement of your house."

"Oh my God!" she responded as her hand flew up to her mouth. "So, y'all came to rob me?"

"No, it's not like that. The last thing we wanted to do was hurt you. This money was given to Jerusalem to continue the mission that his leader started. Unfortunately, his leader was killed in a prison riot. Before he died, he told Jerusalem where the money was hidden."

"How was he able to hide fifty million dollars in my basement without me or anyone knowing about it?"

"Because he owned the house."

"What are you talking about, YaYa? It's like you're talking in riddles. My parents owned this house and left it to me in their will. My mother was killed. My father did life in . . . Oh my God! Oh my God! So you're telling me that . . ."

"Yes, the drug lord was your father, Kaleef."

Khadijah cried. "So all of this time, this was a game to you? You claimed to love me and claimed to care about me and all of this time you were using me to get to the money that my father had hidden in the basement?"

"No, baby. No. I love you sweetheart."

"You lied to me. You played games with my heart. I feel betrayed. I can't believe this is happening to me."

"Baby, please listen. It's not like that."

"What the fuck you mean, it's not like that? All of this has been a lie from the start." Khadijah's hands were moving all over the place. "You used me. You played me as a pawn in your little chess game. I trusted you. I trusted you around my son. I invited you into my home. I gave you my heart, my body, my soul and you just used me. Look at this house. Look at all the different cars in the yard. No wonder this is the very first time you decided to bring me here. You knew I would have figured it all out. No way could an electrician afford all of these expensive things or expensive gifts you gave me. What were the gifts for? To bait me in so when you finally told me the truth . . . you can buy me?"

"No, that was from the heart. I love you, Khadijah. It was from the heart. I love you more than I ever loved a woman in my life."

"I don't believe you. I can't believe a word that you tell me. You're nothing but a liar. A drug dealer. A killer. You're just like my father. I hate him. He's the reason my mother was killed. It was due to the same lifestyle that you are trying to impose on me. I don't want anything else to do with you or the life that you live. I want you to stay away from my son and me. We want nothing else to do with you."

At that time, YaYa's phone rang and he saw that it was Jerusalem. YaYa answered. "Hello. Hell is low."

"What's going on, YaYa?" Jerusalem asked.

"Fuckin' Haitians tried to kill me and Khadijah. I killed all three of those motherfuckas."

"Yes, they just tried to kill me, too. Baby Stone saved my life."

"Have you heard from Malachi and Pinky?"

"I have different messages on my phone but haven't had time to hear them because I had so much stuff going on. I think a few calls are from Pinky. Calling me from her club."

"We need to find out if Malachi is all right. I'm about to get off the phone with you and try to reach him. We'll be over to your house after I reach him," Jerusalem said. "Is Khadijah all right?" he asked before hanging up."

"Physically, she's all right, but mentally, she's not. I had to tell her the truth about everything."

"It was about that time, fam'. It's just messed up you had to tell her this way. Soon as I catch up with Malachi and Pinky, we will be over there."

"Peace."

"Peace," Jerusalem said as they disconnected the call.

YaYa looked at Khadijah who was crying non-stop. "I need to use your restroom," she said in between the tears.

"It's one right down the hallway to your left. Let me show you."

"I don't need you to show me anything. I can find it," she snapped, heading to the restroom.

His phone rang. It was Malachi. "You all right?" YaYa asked.

"Yeah, I'm good. I just got off the phone with Jerusalem, and I'm on my way to your house as we speak," Malachi responded. "Fucking Haitians tried to kill me too. They shot me in my chest, but I had on my vest. I got up and got with those motherfuckas. They are no longer here, believe that. Pinky called and said that Haitian Black paid her a visit. He thinks that we are all dead."

"Well, he's in for a surprise."

Malachi said, "Now, you see what I was talking about. We should have brought it to that motherfucka before he brought it to us. Where would the Black Senate be if he'd been successful and had all of us killed?"

"Well, everybody is fine. I'll see you when you get here," YaYa replied.

He hung up, but his phone rang again and he answered, knowing it was Pinky. "Oh my God! YaYa, it feels so good to hear your voice."

"Yes, I'm all right," he said.

"Malachi told me what happened. Don't you know that motherfucka came to my club bragging that all three of y'all were dead? I didn't know what the fuck to think."

"Everything is all right, princess. Are you okay?"

"Yes. I'm fine now that I know all of y'all are okay."

YaYa ended his call with Pinky. Khadijah hadn't returned from the bathroom. He called out her name a few times, but didn't get an answer. Again he called out her name and rushed to the bathroom and turned the knob. The door didn't bulge. He kicked the door in. Khadijah wasn't there. She had slipped out the bathroom window.

He ran through the house and out the front door to the lawn, but she was nowhere in sight.

CHAPTER TWENTY-SEVEN

Haitian Black paced back and forth. Nine of his top soldiers were seated around him. He gulped down straight hard liquor from his bottle to ease his paranoia. He picked up a blunt and took a few puffs and stared into their blank faces. "What the fuck happened? Can anyone in this room, mon, properly execute the hit on those three bumbaclots? How is it possible that my men missed all three of our targets? Now my life and everybody's life in this room is in danger; along with my business."

His eyes glazed over from all the liquor. He bent down behind his desk and opened up a safe. In anger, he retrieved five ten thousand stacks and slammed them on the desk. "I have fifty thousand stacks for the heads of each one of these three men: Jerusalem, Malachi, and YaYa. That's a hundred and fifty thousand dollars for all three of them motherfuckas. And a bonus for the ones who bring me the death of one of these men before the week is over. There's no room for any mistakes. And I won't stand for another miss."

The men shifted in their seats. Haitian Black continued,

"And if you miss. It's best that you not return in my presence alive, or you will meet your fate. Do I make myself clear?"

One of the assassins glanced at the surveillance monitor and spotted Jerusalem standing alone at the edge of the entrance of the warehouse. "Look, boss." He pointed at the monitor. "Isn't that one of them there?"

Haitian Black walked closer to the monitor to make sure his eyes weren't deceiving him. He smiled when he recognized Jerusalem's face. "Well, well, what do we have here? His balls are too big for his britches. Everybody grab their weapons."

They dispersed and returned with high artillery automatic weapons. He held his hand up for them to pause. "This could be a trap, so make sure that when we walk outside the building we survey the area. If this bumbaclot makes one false move, execute him immediately. Do I make myself clear?"

The room was silent.

He repeated, "Do I make myself clear?"

They nodded.

"Don't anybody make a move until I give an okay."

Haitian Black exited the warehouse in a fast-pace with his dreads hanging wildly as he came face to face with Jerusalem. He pointed at two other assassins and pointed at the edge of the driveway entrance. They each walked to the edge of the entrance with their weapons drawn while the other assassins surveyed the rest of the area.

"Jerusalem," Haitian Black called out.

Jerusalem showed no sign of fear and responded, "Haitian Black."

"You have extremely large cajones to show up here alone. I see you're mighty brave knowing that you escaped death from my hands. You did the worst thing you could possibly do—evoke my rage. You and your organization axed me out without any notice. What you thought I was going to sit back and allow that . . . when I gave you my loyalty and friendship. In return, you turned your back on me. What makes you so confident and so certain that you would be able to escape death for a second time?"

Jerusalem stared back with his signature crooked smile. "I have no worries. Because I feel the spirit of my ancestors' protection around me."

Haitian Black laughed, not fully understanding the logic behind Jerusalem's statement. He looked at his assassins. "Do you hear this? He's talking about his ancestors' spirits." He made a ghost sound. "Whooooo. I guess it's ghosts here. You sure they able to save you. You piece of worthless shit. To have as much power as you have, you still living a fucking illusion talking about spirits, ancestors, and ghosts. You have to be a crazy man."

"If that's what you think. I came here to make you an offer," Jerusalem responded.

"What kind of offer is that? That you think that you can make to Haitian Black." He spoke about himself as a third party.

"I came here to see if we can prevent an all-out war. That would benefit you and me from causing more bloodshed. It also puts money in your hands, instead of the blood of many men."

Haitian Black looked as if he was in deep thought. "It's possible."

"I came to make you a business offer."

"You came to make me a business offer?" Haitian Black responded. "You stupid bama you are. How can you come make me a proposition? If it weren't for me, your ass would still be in the projects nickel and diming . . . robbing and stealing. I've had many chances to take everything you had; instead, I made you a rich man. Now you think I'm inferior. You think you can come to my place, in front of my men, and make me some damn offer? What do you expect? For me to be your chauffeur . . . your bodyguard . . . your valet parker . . . or your shoe shine boy. I'm going to make this plain. Fuck your offer. Fuck your proposition. Fuck your organization. I want your life and the demise of the Black Senate."

Seeing that there was no compromising with Haitian Black, Jerusalem was prepared for his arrogance and stubbornness. He wanted to avoid further bloodshed, but Haitian Black was leaving him no choice. Jerusalem rubbed his bald cranium. It looked as if he was in a state of confusion, but he was giving a signal for the Black Senate Black warriors to open fire.

The Black Warriors were all in position. They were located on top of the roofs of other warehouses, their automatic weapons with scopes attached to them, drawn and ready to shoot at Jerusalem's command. Their weapons had long distance range and were all aimed at Haitian Black's assassins that were planted near the entranceway and located throughout the outside of the warehouse.

Upon getting Jerusalem's signal, they simultaneously opened fire and successfully hit their targets. Haitian Black's men fell to the ground, one by one. He trembled as bullets flew past his head and body, killing everyone around him except him and Jerusalem. Jerusalem stood still in front of Haitian Black, admiring the Black Senate's handy work.

The bullets ceased. Bodies lay throughout the premises

bleeding and meeting their doom. Haitian Black's body trembled as if he were naked and stuck in the North Pole.

Jerusalem said, "Haitian Black, look at me. I'm not going to kill you, yet. Instead, what I will do is make you my final offer and that's a high position in my nation of Black Senates. If you refuse my final offer, it's best for you to go back to Haiti and never return. If I run across anyone that resembles your face, I'm not going to hesitate to kill them wherever I might meet them." Jerusalem retrieved a business card out the pocket of his long, black leather trench coat. "You have seventy-two hours to contact me. After then, I will know that you have refused my final proposition."

Haitian Black eyed the business card Jerusalem held out. He knew he'd been defeated and slowly reached out his hand and couldn't control the trembling as he took the card from Jerusalem's hand.

Without saying a single word, Jerusalem turned and, walked away, his leather coat blowing in the Chicago wind.

CHAPTER TWENTY-EIGHT

Egypt sat in front of the vanity mirror in the bathroom of her luxury condominium, putting on the final touches of her make-up. She stood and viewed herself in the full length mirror in her bedroom. The silver beaded floor length evening gown made her look like a Black Cinderella. While putting on her glass slippers, she heard Etheria's loud outburst coming from the next room.

Etheria continued to shout and curse over the cell phone. She tuned him out and thought about Jerusalem. Since the night they met, she'd thought about him constantly and found herself fantasizing how it would be to spend an eternity in his arms. She knew just from the short time they'd spent together that it was something special about Jerusalem. He was no doubt, one of a kind. Looking into his eyes was like looking into his soul.

She eased the thoughts of Jerusalem to the back of her mind and walked into the living room.

"You disloyal son of a bitch! You're a dead man," Etheria said to the person on the phone, before ending the call.

Egypt hoped the sight of her would help ease the tension in

the room. She stood near Etheria and waited for him to give her a compliment. He barely glanced at her and paced back and forth. "Etheria, is everything all right?" Egypt asked out of concern.

"No, I'm not all right!" he yelled. "What the fuck am I going to do now? This motherfucka has walked away from our partnership causing me to lose a lot of money and giving me a headache. How am I supposed to explain this to your father that I have lost one of our biggest clients?"

"Etheria, everything is going to be okay." Egypt tried to console him by gently rubbing his arm.

"That's just like a typical woman. Thinks everything is fine and dandy in their world. You don't know what the fuck you're talking about because everything is not going to be okay." He jerked his arm away.

"Don't you ever talk to me like that," Egypt responded. "I don't care what you're going through. I don't know what your problem is, but don't take it out on me."

"You just get on my damn nerves with your nonchalant attitude. Daddy's little Princess! You're not living in the damn real world. You don't have this weight on your shoulders like I have. You don't have the responsibilities that I have. All you do is sit around and wait to be pampered, with your spoiled ass. I don't need you telling me shit about everything is fine . . . everything is going to be okay. What I need you to do is stay in a woman's place and keep your mouth closed."

Egypt slapped Etheria. "You arrogant, disrespectful bastard! I thought I was being a woman by trying to console my man. You heartless son of a bitch. You can't see that because your head is always stuck up your ass. You can't see what you have standing next to you. I'm my own woman—with my own thoughts—with my own opinions. You or no one else can stop me from voicing my opinion. You're too busy worried about money that you never took one minute to notice me standing here. You haven't given me not one compliment because your mind is always other places. It's never on me . . . on us. I've had about enough."

"What are you telling me, Egypt?"

"Let's just go because we don't want to be late for my father's banquet," she responded, as she walked to grab her mink coat.

***

National and local dignitaries, which included senators, governors, mayors and high profiled celebrities, filled the ballroom of the five-star hotel. The men wore tuxedos and the women were dressed in their finest evening gowns. Chatter and laughter filled the room.

As soon as Egypt and Etheria entered the ballroom, Etheria grabbed a glass of champagne from one of the waiters trays. Egypt rolled her eyes but kept a fake smile plastered on her face. She scanned the room in search of her father. She noticed Etheria had replaced his original glass with another glass of champagne.

She said to Etheria, "There's my dad. Come on."

They made their way through the crowd of people surrounding her dad, King Geoffrey Toure. King Geoffrey, wearing a white tuxedo and a black bow tie, appeared to be enjoying his time in the spotlight as the guest of honor. Everyone wanted to be near him. With the thick mustache, he resembled George Washington Carver.

King Geoffrey looked up in Egypt's direction. A huge smile crossed his face. "Make room for my beautiful daughter, Egypt, the love of my life."

Just like that, the crowd of people dispersed and made an opening for Egypt. Egypt, with Etheria on her heels, glided toward her dad. They hugged. Egypt gave him a quick peck on the cheeks.

He whispered, "You're late."

Egypt looked in Etheria's direction.

King Geoffrey shook Etheria's hands. "Good to see you, son. Glad you two finally made it."

Etheria smiled. "I'm glad I'm here to help celebrate this evening with you."

King Geoffrey patted Etheria on the back. He turned his attention back to Egypt. "So, how have you been enjoying yourself here . . . in your favorite city?"

"It's been pleasant," she responded.

"Are Sherena and her father coming?" King Geoffrey asked.

"They should be here any minute now."

"I can't wait to see my old friend, Mitchell and my goddaughter. It's been a couple of years since I've seen those two. Have you gotten a chance to spend some time with Sherena?"

"Matter of fact, I did," Egypt responded. "A couple of weeks ago, she was instrumental in me having one of the best times of my life."

"That's wonderful. Keep the details to yourself because with the two of you together, I'm sure it's something I don't want to know."

Egypt laughed. "Father, I've been a good little princess."

"I'm sure you have," he teased.

King Geoffrey looked at Etheria. "Etheria, have you been keeping a watchful eye on my baby girl?"

"Yes, I've been trying. You know Egypt when she gets with her girlfriend. I have no control over her." He gave Egypt a fake smile.

Several waiters walked up to them. One had a tray of drinks and another a tray of fruit and hors d'oeuvres. While Egypt and Etheria were helping themselves to the hors d'oeuvres, Gregory Wilson, the mayoral candidate, walked up and greeted King Geoffrey. "I have two gentlemen I want you to meet. This is YaYa Johnson and Jerusalem Williams."

King Geoffrey responded, "How are you gentleman?"

"Nice to meet you, King Geoffrey." Jerusalem was the first to respond, followed by YaYa.

"Please. Just call me Geoffrey. It sounds better here in America."

Jerusalem responded, "That's fine with me."

YaYa nodded in agreement.

Wilson said, "These are two up and coming entrepreneurs. They are doing big things and giving millions of dollars for my campaign run. They are very good friends of mine."

King Geoffrey said, "Congratulations on your success. I love to see aspiring young men reach their goals and touch their dreams. I learned from coming here to America throughout the years, all it takes is ambition and a vision and you can achieve any and everything that your heart desires." He paused and excitedly said, "I have someone I want you two gentlemen to meet. My daughter and my future son-in-law, Egypt and Etheria."

Egypt and Etheria walked near King Geoffrey. Egypt almost dropped her saucer of fruit when her eyes met Jerusalem's eyes. *It couldn't be.* The object of her daydreams was standing next to her father.

"Egypt, this is Jerusalem Williams and his associate YaYa Johnson. And of course, you know Wilson."

Jerusalem smiled and said, "Nice to meet you." Egypt wasn't sure of how she needed to respond, but

she went along and hoped she could hide her nervousness. She willed her hand not to shake as she extended her hand toward Jerusalem. As they shook hands she saw the twinkle in his eyes. She immediately removed her hand and then shook YaYa's hand.

King Geoffrey then introduced them to Etheria. "Etheria, this is Jerusalem Williams and YaYa Johnson."

Etheria's eyes flashed black as he reached to shake their hands. Etheria thought, *This got to be the same motherfuckas that Haitian Black mentioned.*

King Geoffrey cut his eyes as Etheria grabbed a drink from a passing waiter. He noticed that Etheria had been drinking more than normal. Not wanting to make a scene, he didn't bother to mention it to Etheria.

Egypt also felt like she needed a drink. She stopped another waiter and retrieved a flute of champagne. She took a sip and tried her best not to look at Jerusalem, but failed.

King Geoffrey said, "Since my daughter and Etheria are helping themselves to the champagne, let us all have a drink together." He raised his hand and beckoned the waiter.

The waiter walked up with a tray full of glasses filled with champagne. They all retrieved a glass from the tray.

King Geoffrey said, "Let's make a toast. This is to new acquaintances and possibly new friendships amongst us all."

They clinked their glasses. Egypt and Jerusalem's eyes locked.

King Geoffrey addressed Jerusalem. "You seem very interesting to me. Tell me a little bit more about yourself. What is your business venture?"

Jerusalem said, "My business partner, YaYa, plays a big part in my success. I don't think I would have made it this far without him."

YaYa smiled. Jerusalem continued to share with him and the captivated audience, things about his legitimate businesses such as his real estate company, Meru, which was located in downtown Chicago, his clothing line, and record company. Egypt admired his perfect speech and his posture.

Etheria couldn't help but feel some type of jealousy at the exchange between King Geoffrey and Jerusalem and excused himself. "I see someone I need to talk to."

He left, leaving Egypt alone with her father and the other men. Etheria, never slowing down his pace, walked by a waiter and grabbed another drink.

Wilson interjected into their conversation and said, "Jerusalem's been doing a lot of positive things in the community. Building parks inside the urban community and funding charter schools, homeless and women shelters. He opened up youth centers in neighborhoods throughout the inner city. Also, he's opened up medical clinics for the more unfortunate people."

Egypt couldn't help but admire Jerusalem even more after

hearing all that Wilson said to her father about Jerusalem. She thought, *Where has this man come from? He's doing so much for his people.*

Thirty minutes later, King Geoffrey spoke to a captivated crowd as he gave his speech after receiving his Humanitarian Award. At the end of his speech, he thanked everyone and exited the platform. Egypt hugged and kissed him on the cheek. The live band played contemporary music and the socializing started back up.

Egypt spotted her best friend Sherena, dressed in an elegant black velvet form-fitting evening gown with a long slit in it.

"I'm glad you made it." Egypt walked over to her and hugged her.

I wouldn't have missed it for the world. We've been here, but didn't want to distract you from King Geoffrey's speech by coming up to the table where you were seated," Sherena responded.

"Where's your dad?" Egypt asked.

"There he goes over there, most likely trying to get new clients. You know it's always business with him." Sherena glanced across the ballroom. Her eyes fell on Jerusalem and YaYa speaking with other people. "Is that who I think it is? Is that the guy we met a couple weekends ago at Club Royalty?"

Egypt responded, "Yes, it's, Jerusalem." She let his name roll off her tongue.

"Girl, where's Etheria?"

"I haven't seen him since before my dad got his award." She scanned the room and noticed Etheria in a deep conversation with a group of women. She pretended as if nothing was wrong.

Sherena said, "Girl, have you talked to Jerusalem yet?"

"Not really. Mr. Wilson actually introduced him to my father. We played it off as if we had never met."

"How did you make it through that without giving yourself away?"

"Let me tell you, it was hard. There's something about that man."

"Yes, he is so fine." Sherena said.

Egypt said, "There's more to him than meets the eye."

"I can believe that. So what are you going to do? You going to continue the night without saying anything to him? Because I know you've been thinking about him."

"Yes, I have," Egypt agreed. "More than you can ever imagine. I can barely stand when he's near me. I get so weak. Being in his presence hypnotizes me, and I forget about everything around me. It's like I'm almost lost in a trance."

"Girl, you seem like you're in love and y'all haven't even done the nasty."

"Please. I'm not in love. At least I don't think so. I've never felt real love, so I don't know how it feels. But I know that it's something strange happening inside of me when it comes to this man."

"Things like this don't happen every day. Just follow your heart. I know from experience that your heart will never guide you wrong."

"It's like my heart is doing tap dances as we speak."

Etheria staggered his way through the crowd toward Egypt and Sherena. Etheria said, "Hi Katrina."

"It's Sherena!" she snapped.

"Katrina . . . Sherena . . . whatever," he said as the words slurred from his drunken mouth. He looked at Egypt. "I'm feeling kind of bored and tired. And I'm ready to leave."

The two women Etheria had been talking to earlier were talking to each other. They glanced at Egypt. One woman giggled as they walked toward the exit door. Etheria took his eyes off Egypt to watch the women vanish from the ballroom.

Egypt said, "If you must go, leave. That's fine with me. I'm staying here and enjoying the rest of the night with my father and my friend."

Sherena twisted her mouth sideways. "How you like those apples?"

"That's fine with me," Etheria responded. "I'm going to my hotel. I guess I'll catch up with you at your condo tomorrow." Etheria walked between Egypt and Sherena, giving Sherena the evil eye.

She stared back at him as she rolled her eyes. "Girl, how do you put up with that arrogant, egotistical asshole?"

"It's harder than you can imagine," Egypt responded.

"If I were you, I would give him a Jackie Chan karate chop to the throat. Like woo." Sherena used her hand to demonstrate. "And a Bruce Lee Kung Fu kick in his ass."

"Girl, you're crazy." Egypt laughed.

"I don't know about you, but I'm going to talk to the two finest gentlemen in the room. You can stay here and look like a mannequin if you choose to. Sherena is here and the party has just begun."

She stopped by a nearby waiter and got a drink off the tray. Egypt followed suit but didn't get a drink as they made their way toward Jerusalem and YaYa.

Egypt whispered loudly. "Sherena, Sherena . . . stop, come back here."

Sherena ignored her. Egypt felt like she had no choice but to follow her because she didn't know what would come out of Sherena's mouth.

Sherena stopped in front of Jerusalem and YaYa. "How are you gentlemen doing this evening?" she said.

Jerusalem smiled slightly and responded, "Fine."

"You got that right. If you don't remember me, I was one of your guests at your birthday party."

"Yes, I remember. How can I forget?"

"Me and my friend were standing on the other side of the room and saying to ourselves how handsome you two gentlemen are looking tonight."

By this time, Egypt was standing near them. She elbowed Sherena, who grabbed the spot where Egypt elbowed her. "Here she is here."

Jerusalem flashed a smile and stared at Egypt. He couldn't help but laugh at Sherena's humor.

"Egypt, you remember Jerusalem, don't you?" Sherena asked.

"Yes, I do," Egypt responded in embarrassment.

"Jerusalem I know you haven't forgotten about my friend Egypt. Have you?" she asked.

Jerusalem never removed his eyes off Egypt. "I definitely haven't."

"Well, I see your hands are empty. I'm the only one with a drink. Isn't this supposed to be a party?"

"No, it's not a party. It's a banquet for my father," Egypt responded.

"Well, it's a party now, so let's all have drinks. Where's a waiter?" Sherena looked around. She saw a waiter and said,

"Hey waiter, we need you." She waved her hand and called the waiter over to them. "My friends here need a drink to loosen up."

The waiter nodded and held out the drinks as the other three grabbed a drink.

Sherena said, "Should we drink up or give a toast?"

"Let's toast," Jerusalem said.

"What should we toast to?" Sherena asked, pausing. "I know. I know. Let's toast to destiny. Because she always comes around."

"I can't agree more," Jerusalem said, putting his attention back on Egypt.

They clinked their glasses and took sips from their drinks.

Jerusalem said, "Egypt, you sure look beautiful this evening. The dress you're wearing is gorgeous."

Egypt said shyly, "Thank you. You look very nice in your tuxedo."

YaYa, who had been standing there silently, glanced at his friend. "Why are you so quiet? Are you the strong and silent type?" Sherena said to YaYa.

"No. I just don't have too much to say right now," YaYa replied. Although Sherena was a very attractive woman, he wasn't interested. YaYa was still feeling the pain of losing Khadijah.

Sherena, leaving YaYa no choice, grabbed his hand. "Let's go see what's on this beautiful buffet."

Before YaYa could resist, Sherena led him away.

Egypt stood alone with Jerusalem and felt at a loss for words. Not because she didn't have anything to say, but because she was nervous as she looked in every direction but at

Jerusalem.

"So you're a princess, huh?" Jerusalem asked.

"I guess you could say that," Egypt responded.

"And you have a fiancé?"

"I guess you could say that too."   .

"Well, you weren't acting like you had a fiancé when you were dropping it like it was it hot at my birthday party."

"I was not dropping it like it was hot."

"Well, you weren't acting like you had a fiancé when you slow danced with me all through the night."

"I just came out with my girlfriend to have a good time. It was innocent."

"Are you sure that it was innocent? Tell me this, Egypt. Have you thought about me constantly the way that I've been thinking about you?"

"To be truthful with you, I have."

"Do you want to go somewhere, where we can talk?" Jerusalem asked.

"I would like that."

"Let's grab our coats and go take a walk together."

"Meet me at the exit door while I go tell my father that I'm leaving."

"You're not going to disappear on me again, are you?"

"No, I promise."

Egypt said her good-byes to her father, and she waved at a distance at Sherena, whowaved back and gave her the thumbs up.

CHAPTER TWENTY-NINE

"So where are we going?" Egypt asked, standing outside of the luxury hotel dressed in a white mink coat and hat with matching white leather gloves.

"Let's just walk," Jerusalem replied. He too was dressed appropriately for the Windy City weather in a wool trench coat, a mini godfather hat, and black leather gloves. "I want to get to know you. Walk with you and talk with you without the music and crowd of people around us."

They walked in a slow steady pace down the sidewalk on Michigan Avenue in the cold Chicago air.

Egypt asked, "What do you want to talk about?"

"I want to know everything you feel comfortable telling me.

I want to know your favorite color; your favorite song; your happy or sad moments. Your favorite food. Your favorite movie. I want to know everything there is to possibly know."

Egypt felt comfortable with Jerusalem as they exchanged information about their favorite things. She shared with him her life story. She shared her feelings about the loss of her mother and how she really felt about her arranged upcoming nuptials with Etheria. She admitted she didn't want to marry him.

Jerusalem told Egypt about his childhood, his prison time, and becoming a well-known entrepreneur. They shared some of their deepest secrets, knowing that their secrets were safe with one another.

Time flew by as they talked. A few hours passed without them realizing it. Jerusalem noticed a horse and carriage half a block away. He grabbed Egypt's hand in his and said, "Let's take a carriage ride."

"That would be nice. I've never been on a carriage ride," Egypt said excitedly.

Jerusalem took off his hat, bowed, and said, "After you, my beautiful princess."

Egypt smiled. Jerusalem took her hand and helped her into the carriage.

The middle-aged driver looked back, smiled at the two, and thought what a beautiful couple. He asked, "Where are we going tonight? Would you like to go down Lake Shore Drive along the lake or down Rush Street?"

"Just ride us until I tell you to stop," Jerusalem responded.

The driver tipped his hat. Jerusalem placed his arm around Egypt's shoulders and drew her closer. Being in his arms made Egypt feel protected. She didn't want to be anywhere else in the world at that moment, but in his arms. They rode around the area looking at the beautiful sights of downtown Chicago.

After riding around for over an hour, Jerusalem told the driver, "This is far enough."

The driver stopped the carriage. Jerusalem reached into his

pocket and handed the driver a wad of money, knowing that it was much more than the cost of the ride. The driver said, "Thank you, sir."

The driver opened the door. Jerusalem exited first and then assisted Egypt down from the carriage.

Egypt and Jerusalem walked back in the direction of where they originally started.

Jerusalem said, "So, you said Prince is your favorite artist?"

"Yes. I love the songs that he makes."

"Would you mind going to his concert with me?"

"I would love to go," Egypt responded.

"He's one of my favorite artists too," Jerusalem admitted.

"Are you just saying that? Because you don't look like the Prince type."

Jerusalem began to sing, "Until the end of time, I'll be there for you. You own my heart and mind. I truly adore you . . ."

She smiled then giggled at Jerusalem as he sang Prince's song.

Jerusalem stopped and looked into her eyes. "Your smile outshines the moonlight to me." He looked up toward the bright, moonlit sky.

Egypt looked back at him, starry-eyed. "I want to spend every moment that I can with you. I want to be the one that you call when you feel alone. I want to be the one to put my arms around you when you need protecting," he said.

"I want the same thing you want," Egypt responded.

At that moment, Jerusalem wrapped his arm around her waist and pulled her close. Egypt placed her arms around his broad shoulders. No other words needed to be said. Their lips connected. Jerusalem eased his tongue inside of Egypt's eager mouth. The rest of the world didn't exist. It was just the two of them. Egypt felt as if she were floating on a cloud as their tongues danced. Jerusalem felt his heart tug the moment his lips touched Egypt's. Jerusalem knew then that he and Egypt were connected for life. Egypt also knew it. They stood in the middle of the sidewalk wrapped up in each other's arms. People passing by gawked at the couple.

Someone yelled out, "Lips . . . lips . . . kiss . . . kiss . . . go get a room and see if you hit or miss."

Egypt was the first to pull away. Jerusalem said, "Looks like we got caught up in the moment."

"You don't say," she said.

They continued to walk and talk and share small kisses in between their conversation. Egypt glanced at her watch and realized that she had lost track of time and made Jerusalem aware that time passed by without his knowledge. He flagged down a passing cab. The cab stopped, and Jerusalem handed the driver five one hundred dollar bills and instructed, "Take this young lady where ever she wants to go."

Egypt slid inside the back of the cab. Before Jerusalem closed the door, he bent down and gave Egypt one more kiss. The driver looked in his rearview mirror and smiled.

Jerusalem reached into his pocket and took out a small business card. "This has every last one of my numbers on it. I hope to hear from you before the day is over with."

"I promise you, you will."

He closed the door of the cab, moved back, and watched the cab driver take Egypt away.

Euphoric, he walked back toward the hotel and reminisced about the evening that just took place.

***

Egypt exited the cab at Etheria's hotel. She wanted to inform him of her plans. She wasn't going back to Africa with him and would be extending her stay in America. She entered the hotel and went straight up to the penthouse suite.

On the elevator ride up to the penthouse, her mind drifted back to her time with Jerusalem. The sound of the elevator brought her back to the present as the doors opened right outside of Etheria's penthouse suite.

Egypt knocked on the door. She stopped when she noticed the door moving. Someone was opening it from the other side. To her surprise, the same two women she'd seen earlier at her father's banquet slid out the door and past her. The women looked as if they had been up all night. Egypt stared at them but shifted aside. They mumbled some words, but she ignored them.

Without seeing any sign of Etheria, Egypt entered. Several empty bottles of champagne lay scattered throughout the suite. She continued toward the bedroom. The door was wide open. She could hear his snores before she entered. He lay naked on top of the plush white comforter passed out.

"Etheria," she said several times before he woke up.

With half-opened, bloodshot eyes he said, "Egypt, how did you get in my room?"

"Your guests let me in."

"My guests?" Etheria sounded confused.

"Yes, your guests. You low-down, no good bastard. What we had or what we thought we had is over." She turned and walked out the room.

Etheria jumped out the bed naked, not realizing he didn't

have on any clothes.

She headed toward the door. "Don't you think you should at least put some underwear on?"

Etheria looked down at his nakedness, stopped, and then hysterically started looking for his pajama bottoms. He hopped on one leg as he attempted to put on his pajama bottoms without falling down.

Egypt headed straight to the elevator. She pressed the down button and impatiently tapped her foot. The doors opened and she entered. She could hear Etheria calling out her name. His voice got louder and louder. Repeatedly, she hit the first floor button. He rushed out the front door and toward the elevator.

"You can explain this to my father or I can," Egypt shouted.

"Wait, Egypt!" Etheria called out, just as the elevator closed. He pounded on the door in frustration.

CHAPTER THIRTY

Jerusalem sat behind his mahogany desk on the top floor located in one of the downtown buildings where his real estate company was located. He finalized a quarter of a million dollar sale with one of his top salesman over the phone. He heard a knock on the door as he was ending the phone call. "Come in," he said.

Vanessa Long, his secretary, a young African-American woman, entered. "Mr. Williams, sorry to disturb you, but there's a gentleman out here to see you. He says that it's very important that he talks to you, but he doesn't have an appointment. He's adamant and says it's urgent that he speak with you."

"Let him in," Jerusalem responded.

She opened the door and said, "Mr. Williams can speak with you now."

Haitian Black entered the office. Vanessa walked out and closed the door behind her.

Jerusalem looked at his unexpected guest. He motioned with his hand and said, "Have a seat."

Haitian Black unbuttoned his black leather coat as he sat down, revealing black slacks, a blue shirt, and a pinstriped tie.

Jerusalem said, "I'm glad you came. I know this was a difficult decision, but I think it'll work out for the both of us. I see no reason for us to continue to be enemies when we can combine forces and make a powerful business."

"I agree," Haitian Black said humbly. "I couldn't agree with you more. I've learned a valuable lesson, Jerusalem. I must say, I did let my greed get the best of me. I wasn't as fair as I could have been. I know that I was the cause of our partnership coming to an abrupt end. My desire for power took control of my state of mind and corrupted my decisions. And my decisions weren't as honorable as they should have been."

"I understand," Jerusalem responded. "I respect you for your honesty. I admire you for coming here and saying the things that you're saying to me. I will keep my word also and give you a high position in my organization and a territory that you will run under your command. I will supply you with everything that you need. Whatever you buy from me, I will also give you the same amount on consignment. That will help you to rebuild your organization. Here today we swear to be allies."

They both stood and shook hands to seal the deal.

Jerusalem said, "If there's anything you need from me, I'm here for you. I wish you success."

"Thank you, mon," Haitian Black responded, right before he walked out of Jerusalem's office.

Jerusalem's phone rang. He saw an unknown number on the display, but he answered the phone and smiled when he heard Egypt's voice on the other end. "Hi beautiful."

"Hi, Jerusalem," she responded.

Jerusalem leaned back in his chair. "I've been anxious to hear from you. I'm glad you finally called me. I was wondering if you would."

"I can't deny that you're a hard man to forget about. You've been on my mind since we departed earlier this morning."

Jerusalem turned his chair around and looked out the window. "And the time that we spent together last night has also been filling my thoughts. Can I see you tonight?"

Egypt responded, "I would love that. What do you have in mind so I'll know how to dress?"

"It's nothing too big. Dress casual. Something relaxing."

"I'll see you tonight. Around seven would be fine?"

"I'll see you around seven and not a minute later. Where should I pick you up at?"

She gave him the address to her condominium, and they ended their call.

Hearing Egypt's voice over the phone made Jerusalem think about how sexy her voice was to his ears.

***

Jerusalem's limousine pulled up in front of Egypt's condominium. He dialed her number from his cell phone. Minutes later, Egypt exited the building wearing designer jeans, heels, and a purple cashmere sweater under a tan cashmere coat with purple gloves.

Egypt's mouth dropped open in surprise, seeing Jerusalem step out of the limousine wearing a white and black tuxedo, with black pants and a white tuxedo jacket with a white bow tie..

"What's going on? You told me to dress casual."

"What you have on is fine? You look beautiful. Besides, I wanted to see how you looked in casual clothing. I love how your body fits in those jeans. Shall we go?" He held the door open.

Egypt entered the limousine with a puzzled look on her face. "What's going on? I feel so underdressed."

"Just be patient. You'll see."

The limousine pulled up outside of a downtown exclusive women's boutique where only the rich and powerful shopped. The limousine driver opened the door. Jerusalem led Egypt inside. A cheerful young sales clerk immediately greeted them. "Hi, I'm Ginger. May I help you?"

Jerusalem responded, "We want to try on evening gowns."

"May we take your coats while you shop?" another sales woman came over and asked.

Jerusalem and Egypt handed the sales woman their coats. They followed Ginger to the section of the boutique filled with exquisite designer dresses in all colors and lengths.

"You look to be about size seven, am I correct?" Ginger asked Egypt.

"You're correct."

"Any particular color?" Ginger asked.

"She'll look good in any color, let's see a variety," Jerusalem responded.

Ginger and Egypt picked out several dresses as Jerusalem stood in the background and watched.

He sat outside of the dressing room while Egypt tried on different evening gowns and modeled them for him.

She looked good in each one, but one gown caught

Jerusalem's attention. She looked breathtaking in the black evening dress with one strap across the shoulder that ran underneath her arm and connected to the hip, exposing some of her body.

Egypt twirled around to show him how the dress looked at different angles. "You like?" she asked.

"Like? I love it. Well, minus your undergarment," Jerusalem responded.

Ginger said, "Looks like we have a winner."

Egypt hesitated. She ran her hand down the long split revealing her long legs. "Don't you think it reveals a little too much?"

Jerusalem responded. "No, that dress was made just for you. You look perfect in it. I can't imagine anyone else wearing that dress, but you."

Ginger nodded in agreement.

Egypt stood and admired herself in the floor-length mirror. She looked up into Jerusalem's eyes and saw admiration. Then she looked at Ginger. "This is the one I want."

Jerusalem looked at Ginger. "We'll need shoes to match the dress."

"I have the perfect pair. I promise you won't be disappointed," Ginger said.

"Wait, there's something else I'll need," Jerusalem said.

He whispered something near Ginger's ear. She left them alone as she walked to another section of the store.

Ginger returned with not only a pair of beautiful silver and crystal beaded heels; Ginger carried an ankle-length mink coat.

Jerusalem bent down and placed the shoes on Egypt's feet.

Egypt seemed to enjoy the special treatment as some of the sales people looked on in envy.

"I have one more gift for you." Jerusalem stood and retrieved a long, black velvet box.

Egypt's eyes lit up at the exquisite diamond and pearl necklace. "It's beautiful."

"Not as beautiful as you." He removed the necklace from the box and placed it around her neck.

"I'll cherish this forever," Egypt responded as her hand touched the necklace that now adorned her neck.

"Will there be anything else, Mr. Williams?" Ginger asked.

"No, thank you. You've been very helpful." He retrieved his credit card from his wallet and handed it to Ginger. "Give yourself a two hundred dollar tip."

"Sir, that's awfully generous of you, but I get paid on commission and my boss frowns on us taking tips."

Jerusalem reached into his pocket and pulled out several stacks of hundred dollar bills. He placed them in her hand. "Consider this between me and you."

Ginger's eyes lit up with excitement. "Thank you so much, Mr. Williams. If there's anything you ever need, just call the shop and ask for me. If we don't have it, I'll make sure I locate it for you."

She left them alone. Egypt slipped her arm through his. "That was very generous of you."

"If she was my sister, I would hope someone would treat her the same way."

"Some people treat sales clerks and the help as if they are beneath them, but not you."

"We're all put here to do a job. One job isn't better than the other. We all belong to Allah."

Ginger returned with Jerusalem's card and receipt. She smiled as they left out of the shop, but some of the other sales clerks looked on with envy.

Less than an hour later, they sat at a table in a five-star restaurant, located on the top floor of a downtown high rise building.

The restaurant required reservations, and on a normal day, was filled to capacity. The sign on the outside of the door read, "Closed for two hours."

The chef brought out their dinners. After a playful banter of getting to know each other over dinner, the conversation shifted.

Jerusalem stared into Egypt's eyes. "I love your accent and tone of voice. I think it's beautiful the way you pronounce your words. I can listen to you talk for hours at a time."

Egypt batted her eyes. "I know sometimes I can talk a little too much." She smiled.

"No, I find you very interesting. Being the daughter of a king, I'm sure you've travelled across the world and met many powerful people. Maybe even studied many different cultures."

"Yes. Ever since I was a young girl, my father sent me to learn different theologies and ideologies. I learned to speak five different languages fluently. I went to various schools across the eastern and western continents. I finished my education in the U.S. I have a master's in political science and a bachelor's in sociology. I should be ready to take my final exam in criminal law by next fall."

"That is some amazing accomplishments, especially in such a short period. You've yet to see your thirties, and you already have three different degrees in major subjects. You are a beautiful, intelligent Black woman."

Egypt smiled. "Thank you. That's very nice of you to say. Knowing your background, I can only imagine your struggles. I know it wasn't easy for you with all the odds against you, but I guess it made you the man you are today. You're a handsome, young, noble Black leader; a strong example for your people."

"If you're trying to get me to like you, it's a little too late, because I already do. I like you a lot. Even more each moment that I spend with you," Jerusalem responded.

"I feel the same. I like you a lot too, Jerusalem."

"So tell me, Ms. Master's, Bachelor's, Criminal Lawyer, which is your favorite subject out of the three degrees you have."

"Well, I haven't received the third one just yet. But I think all three are important to know and have had studied. But since you want me to choose, I will say that political science is very intriguing."

Jerusalem asked, "Why do you say that?"

Egypt responded, "I think we should be educated on politics and know more about the politicians that lead us and know what their real intentions and motives are. I think that we have the option to live in two ways. We can follow, or live our lives according to the dictation of others, or according to our own light. It's easy and convenient to follow others. Your parents will be happy if you followed them, their ideas, and their way of life; even though, it may be worthless. Their lives have not made them blissful or illuminate. They live in misery, and still their egos insist that the children should be obedient. Politicians can be the same way. They try to force society to live according to their ideas, and they have the masses fooled like they are doing public service. All they are doing is destroying the freedom and peace of the people. They are creating a false humanity. Insincere human beings. A gardener should be judged by what he reaps. To impose certain superstitions, certain structure, or character on any person makes that person a hypocrite. Sincerity is to live according to your own light. Not to live a double life. The new man is absolutely a necessity now because the old man is so decayed and ugly, rotten."

Jerusalem responded, "You are absolutely right. That's why we must follow our own voice. Some feel if they follow his own voice, that he's going against his parents, against society or against the leaders of this world. The conscious these people create in us is pollution. The police officer inside of us . . . the priests that's inside of us . . . the preacher that's inside of us . . . the reverend . . . the minister and the politician who go on condemning us. They all say, you should not do this . . . this is not right. This is wrong. You are a sinner if you do this . . . building guilt inside of us. It's like torture, making it hard for us to rest. It's making us miserable . . . afraid. They always want us to feel afraid and feel guilty because the more afraid and the more guilt we feel, the more control they have and the more we fall in their grips. How can we be joyful, happy, and cheerful in a society who's constantly condemning us?"

"And making us all schizophrenic," Egypt interjected. "You are well knowledgeable when it comes to politics yourself."

"A little. But you can school me anytime." Jerusalem drank some of his wine.

Music began to fill the air as the pianist played a lovely, slow melody. Jerusalem stood, picked up a purple flower from one of the bouquets on the table, and handed it to Egypt. She took a quick whiff of it. He held out one of his hands. "Would you like to dance with me?"

"I would love to." Egypt and followed Jerusalem to the center of the dance area.

They slow danced to the soft music. Through the huge glass window, they watched the first snowfall of the season. They looked into each other's eyes, and Jerusalem took the opportunity to kiss her soft lips. The soft, intimate kiss sent shocks through both of their bodies. It felt like they were connected for life.

Their kiss ended and they continued to dance. Jerusalem asked, "Have you ever thought about just running away and getting away from everything for a while?"

"I think about it all of the time."

"Well, let's run away together."

"And go where?"

"Wherever our hearts and our desires take us. I have a private jet to take us anywhere we wish."

"When do you want to leave?"

"How about now?" Jerusalem responded.

"Now?"

Jerusalem said, "Yes, now. Let's just go pack a few things, grab our passports, and we'll just shop wherever we go for the rest."

"Oh Jerusalem, I would love that. It's been awhile since I've done anything this spontaneous."

"That's another reason why you should do it. Live a little," Jerusalem said.

"But everyone's going to be looking for me. I don't want to worry my father."

"You can tell your father you're on extended vacation. Come on. Please." Jerusalem pled with his eyes.

Egypt looked away in deep thought. After a minute, she looked at Jerusalem and said, "Okay. Let's do this."

"Everything has already been taken care of here. Let's grab our coats and let's go see the world."

He grabbed Egypt's hand and led her toward the front of the restaurant, and the staff watched the excited couple vanish out the front door.

CHAPTER THIRTY-ONE

Jerusalem waited outside of Egypt's condominium while she located her passport and packed up a few personal items.

He made a few phone calls. "YaYa, I can trust you to call me if anything comes up," Jerusalem said.

YaYa responded, "You haven't had a real vacation since you've been home. Go. Enjoy yourself. Malachi and I got this covered."

"Have you caught up with Khadijah?" Jerusalem asked.

"She came over and told me she was pregnant. She's worried about keeping it because of my lifestyle. Her son's father was killed in Iraq, and she's afraid she might lose me."

"I'm sure after you talk with her tonight, you'll be able to sooth her fears."

"I'm sure everything will be fine." YaYa went on to talk about business.

Jerusalem smiled as the limousine door opened and Egypt entered. "I got to go. But call me if you need me." He ended the call with YaYa.

Egypt said, "You didn't have to get off the phone."

"When I'm with you, I like to give you my full attention."

Jerusalem reached over and grabbed Egypt's hand. They chatted while the driver took them to the airport.

The following day, Jerusalem sat behind his mahogany desk after a fine dinner in the dining area of the cruise ship. Jerusalem said, "I have a surprise for you."

He led Egypt into his chambers. A trail of rose petals went from the door to the bedroom and bathroom. Jerusalem led Egypt to the bathroom and opened the door. More rose petals were on the floor and led straight to an oval porcelain bathtub filled with lots of bubbles.

Egypt smiled and thought, *How romantic.* Jerusalem slowly undressed her. Egypt trembled slightly. She felt nervous because she had only been with one man. That one time with Etheria was not a good experience.

Jerusalem helped her into the tub. The warm water felt good to Egypt's body as she slid down into the tub. The bubbles rose to the top. Jerusalem picked up the soft mesh sponge and gently bathed her. Egypt exhaled with each one of his touches.

Afterward, Jerusalem dried her off and led her to his bedroom filled with lit candles and an assortment of flowers. A sexy lace see thru purple lingerie lay across the bed.

"I bought this for you to wear. Why don't you put this on for me while I go take a bath?"

Jerusalem returned after his bath wearing silk pajama bottoms and no shirt. Egypt stood on the side of the bed. Jerusalem was able to get a perfect view of her wearing the lingerie. He stopped at the door and stared at Egypt with lust in his eyes.

"Damn, you're beautiful," he said.

Egypt smiled but didn't say a word. Jerusalem walked near her. He took her hand and turned her slowly so he could view her curves in the lingerie. Pulling out a silk scarf out of his pajama pocket, he turned her and blindfolded her. He whispered in her ear, "Do you trust me?"

She nodded before she responded, "Yes."

Jerusalem laid her gently on the bed and then slowly removed her lingerie one piece at a time. He picked up a yellow rose and held it up to her nose. She sniffed it. He rubbed the rose across her nipples. Her nipples hardened. He rubbed the rose down her stomach and her thighs. He picked up a red rose and repeated the motions.

Reaching on the side of the bed, Jerusalem dipped his finger in some melted chocolate and placed his finger inside Egypt's mouth. She sucked the chocolate off his finger. He covered her mouth with his, dipping his tongue in and out of her mouth.

He dipped his finger in the chocolate again and rubbed chocolate near her ear all the way down to her belly button. Slowly, he licked the chocolate from her neck. He kissed her neck and kept doing the same motion until he reached her nipples. . As he swirled his tongue around each hardened nipple, Egypt moaned softly, as desire filled her body for more.

Jerusalem licked down her stomach, including the diamond in her belly button. He removed his pajama bottoms and placed himself in between Egypt's legs. She reached for the blindfold. He stopped her from removing it. "No, not yet."

He eased his head down in between her legs, licking and sucking the walls of her sweet neatly shaved pussy. Egypt arched her back. She'd never felt the type of pleasure she was experiencing with Jerusalem.

Jerusalem dipped his tongue in and out of her causing her legs to shake. She grabbed his head and shouted out in ecstasy. He eased up and removed the blindfold from her eyes. Their eyes locked. Love radiated between them.

The sight of Jerusalem's long, thick shaft caused Egypt's heart to skip a beat. She was nervous because she was concerned about the size. She didn't know if she would be able to handle his size, but was willing to try it. Her pussy moistened even more as she rubbed and stroked his stiff penis with her hand.

Egypt lay back on the bed and glided Jerusalem inside her one inch at a time. He gently entered her until her body accepted every inch. Her legs wrapped around his back as he slowly stroked her. Egypt closed her eyes. Egypt fit Jerusalem like a glove. They were a perfect fit.

Their moans were harmonious. Jerusalem rolled Egypt on top of him without exiting her. She leaned down and whispered in his ear, "I've never rode a penis before."

"Don't worry, I'll teach you. Just move like we slow danced the first night that we met."

Egypt fell into a slow rhythm on top of Jerusalem as if it was natural. She slid up and down and round and round on his dick. Jerusalem held her by the hips. Egypt felt her body convulsing. She leaned down and kissed Jerusalem as she exploded all over him.

Jerusalem pulled out of her and gently laid her flat on her stomach. He entered her from the back. She moaned with pleasure as he stroked her faster. She screamed out his name with pleasure.

He stroked her deeper and deeper and felt himself coming to a climax. Moving her hair aside, he sucked on the back of her neck and exploded like a cannon as they climaxed together.

His body fell limp on top of Egypt. Caught up in the beautiful experience they just shared, they were both breathing heavily. They made love through the night as they headed back to shore.

By the end of their trip, they were closer and the bond between them sealed. Jerusalem knew he'd met his soul mate and Egypt knew in her heart that she'd found her king. They were inseparable.

CHAPTER THIRTY-TWO

A month after Jerusalem's trip with Egypt, different leaders of the Black Senate from all over the city and other states such as California, Texas, Georgia, and Louisiana were in the city for the annual meeting held in the projects. The leaders, with their generals beside them, all wore black street attire and the Black Senate signature chains around their necks.

They came by various forms of transportation. Most parked their cars in nearby parking garages, some caught cabs or travelled via the L train because no one wanted to draw too much attention.

Malachi had security beefed up. He had soldiers on rooftops and entrance areas of the projects. One of the members of the local Black Senate led the visitors to a secret location, which happened to be the basement of one of the project buildings.

Jerusalem, Malachi, YaYa, and Pinky sat behind a long black table facing the members of the Black Senate. Each one of the members of the Black Senate from the city and various states stood in the area directly in front of the three Kings and

Pinky. The leaders discussed economics and ways to improve the economy in their local communities. They presented plans on how to create more jobs and financial security for the people who lived there.

There were discussions about small business loans with low interest rates to Blacks who were starting small businesses. They also talked about the judicial system and resolutions on helping members of their organization that had been in prison. Programs were put in place to help fund good attorneys and fund organizations that helped ex-cons once they were released from prison. The programs were also designed to help with housing and job placement.

After each leader presented their economic plan, they handed Pinky, who was the Black Senate's treasurer, a bank moneybag, which held two percent of their earnings. The money funded the Black Senate's overall agenda.

The meeting ended and all of the leaders and members in attendance socialized. It was a reunion for some and a first meeting for others. Malachi and YaYa walked up to Jerusalem.

Malachi said, "I was waiting on you to return so we could discuss this small problem we have."

Jerusalem responded, "What is it?"

Malachi said, "Tiny and Mice."

Jerusalem stopped looking around the room and looked directly at Malachi.

Malachi continued, "They've been taking advantage of their authority. Disciplining some of our soldiers without any mercy or just cause. I've been hearing rumors on how they've been beating some with bats because they say they violated one or two of the laws. Even breaking some fingers and beating some so bad that they were hospitalized. Some of our top soldiers have turned coat and ran to the Majors for protection. Some of our top soldiers like Monkey Man, Top Dog, and Oak Tree have left our organization and joined the Majors with some more of our soldiers whose names I can't recall right now."

Jerusalem stared at Tiny from a distance. With fire in his eyes, he watched Tiny and Mice talk to some Louisiana generals. "You know what you need to do. Take care of that ASAP. I have other business to take care of. I'll catch up with you guys later."

Jerusalem spoke with people as he made his way through the project building.

Malachi walked up to Tiny and Mice. "I need to talk to you two. Come with me."

Tiny and Mice looked at each other and then followed Malachi out of the building. He led them to the side of the building out of sight from the others.

Tiny spoke first. "What is it you want, Malachi?"

"It's about your future with the Black Senate. It has expired."

Mice stuttered, "Expired? Whatcha mean?"

"It's over," Malachi said with authority. "Y'all both have been in violation. Using your authority in the wrong way. I know that's due to your drug and drinking habits."

Tiny stuttered, "I-I-I don't have a drug problem. I have it under control."

"It's too late. Either y'all can die in honor, or I can give your mothers a closed casket. You choose."

Tiny and Mice both wore fear in their eyes. When Malachi was like this, there was no negotiating. Once Malachi got an order, he wouldn't stop until it was fulfilled.

Tiny said, "I want to die like a Black Senate."

Mice repeated Tiny's words.

"Well, y'all lead the way," Malachi said.

Tiny and Mice walked through the alley and ended up behind the Metropolitan High School. Their pace was slow as if they were walking down death row knowing that this would be their last walk.

Malachi said, "This is far enough."

They stopped and glanced at each other.

"I'll make this quick and painless as possible. Any last words? You have thirty seconds," Malachi said.

Neither said anything. They kneeled side by side. Tiny removed his Versace shades, folded them and placed them on his left side. Mice removed his fitted cap and placed it on his right side. They each closed their eyes. Malachi imagined them making peace with their maker. Thirty seconds later, Malachi shot Mice first in the back of the head, ending his life. Mice's body fell down on the ground. He then placed one shot into the back of Tiny's head and he fell on the ground.

"RIP" Malachi said aloud and walked away leaving their bodies to be discovered by some unfortunate person later.

***

Jerusalem pulled up in his Lexus SUV to the Majors hangout. Some of the Majors looked at the car suspiciously and some grabbed their gun as they watched Jerusalem exit the SUV alone. His medallion was the first thing noticed.

He walked up to the gang of men. "I want to speak to your leader. Will one of y'all go get Monster?"

One of the younger boys ran around the corner as fast as he

could and returned with Monster. Word of Jerusalem being there spread like wildfire. Not only did Monster, a six-feet-six muscular man, wearing a leather coat appear, but also so did Frog and other former soldiers of the Black Senate.

Normally, Monster's presence would intimidate an ordinary man, but Jerusalem faced him with no fear. Monster walked up to him. "What the fuck you doing on my turf? You know you're way out of bounds, Jerusalem. This is Major territory. If you think you're coming to take something from over here, it's not happening."

Jerusalem stared up at him. "I don't want your territory, but you do have something else that belongs to me."

"And what is that?"

"You have a few of my soldiers."

"They are Majors now. They weren't being treated right. They came to the Majors where they could get love and be respected as a man."

"What happened to them was out of my control and I didn't know about it. That situation is being taken care of as we speak."

"You think you can just come over here and take my men."

"You and I know that you don't want to war. You know if anything happens to me that it would never stop raining bullets. It wouldn't be good for your organization. But what we can do to settle this, you and I can go chest to chest, man to man."

"I don't have a problem with that. If I win, I'll keep your men," Monster responded.

"If you win, I won't bother you again," Jerusalem said,

removing his coat and his medallion. He took off his holster that carried two nines and placed it the front seat of his SUV.

The gang of men made a circle around Monster and Jerusalem as they squared up. Monster threw powerful blows but was unable to hit Jerusalem because he was too fast. Jerusalem was bobbing and weaving as if he was a trained boxer. Everybody heard about Jerusalem's knuckle game but had never seen it in person. Jerusalem caught Monster with a right hook and a jab, with lightning fast speed and power, making connections.

Monster was unable to hit Jerusalem with any power blows as Jerusalem made more contact with Monster's body, hitting him with ones and twos and threes combos. Jerusalem knocked Monster unconscious.

Jerusalem walked back toward his SUV, and the gang of men spread out as he walked through. He reached into the SUV and grabbed his holster. He placed it on and then grabbed his medallion and coat and placed them back on.

Monkey Man, Top Dog, and Oak Tree walked through the crowd of men, opened up the doors of the SUV, and entered.

Jerusalem rode away with the men he came there for.

CHAPTER THIRTY-THREE

Egypt eased into the passenger seat of Sherena's BMW located in front of her condominium. "Girl, look at the glow on your face. What's been going on with you? Where have you been?" Sherena asked as she pulled off. "I've been trying to reach you for weeks."

Egypt smiled and responded, "I've been having the best time of my life. Jerusalem is so great, that it's unbelievable. He's been catering to me. He's been showering me with gifts. He's been taking me places that I could only dream of."

"Ooh girl, have you given Jerusalem some?"

"What do you think?"

"By the look of the glow on your face and that big ass smile, yes, you've done the nasty."

"I sure have, girl. He knocked it out the park with that big ol' baseball bat he had."

Sherena said, "Stepping up to the plate with his Louisville slugger is King Jerusalem. Egypt winds up and throws a fastball. Pow. It's out of here."

"Girl, you're so crazy. But anyway, back to what I was saying. It was amazing the way that he kissed me, touched me, and licked me all over. The way he took his time and pleased my body. I didn't know making love could feel so good. To top it all off he's a great kisser. I couldn't get enough of his kisses."

"Egypt, are you in love?"

"Yes, very much so."

"You go girl!" Sherena gave her a high-five with her right hand while keeping her left hand on the steering wheel.

Egypt beamed with pride. "Thanks."

"I'm so happy for you. Because Etheria is garbage."

"Compared to Jerusalem, he is burnt garbage. Since we've been back from our trip, he's taken me to his mansion and I met his mother, Mama Sherry. She is so sweet and nice. We've been riding horses together, taking long walks, and I met this little seven-year-old that he's adopting. He is so cute. His name is Javian, but he kept on insisting that I call him Baby Stone. He said I was the only one besides Mama Sherry and Jerusalem that could call him Javian. He is hilarious. He showed me videos from cameras he's set up throughout the house where he's filmed playing tricks on Mama Sherry. Shampoo in toothpaste. When she brushed her teeth and realized it was shampoo, it bubbled up and she started spitting out bubbles. It was the most hilarious thing I'd ever seen."

Sherena stopped at the red light. A car hit them from the back. They screamed. They turned around to look. An old man in a station wagon was the culprit. Sherena got out of the car to make sure the man was okay. While she was checking on the old man, a van pulled up on the side of the car. The side door of the van opened. Two men dressed in black with their guns drawn snatched Sherena before she could respond. Egypt attempted to lock the passenger door but to no avail. The other man yanked the passenger door open and pulled Egypt out of the car kicking and screaming. He threw her in the van alongside Sherena.

***

Haitian Black looked at his surveillance camera and to his surprise, he saw Etheria standing there. He grabbed his gun, walked to the elevator, and walked to the entranceway of the warehouse. Thinking that Etheria came to cause problems, he braced himself. He drew his gun as he opened the door.

Etheria ignored him and walked past him. "Put that shit away. I got bigger problems than your stupid ass and I need your help. You owe me a favor. The least you can do is help me this one last time."

Haitian Black continued to hold the gun on Etheria.

"You help me with this and then all debts are paid."

Haitian Black eased the gun down. He decided to see what was on Etheria's mind.

Etheria's cell phone rang and he answered. The man on the other end said, "We got her, boss."

He responded, "Bring her ass to Haitian Black's garage." He clicked the phone off and looked at Haitian Black.

"What's the fuck going on, mon?" Haitian Black asked.

"It's my fiancé. She left me. She's ruining my life, and I can't let that happen. I got too much invested in this relationship to lose her now. She's about to fuck up everything. She's been running around with that bastard Jerusalem."

"What you need me for?" Haitian Black responded.

"I've kidnapped Egypt. I need to use your place until I figure all of this out."

The men pulled up in the van with Egypt and Sherena. The three men exited the van and pulled both ladies out. They were blindfolded and their mouths were gagged with cloth.

Etheria motioned the men to follow him to the elevator. Haitian Black reluctantly went along with Etheria and his plan. Etheria pressed the second floor button. They went to an office. The two men sat each one of the women down in separate chairs. Etheria removed Egypt's blindfold and the gag from her mouth. The other man removed Sherena's at the same time.

Their eyes showed shock as they looked at Etheria.

Egypt spoke out. "What is this? My father will have your life if you don't let me go immediately."

"Shut the fuck up!" Etheria slapped Egypt. "I'm not bullshitting with you anymore. You're trying to ruin my life and I'm not having it. I will kill you first. And if it comes down to it, I will kill your father."

Egypt, with fire in her eyes, stared at Etheria.

"If you want to see your father alive, you'll do as I tell you. I have men who are loyal to me. They are ready to assassinate your father at my will, and I don't think you want that. You think you'll be able to live with that. Having no one, I don't think you can. So it's best for you to play by my rules."

"Etheria, you've lost your mind!" Egypt shouted.

"I have a minister coming to marry us. You will marry me and sign the marriage license. Do you understand me?"

Egypt spit at him. "I will never marry you, so you can save your threats. 'Cause if anything happens to me or my father, everyone from our nation will be out to kill you. You wouldn't be safe anywhere in the world."

"Not if I kill Jerusalem. How would you like that, darling? I know where you've been and who you've been fucking with. You've been running around in the streets with this low-life peasant."

"He's more of a man than you'll ever be," Egypt said.

He placed his hands around her neck. "You watch what you say to me, you little spoiled bitch."

Etheria turned to one of the men and said, "Find out what's taking the preacher so long?"

Haitian Black, who had been pacing in the background, said, "I got to take a piss."

Etheria didn't respond, so

Haitian Black went to the nearby bathroom. He flushed the toilet as if he really did use the bathroom. He turned the water on the faucet and while it was running, he sent Jerusalem a text message with details on how to enter the warehouse unnoticed. Afterward, he returned to the room where everyone was still located.

One of Etheria's men said, "The Reverend said it will be forty-five minutes to an hour before he can make it. He got caught up in traffic."

Etheria snatched the cloth out of Sherena's mouth.

"I'm glad you came along for the adventure," he said, "'Cause I can use your little smart ass. You can be a witness. If you refuse, I won't hesitate to kill your ass first. I've wanted to dispose of your messy interfering ass anyway. 'Cause I know you've been filling Egypt's ears full of negativity about me."

"I was absolutely right about your evil, rotten ass," Sherena responded.

"I don't have to listen to you." Etheria stuffed the cloth back in her mouth. "Just remember what I said. And I'm not playing with your ass."

Etheria looked in Egypt's direction. "Since we got time to waste, why not start the honeymoon early. Bring your ass with me."

He grabbed her by the hair and pulled her up. "Y'all keep an eye on that other bitch."

Etheria dragged Egypt to another room and threw her on the bed.

Egypt shouted, "Etheria, no! Don't do this like this. I'm going to marry you. I'm going to give you what you want. Don't do this."

"Shut the fuck up! I am in charge, and I'm calling the shots here now. It's too late for that shit."

He bent down and kissed her. She bit him. He reached back and slapped her. Anger filled her eyes as she stared directly in his eyes. Tears formed in the corner of her eyes while he tore her clothes off. Etheria held her down with one hand and used the other hand to unbutton and then unzip his pants. He pulled his pants down, exposing himself. A wicked smile swept across his face.

Egypt attempted to shift her body, but his weight was too much. She screamed out. He placed one of his hands over her mouth. Just as he was about to penetrate her, rapid gunshots were heard outside of the room.

"What the fuck!" Etheria jumped up, almost tripping over his pants that was down to his ankles.

While pulling up his pants, Jerusalem burst through the door, startling him.

***

The sight of Egypt tied up on the bed naked infuriated Jerusalem. His attention was now directly on Etheria. Before Etheria could say a word, Jerusalem placed his smoking gun on a nearby shelf and caught Etheria with a right hook to the chin knocking him to the floor. Dazed and trying to recover, Etheria remained on the floor. Jerusalem kicked him in the stomach with his Timberland boots. Etheria winced in pain.

"Get up, you weak piece of shit!"

Etheria rose up and tried to catch his breath. He swung wildly at Jerusalem, who weaved back, dodging the punch. He let out a flurry of punches, accurately connecting to Etheria's face and upper body.

Barely concious, Etheria lay on the floor bloody. Jerusalem removed his jacket, covered Egypt's naked body, and untied her.

Egypt wrapped her arm around Jerusalem's neck and cradled her head on his shoulder. "Everything's all right now. I'm here, baby." He grabbed her face. "Are you okay?"

Tears flowed down her cheeks. "Yes, I'm okay. I'm glad you made it in time. That bastard tried to rape me. But you made it just in time."

She stood up, then went over to Etheria, and kicked him several times in the stomach. Jerusalem located her underwear and pants and handed them to her. She slipped them on. He grabbed Etheria by the collar and lifted him up, placing a gun to his head. "Bring your ass up in here."

Jerusalem dragged Etheria to the other room. Egypt followed.

Haitian Black was kneeled down consoling Sherena with the

dead Africans lying bloodied on the floor.

Jerusalem walked up to Haitian Black and they embraced. Jerusalem said, "Thanks for having my back."

"No problem, mon."

Etheria yelled out, "You low-down backstabbing motherfucka. I knew I couldn't trust your ass."

"Fuck you, mon. I never liked you anyway. You're rotten and no good. You're getting what you deserve."

Sherena walked over to Etheria and kicked him in the nuts. He bent over and whimpered in pain.

Jerusalem said to Haitian Black, "Tie his ass up."

Haitian Black did as instructed.

"Contact your father," Jerusalem said as he handed Egypt his cell phone.

***

King Geoffrey flew in from New York as soon as he got the phone call from Egypt. With several of his men walking behind him, King Geoffrey followed Haitian Black inside of the warehouse.

Sitting in a chair tied up and bloodied, Etheria made eye contact with King Geoffrey.

Egypt and Sherena ran up and embraced her father before he made it to the room.

"Dad!" Egypt said.

He shook Jerusalem's hand. "Thank you for rescuing my daughter. Anything you need, please come to me. I am forever grateful to you. And thank you for leaving me Etheria to deal with."

He ordered the men to take Etheria. They pulled him up out

of the chair. King Geoffrey stared at Etheria with death in his eyes. Etheria knew it was a stare of death.

King Geoffrey turned toward Egypt. "You and Sherena come with me."

Egypt walked over to Jerusalem and embraced him. "I love you so much," she whispered in his ear.

"I love you too, princess," he responded. "Know this. I will give my life for you."

Sherena went up to Haitian Black and kissed him on the cheek. "Thank you."

Egypt broke the embrace with Jerusalem and left the room with Sherena and King Geoffrey. Jerusalem and Haitian Black stood side by side.

Jerusalem turned and looked at Haitian Black. "I think she likes you."

"What's there not to like, mon?" Haitian Black responded with a hearty laugh.

CHAPTER THIRTY-FOUR

Over the next several months Jerusalem and King Geoffrey grew closer. Jerusalem visited Nigeria on many occasions. Whenever King Geoffrey visited the United States, Jerusalem would be one of the first people he contacted. Jerusalem received King Geoffrey's blessing to continue the relationship with Egypt.

With the weather now getting warmer, Jerusalem planned a picnic near the harbor for Egypt. While gazing at the water, a yacht passed by, and under the moonlit sky, she noticed the people on the yacht held up lighted signs that spelled out "Will you marry me?"

Jerusalem pulled out a black velvet box and opened it, displaying a fourteen carat princess cut diamond ring.

Egypt responded, "Yes, Jerusalem. Yes, I'll marry you."

He slipped the ring on Egypt's finger. They kissed under the moonlight as the people on the yacht cheered.

***

Jerusalem became second in command of King Geoffrey's heroin business. He now controlled the majority of the supply throughout the north, south, and east. Jerusalem knew that he could be as powerful as the Italian Mafia, but needed to figure out a way to keep his political connections with Gino, known as one of the godfathers.

An hour later, Jerusalem pulled up in front of Gino's two-story mansion. He exited his SUV carrying two suitcases. Gino's bodyguards greeted him outside of the door. Without saying a word, they patted him down. He opened up the suitcase and they checked to view its contents.

One of the bodyguards opened the door. A maid then greeted Jerusalem and led him through the house to the patio.

Gino was leaned back in a chair smoking on a Cuban cigar. He looked up in Jerusalem's direction. "Welcome. Have a seat, my friend."

Jerusalem sat on the other side of the patio table placing the suitcases down beside him.

"Can I offer you any refreshments?" Gino asked.

"No, thank you," Jerusalem responded.

"I can't help but notice the two suitcases you brought with you. You brought me a gift, or are you moving in?" Gino picked up his glass and drank some of the lemonade.

"No, I won't be moving in, but I have brought you a present. Not only for you, but for some of your other associates."

"What have I done to deserve such a gift coming from you?"

"I just wanted to show my appreciation for all you've done for me over the past few years. I appreciate the knowledge you've shared with me. You've taught me how to be a successful businessman and how to carry myself in many situations. I couldn't have made it this far without your guidance. But as you can tell, I'm an authentic type of man and sometimes, a man has to finish his journey alone. I hope that you understand, and I hope we can also keep our friendship."

"So what are you telling me, Jerusalem? That our business relationship is over? Are you unhappy with the way you and I conduct business? I thought I was being good to you and fair."

"It's not that. You were fair in every way. But there comes a time for a man to make his own moves and be able to expand as far as his vision can take him. So I brought you this gift." Jerusalem placed both suitcases on the table. "It's five million in each suitcase. Five million for you and a million for each one of the other five families to show my gratitude."

"Tell me, Jerusalem, what is this new adventure you're on, now that you don't need my help? As far as I know, I'm the only one in Illinois who can supply you. You must have met some heroin god."

"No, I just had to travel a long way to meet the Wiz. He gave me a new blueprint to build a bigger and more powerful empire. Being a businessman, I couldn't pass that opportunity up. With you being a businessman also, I know you'll understand. We can continue our business in a different way. I can give you and your associates a key of heroin; let's say fifty thousand a key."

"Fifty thousand a key. It seems like you're trying to corner the market. Not even my associates or I can compete with those prices. Me being a businessman, I have to consider your offer, but before I do that, I have to take it up with my associates. My concern is how the other heads of the five families will feel about losing your business. I don't think they will be too happy even with the gift. Because they were making more than a million apiece from you."

"Well, I'm willing to bring y'all a million dollar a piece every six months to keep your friendship and political connections," Jerusalem said.

"That might be possible, but I'm not sure. Knowing my associates, they will wonder why and want to know your motives. You know my friend Kaleef tried to rise above the Italian mob, and my friends weren't too happy about it. Kaleef ended up doing life in the federal penitentiary because he wasn't under our protection any more. I hope you understand what type of position you're putting me in. I wouldn't want anything like that to happen to you."

"I've learned that you can only control your destiny and not your fate. Like I said, I am an authentic man. Sometimes I have to stand alone. Stand on what I believe in. With all due respect, Gino. I believe that this is the best move for me right now. "

"I understand. You've never had a drink with me. Have a drink with me this day."

"No, I'm fine, with all due respect."

"Mary, bring me a bottle of wine and two glasses," Gino yelled.

Jerusalem said, "I'm fine, Gino."

"I insist, Jerusalem. Let's end our friendship with a toast. Plus, you brought me a beautiful gift, so why not?"

Mary walked out on the patio with the bottle of wine and two glasses. Gino stood up, took the bottle from Mary, and poured wine into both glasses. He sat one glass in front of Jerusalem.

Jerusalem picked up the glass and stared directly into Gino's eyes. Gino raised his glass. Jerusalem hesitated for a few seconds, stood up, raised his glass, and toasted with Gino. With one single gulp, they both finished their glass of wine.

"Come here, Jerusalem. Give me a firm shake and a hug."

Gino grabbed Jerusalem and kissed him on both cheeks. "You've turned into a great businessman. I couldn't be prouder. You've reached above my expectations. Now I might have to buy from you. I'm proud of you."

Jerusalem gave a fake smile. "Thank you, Gino. If you would excuse me, I have other business I must handle. I'm already a little late."

"I understand. Have a nice day."

Jerusalem returned to his SUV and called YaYa as he drove away. YaYa answered. "It's done," Jerusalem said, hoping he wouldn't have to regret his decision.

CHAPTER THIRTY-FIVE

Jerusalem walked through the projects passing by his army of Black Warriors with a face of stone. You couldn't help but notice the look of vengeance. Many were going to pay for the demise of his brother and his comrade.

He walked to the front of his soldiers, stood, and stared for a minute or more before he began to speak with Malachi, who was standing on his side. Everyone could feel the absence of one of the three kings.

It made the realization of the death of YaYa more real. The three bad black brothers—the three kings—were now only two. Things would never be the same. YaYa's death signified a dramatic change was about to take place.

Jerusalem, in a voice sounding like thunder, said, "I put this on the virgin Mary. I got no love for you that is scary. If you eating with me, your mind had better be military. Remember King YaYa's obituary. We are united and ready to take these devils to war. I'm calling out for all the lords of the battlefield. I can see the lights on top of the holy hill. It's time for a real warrior to come and lead us. I'm calling like the one that came after Jesus. So where my warriors that's ready to ride or die? Don't let your slugs fly until you see the white of their eyes. Hear my war cries. Where are my warriors?"

They yelled out, "The Black Senate."

Jerusalem repeated, "Where are my warriors?"

They yelled out again in unison, "The Black Senate."

"Everyone follow me," Malachi ordered.

The army of Black Warriors followed Malachi to two vans parked at the very back of the projects. D-Dog, Top Dog, and Monkey Man passed out automatic weapons and ammunition to each one of the soldiers.

Jerusalem stood and watched from afar. His warriors were ready to put their lives and freedom on the line. The city of Chicago was about to witness terror like they had never seen before. The enemies of Jerusalem was about to feel his wrath.

***

Hawk and Catfish cruised the Westside of Chicago looking for a prostitute to harass. They wanted to get their dick sucked for free. They spotted a beautiful, exotic, and sexy Black woman they'd never seen before walking the strip. With little to no clothes on, China Doll noticed them staring as they passed and made a U-turn.

She stopped walking as the car pulled up beside her and rolled down the passenger side window.

Catfish was the first to speak. "Hi, sexy."

"Hi," China Doll replied.

"Can we have a word with you?" he asked.

China Doll looked around.

"You don't have to worry," Catfish said. "We're not here on business, so you can relax."

"What do you cops want to talk to me for?" she responded. "I'm just taking a walk to get some fresh air. That's not a crime, is it?"

Hawk, with little patience blurted out, "Look, bitch, don't try that shit with us. We know you out here selling pussy. Don't make me get out of this car and take your ass in for solicitation and whatever else I can think of. I know your pimp wouldn't like to have to come to the precinct and bond your yellow ass out of jail, now would he?"

"Well, what the fuck you motherfuckas want with me?" she responded.

"We want to know how good you are at sucking two dicks at the same time," Catfish responded.

They both laughed.

"What's in it for me?" she asked.

"What's in it for you?" Hawk said. "To be able to walk down the ho' stroll without us taking you in every time we see you, bitch. That's what's in it for you."

Luscious ran up frantically. "Help me! My girlfriend looks like she's overdosed. Help me, please!"

"Calm down, bitch." Hawk said.

"She's overdosing, please!" Luscious said. "She needs some help."

"Help her for me. I got you," China Doll said.

Hawk and Catfish look at each other for a second. "Where's she at?" Hawk asked.

"Right there in the alley." Luscious pointed.

Hawk and Catfish exited the car and walked toward the

alley. China Doll and Luscious followed. Several working girls surrounded the one who was on the ground with foam coming out of her mouth.

"Y'all bitches move out the way," Hawk ordered.

"What did she take?" Catfish asked.

One of the girls said, "We shot up a couple of CCs of heroin."

Hawk looked at the girl with disgust on his face. "You stupid bitch."

China Doll and Luscious walked up behind Catfish and Hawk with razors in their hands. Almost simultaneously, they sliced their throats from ear to ear, as the other gutter girls pulled their knives and jugged the two cops repeatedly.

Hawk and Catfish attempted to stop the blood coming from their throats before finally falling to the concrete.

Pinky appeared from behind a nearby dumpster holding a tech nine automatic weapon as the gutter girls cleared the way for her to walk up to the two cops' bloodied bodies that had been filled with stab wounds and heads barely connected to their bodies.

Pinky stared down at both of them. "This is for YaYa." She unloaded multiple shots to each cops' body. The gutter girls all stood in silence for a few seconds before exiting the alley. Each went their separate ways and disappeared into the urban streets.

For the next couple of weeks, all over the Chicago area, cops were found dead. Some murdered in their cars as they patrolled the streets, others sniped from project buildings as they walked through the Black communities or coming out of convenience stores with cups of coffee and sandwiches; falling to the ground from a single shot to their head from a high-powered weapon.

The chief of police tried to gain control by putting four cops to a car with full body armor with at least one patrol car following the other one, but it didn't stop the Black Warriors from attacking the police every chance they got; wounding some, if not killing them.

Chicago police force was definitely feeling the heat that was coming from all directions.

Jerusalem found himself riding the streets of Chicago with no particular destination in mind. He rode in his Black BMW in deep thought and couldn't stop thinking about the bloodshed that was caused by his hand, knowing that it wasn't over yet.

Gino and the other heads of the Italian mob family had to pay for the death of his brother and some of his warriors that lay dead in their resting place. They all had to pay for the deaths of his loved ones.

Right before Jerusalem woke up from his trance, he noticed he had come to an area that was familiar to him. He hadn't been in the area for many years. His memories flashed back to the time of when Mama Sherry rescued him from the area.

He pulled up to the overpass that was once his home for a little over a year. Homeless families still filled the area with cardboard boxes, old dirty blankets and mattresses to try to make them as comfortable as possible. Jerusalem stared up at the underpass, as the people looked as if they were barely living life. What they did have was a free mind. They didn't have to carry the weight that was on his shoulders. The weight was starting to wear him down. He thought back to some of the things Kaleef told him while he was in prison.

He took a huge gulp from his bottle of imported Cognac and

another pull from his blunt.

Antonio, one of the heads of the five families never changed his routine even though he knew a war was taking place throughout the streets. Antonio sat in his old model Cadillac waiting on his son to exit the junior high school. He made it his business to take his son to school and pick him up and today was no different.

He smiled as he saw his only son walking toward him. His son was always eager to share with him the events of his day. He watched with pride as his son walked in front of the car and waved at him. The eleven-year-old son entered the passenger side of the car.

"Hi, father," the young boy said as he set his backpack down on the floorboard of the vehicle.

"Hi," the man said as he leaned and kissed his son on the cheek. "How was your day?"

He didn't notice the black Crown Vic with dark tinted windows pulling up beside him.

The back window rolled down. Malachi, with a black bandana covering his face and showing only his deadly eyes, pulled out a Mac 11 assault rifle. He unloaded every round into the driver's side of the car, killing the man and his son.

CHAPTER THIRTY-SIX

Jerusalem exited his car and walked toward the homeless people. The noise from the cars on the busy freeway was loud and clear as he looked around to see if he could recognize any familiar faces.

Some of the homeless people walked up to him and asked for spare change. Jerusalem felt his heart tug and began handing out bills in increments of twenties, fifties, and hundreds. The crowd around him grew. One of the homeless men caught his attention. It was something about his eyes. Staring back at him was Harry. Harry was twenty years older, but Jerusalem knew it was him.

"Harry?" Jerusalem asked.

The dark-skinned older man looked confused. He took the money Jerusalem offered, but remained silent.

"It's me, Jerusalem," he said.

"Jerusalem?" The older man looked at Jerusalem in disbelief, but now staring at him more intensely to see if he could recognize him.

"Yes, it's me," Jerusalem responded.

They embraced like two old friends. Tears filled the old man's eyes.

***

Pauly exited his house enraged, yelling at the top of his lungs at his wife. "My mama told me I should have married someone else. You're nothing but a lying bitch," he yelled out other words in Italian.

He got in his car and slammed the door. Still enraged, he put the car in reverse and backed up. His car was cut off at the end of the driveway by a black van. Three Haitians exited the van, along with their commander, Haitian Black. Wearing all black, the men, with their high-powered weapons, shot into the car. Pauly's car drifted backward.

The driver of the van moved and Pauly's car rolled into the street. Haitian Black and the men with him never stopped firing. They didn't stop until Pauly's body slumped over and was no longer moving.

Pauly's wife stood in the front door yelling in horror. Haitian Black and his men got back in the van and sped off, leaving onlookers in shock at the blood bath that just occurred. Some of Pauly's neighbor tried to get a license plate number as the van sped away.

***

Jerusalem smiled for the first time since YaYa's death at the sight of Harry. "How have you been?" he asked Harry.

"I'm okay. You're looking good. Looking like a successful

businessman or something. I have to admit. I thought after not hearing from you or about you, that you were somewhere dead. I've thought about you over the years, and I'm glad you're still alive and doing well."

In a low voice, Jerusalem said, "Everything isn't always what it seems."

"You're alive, aren't you?" Harry said.

"I found out that because you're breathing, doesn't mean you're alive." Jerusalem's voice drifted off.

Harry could tell from Jerusalem's tone and look in his eyes that the young man was dealing with something deep down within his soul. Harry said, "Walk with me."

Jerusalem did as instructed.

"Dilemma is the essential way in which we all are tested," Harry said. "Facing your dilemma is the only way you can defeat it. Dilemma is our destiny. Fight it. Enter into your dilemma with intensity. Live the dilemma. Go through the heat and suffering of it. You must experience it. Don't run from the fire. What is manifesting from fire will burn away all the dirt and pure gold will remain."

By now they were standing with a clear view of the open highway. Jerusalem turned to Harry and said, "Thanks for your words of advice. I want to help you. I want to set you up in a house and get you a job and off these streets. You don't have to live like this." Jerusalem pointed at the background of the area where they stood. "Harry, you don't have to be homeless anymore."

"Thank you, Jerusalem, but no thanks." Harry smiled.

Jerusalem frowned in confusion.

Harry went on to say, "This is my life here. This is how I

choose to live. Happiness is of the internal . . . not of the external. If you're not at one with the whole you, you can never find peace no matter where you try to go. There will always be a conflict on the inside. The moment you stop accepting the challenge of life, you are dead. This, I accept." He pointed. "Whatsoever life brings, even if it's war, that too must be accepted. If life is leading a person into war"—Harry stopped, smiled and looked into Jerusalem's eyes.—"That war must be accepted."

How does he know my internal conflict? Jerusalem wondered.

As if reading Jerusalem's mind, Harry said, "Listen to me, my friend. Success sometimes follows failure. We set our heart on something and it wasn't ever to be obtained. We expected happiness to come after obtaining something and it led to sorrow. The end is always unknown. Invisible life is a journey. This is an invisible unknown. I appreciate your offer to help, but I'm happy here."

"I understand, but here. Take this. Maybe, you can use it." Jerusalem reached into his pants pocket and took out a wad of money. "I don't know exactly how much it is, but I know it should be well over seven thousand."

"That I will accept," Harry said. "I'm no damn fool. Free money. Shit, give it here."

They both broke out in laughter.

Harry said, "I almost forgot. There's been some crazy lady asking about you. Almost every day. She leaves for days and then she comes back and stays for weeks and months. She's been doing that for about nine years now. I don't know what it's all about, but all she says is your name, 'Jerusalem. Where's

Jerusalem? Have you seen Jerusalem?'"

"Where is she?" Jerusalem asked.

Harry looked around at the different faces of homeless people. "I saw her earlier. She must be in her house right over there." He pointed at a homemade cardboard box.

CHAPTER THIRTY-SEVEN

Another one of the heads of the five families exited the movie theater with his wife. He held her hand as they laughed and walked through the parking lot toward their car. "I can't wait to get you home," he said to his wife as she giggled.

An old woman walked toward them. The couple barely noticed her, as they continued to flirt with one another. The closer the old woman got, it was clear that it was a black man dressed up in drag. The man pulled out his .357 handgun and shot the mob boss twice straight in the chest. His wife stared in disbelief. The shooter ignored her as the mob boss's body fell to the ground. The shooter stood over the mob boss and shot a bullet straight into his head.

The wife screamed out. The shooter shot her once in the head, killing her instantly. Her body fell on top of the mob boss. The shooter briskly walked away into the night as he saw a few people coming in their direction.

CHAPTER THIRTY-EIGHT

Jerusalem walked over the homemade tent Harry showed him. Briefly, he stood on the outside of the tent that was made out of old sheets and two by fours and boxes before trying to find out who would be on the other side of it. A part of him didn't want to know, but something inside of him wouldn't allow him to leave. He needed to know what woman had been looking for him for years.

Jerusalem sighed. "Hey! Is anyone in there? Hey, you there?"

"Get the fuck away from my damn house!" the lady yelled out.

Jerusalem's trembled with fear. He could never forget that voice. It had hunted him for years. He pulled the sheet back and to his disbelief, he came face to face with Anna Marie. They stared at each other in silence for a few seconds.

Anna Marie asked, "Who the fuck is you? Get the hell out of my house!"

Jerusalem didn't move. He just stared at his mother. The rage that had been living dormant in him for years started to erupt like a volcano.

Anna Marie noticed by the way he was dressed that he wasn't one of the homeless. She changed her tone. "Who is you? You got some dope? You got that, boy? Do you know where I could get some good heroin? I'm sick. I got an illness. Just give me a fix. Please."

Jerusalem's heart softened as he looked at the condition of the woman staring back at him—his mother. After all of the things she'd done to him, he stilled loved Anna Marie. He breathed heavily as he took slow steps toward her. Each step represented his heart opening up to her. He wanted to embrace her, forgive her, and comfort her. After two decades, his heart owned up to missing her.

"You got some money?" she asked. "Give me twenty dollars. Just twenty dollars. That's all. That's all I need. I'll do anything. I'll suck your dick."

Jerusalem stopped in his tracks and the rage reappeared but stronger than before. "What? What did you say to me?"

Anna Marie repeated herself. "I'll suck your dick for twenty bucks."

Jerusalem clinched his teeth. The anger of her abandoning him and not having a mother for twenty years filled his heart. He was reminded of the little boy who was left alone, homeless and afraid—all at the hands of her—Anna Marie—his so called mother.

He reached behind him, pulled out a forty-five from underneath his shirt, and pointed it straight at her.

She screamed.

"Shut up, bitch!" Jerusalem demanded.

"Don't shoot me! Please don't hurt me," she begged.

He grabbed her by the hair and put his gun to her head. "Bitch, if you make another sound, I'm going to blow your brains all over this piece of shit you call home. You hear me?"

"Yes. Yes, I hear you," she stuttered.

"Get your ass up." Jerusalem helped her up with force. He grabbed her arm, led her to his car with one hand, and placed his gun back behind his shirt with the other. Harry and others watched from the sidelines.

Jerusalem popped open the trunk and forced Anna Marie inside. She whimpered.

"If you make a sound, any sound, I'm going to pull this motherfucka over and blow your fuckin' face off. You hear me?"

Anna Marie nodded in agreement.

He closed the trunk, walked to the driver's seat, and drove away.

***

Another one of the mob bosses rubbed his full belly after leaving his family-owned Italian restaurant. His driver held the back door open and he got inside. The driver got behind the wheel and started driving the mob boss home.

"Hurry up, because I got to piss," the mob boss said.

The driver said, "Boss, there's a car stalled at the light, " as they drove on West Ontario Street near the Hard Rock Cafe.

"Then go around him."

Before the driver could respond, a shadow appeared holding a gun. Bullets flew inside of the car shattering the window, hitting the driver.

"Shit!" the mob boss said as he slid down in the seat. The male figure in the shadow walked to the back passenger side and fired shots. The window shattered and the shooter aimed at the whimpering mob boss and shot him in the heart and then in the head.

***

Jerusalem pulled up to a house on the Westside of Chicago. He popped open the truck and snatched Anna Marie's frail body out.

"Where are you taking me?" she asked, as her arms swung hitting him a few times.

"Shut up!" Jerusalem placed his hand behind her thin neck, led her to the house, and knocked on the door.

A middle-aged woman opened the door. Jerusalem pushed Anna Marie inside of the house. The middle-aged woman closed the door behind them as Jerusalem dragged Anna Marie along.

"Sit your ass down and don't move or say a fuckin' word!" Jerusalem said.

Anna Marie did as she was told.

Jerusalem turned toward Francis, who was the director of Jerusalem's rehab clinics located in various parts of the city. "This is Francis. Francis this is . . . you tell her. What's your name?"

Anna Marie said, "Anna Marie Williams."

"Francis, I want you to keep her here until I return. She needs your help. As you can tell, she's a junkie. Don't let her out of this house and don't give her anything to help with the detox. And also, don't mention my name to her under any circumstances."

"You know not giving her anything during detox might kill her," Francis said.

"Don't give her shit. Let her ass detox cold turkey."

Francis shrugged her shoulders. "I guess you know what you're doing."

"Just clean her ass up. You got funds to get her some clothes and whatever else she might need. I'll be back to check on y'all from time to time. Remember, do not mention my name. Never leave her alone. If she has to be here alone, then handcuff her to the bed."

"Okay," Francis responded.

Jerusalem kissed Francis on the cheek and left the house.

***

The tall, slender fifty-year-old mob boss, Donatella hid out in one of his secret clubhouses. After hearing about the murders of the other mob bosses, he wasn't taking any chances on being next. He smoked more than he usually did because his nerves were bad. He didn't feel safe anywhere and ended up in this clubhouse surrounded by his men.

His attempts to contact Gino remained unsuccessful. Gino fled overseas to an unknown location. All of the mob bosses underestimated Jerusalem and the organization they called the Black Senate. Donnatelle watched them rise to power and was amazed at how they were now more powerful the Italian mob.

Donnatelle's ego wouldn't allow him to admit defeat amongst his men. He hit his chest. "See, I stayed here with y'all. But Gino ran away and he's hiding from them moolies. Them niggas are dead. You hear me! All of them! I want Jerusalem's balls

274

given to me in my fuckin' hands. You hear me!" Donnatelle looked at all the men sitting around him. He hit the table. "You hear me! I want his whole family dead! His kids dead, his mother dead, his wife dead."

One of the men said, "Fuckin' niggas think they are more powerful than us. They think they can come against us. We're Italians. Our bloodline runs from here to Italy. Pure Italian."

Donnatelle said, "They don't know where the fuck they from or where they going. They think they can fuck with us." Donnatelle looked around. He clenched his fists tight. Donnatelle had earned his reputation on being a ruthless killer from his teenage years. He loved the act of war. He built his power on violence and being surrounded by his men reminded him of that. He was not going to hide anymore. He and his men would reclaim their city and destroy the Black Senate.

A blast from a hand grenade blew the front door of the clubhouse open. The Black Warriors, along with some of the Nigerians and Haitians, rushed into the building with their high-powered weapons and opened fire, catching Donnatelle and his men off guard. They shot anything or anyone moving. Gunfire came from every direction, killing anyone sitting or standing.

Donnatelle's attempt to shoot someone with his handheld gun was unsuccessful, the blast from one of the bullets, knocked the gun right out of his hands. Donnatelle held his hand in pain. A Black Warrior shot him multiple times, as his body shook repeatedly with blood oozing out with each shot. None of the Black Warriors or their comrades was injured. They were all wearing bulletproof vests.

Injured and dead bodies lay throughout the club. It was a blood house. The gunmen walked around the room and shot every injured person straight in the head.

The mob family never stood a fighting chance against the Black Warriors and their comrades.

CHAPTER THIRTY-NINE

The next few months went by in a blur for Jerusalem. During that time, he went by the clinic to check on his mother and check on her progress. For the first time in Jerusalem's life, Anna Marie was drug free. She looked healthy and more like the woman on a picture he'd remember seeing as a child.

On this particular visit, Francis had left Anna Marie alone with Jerusalem. Anna Marie talked to him, but she still hadn't recognized her own son.

She said, "You don't have to worry, Mister. I'm never going back to that life. I'm never doing dope again. I love myself now. Thanks to you and Francis. Y'all gave me a new start. I appreciate everything you guys have done for me." She paused. "I'm sorry. I'm just so happy. I've never felt so clean. It's as if I'm a brand new woman. I feel alive."

Jerusalem looked into her bright eyes. Eyes that just months ago looked dead, but now looked lively. "You still don't recognize me, do you?"

Anna Marie studied his face. "No, I don't think so."

"It's me, Mama. Jerusalem . . . your son."

Anna Marie's mouth flew open. She placed her hand across her mouth to smother the moans. Tears flowed down her face like a water fountain. "You're my baby? My baby Jerusalem?" she asked.

"Yes. It's me, Mama," Jerusalem responded.

She jumped from her chair and wrapped her arms around him, crying her eyes out. Jerusalem sat still, unsure of how to respond. He tried to resist hugging Anna Marie but couldn't. He raised his arms slowly, wrapped them around his mother, and hugged her as hard as he could. A dam was open and the tears of all the pain from all the years flowed from Jerusalem's eyes and onto her shoulder.

They both took a seat on the living room sofa as they wiped the tears from their eyes.

Anna Marie was the first to speak. "I came back to look for you, Jerusalem. I kept coming back to the same place hoping that one of those times I would run into you. I prayed every day and night for God to bring my son back to me and you came back. Thank you, God. Thank you."

They hugged each other again. Tears flowed freely between the two of them.

Jerusalem looked into the eyes of his drug-free mother. "How could you leave me, Mama? I was just a baby. You left me on the streets alone to fend for myself. I was only six. Do you know what all I had to go through? Do you?"

"I can only imagine," Anna Marie responded, holding his hand. "I was sick, Jerusalem. That dope had me. I was on that stuff and it took over my life. I didn't care about nothing but a high. I was sick." Tears rolled down her face again.

"You left me to die. You gave me to the wolves for slaughter. Why didn't you love me? I was your child. Your only child . . . your son. Why didn't you ever love me, Mama?" Jerusalem's voice was low, barely above a whisper. He no longer had tears in his eyes. He asked her things that he'd always wanted to know, questions that haunted him over the years, and questions he'd promised himself he would ask her if he ever faced her again.

"I loved you then and I love you now. I've always loved you, Jerusalem. When I realized what I had done, I came back looking for you. You wasn't there. I looked all over for you. I asked people, but nobody knew where you were. I'm sorry, baby. I'm sorry for what I made you go through. Please forgive me. I need you to forgive me. I know it's going to take some time, but please try to find it in your heart to forgive me. I'm sorry. I can't say that enough."

"Why didn't you take me with you? Why didn't you take me to my father? To his family . . . anywhere but where you left me, or is it because you don't even know who the fuck my father is?"

"I know who your father is."

"Who?" Jerusalem asked. "Who is my father? At least give me that much. Who is my father and where is he?"

Anna Marie looked Jerusalem dead in the eyes and softly said, "Your father is Kaleef. Kaleefah Washington."

Jerusalem couldn't believe what he was hearing. "Who?" he asked again.

"His name is Kaleefah Washington. They called him Kaleef. Last I heard he was doing life in the federal penitentiary."

Francis yelled out from the front door. "Can y'all help me get the rest of my groceries?"

Jerusalem looked at Anna Marie and shook his head in disbelief before jumping up off the sofa and rushing past Francis out the door.

Anna Marie yelled, "Jerusalem! Wait! Come back, Jerusalem!"

He didn't come back; instead, he got into his car and sped off. Jerusalem stopped at the liquor store and bought a few bottles of Hennessy. Egypt called him a few times but he ignored all of her calls. He rode around the city drinking and smoking weed like he'd never done before. With no particular destination in mind, he rode around lost in his thoughts.

He answered Malachi's call after five times. "Man, where you at?" Malachi asked from the other end of the phone."

"Here . . . there . . ." Jerusalem responded.

"Why you riding solo? You should have some Warriors with you. You know it's not safe on these streets by yourself."

"Death is certain. You can't run from it. It will find you no matter where you try to hide."

"Be careful."

"Peace," Jerusalem said, right before ending the call. He took another hit of the joint he held in his right hand and continued to cruise through the city.

Jerusalem knew as long as Gino was alive, his life was in danger, but Gino wasn't safe either. Unlike Gino, Jerusalem refused to go into hiding. He was a king and would not fear his destiny. Jerusalem couldn't get his mother's words out of his head. Kaleef was his father.

He parked his car in the park and reminisced about his time with Kaleef. He thought about all of the conversations they'd had. Everything was coming together. It explained the special treatment Kaleef gave him. He recalled all of the things Kaleef taught him as well as the fifty million, which now, seemed more like an inheritance.

Did Kaleef know Jerusalem was his son? Did Kaleef do all of those things out of a guilty conscious? All of those questions and more filled Jerusalem's head. The announcer on the radio broke Jerusalem out of his trance.

The announcer said, "Mayor Elect Gregory Wilson has been found dead in a local hotel from an apparent overdose. More details to follow when we get them. The swearing in ceremony was set for tomorrow. However, the candidate with the second most votes will now be sworn in as mayor. Rest in peace, Wilson. You will be missed. The family has asked that we give them time to mourn their loved one."

CHAPTER FORTY

The next day, Jerusalem sat behind his desk in his empty house watching the news. Earlier, he'd sent Mama Sherry and Baby Stone to go stay with Egypt until he felt it was safe for them to return home. He'd also given the house staff time off because he wanted to be alone.

His eyes were glued to the television. Cameras zoomed over the huge crowd of people as they waited for the new mayor to be sworn into office. The new mayor walked up on the podium and to the lectern. Gino stood behind him with a smug look on his face. Jerusalem took a hit from his blunt and blew smoke into the air. Gino's body jerked as three gunshots from a lone shooter pierced his body. The third shot went straight through his head. People screamed and began running. The cameraman never dropped the camera as viewers watched the events happen live.

"There's the shooter!" one of the officers shouted.

The cameraman turned the camera to face the east side of the crowd. The Black Warrior's attempt to get through the crowd was unsuccessful. One of the police snipers shot him in the back of his head, and he dropped down on the ground.

Jerusalem watched the scene play out like the rest of the city. He hated losing one of his soldiers but was satisfied that he'd accomplished his mission by killing Gino.

After Gino's life ended, it seemed as if Jerusalem should have been happy, but instead he fell into a deep depressive state. Day in and day out, he drank and smoked. He never left his house. So many things weighed heavily on his mind, and he felt like he was losing control.

Pinky, Malachi, Egypt, Mama Sherry, and King Geoffrey all attempted to get through to him, but he wouldn't talk to anyone. Jerusalem became a recluse.

On this particular day, over a week after Gino's death, he sat in his home office at his desk staring out into open space. He swiveled his chair to face the security monitors. He saw the flashing lights of the local police force vehicles, FBI, and other law enforcement agencies as they surrounded his home.

Jerusalem didn't attempt to move. He watched them approach the house. Yet, he didn't flinch when the front door flew off the hinges from the battering ram the officers used. After taking a toke of his blunt, he drank from the bottle of imported cognac as the team of law enforcement agents invaded his house and went from room to room with their weapons drawn.

The doors to his office flew open. Several men ran over to him. Jerusalem stood without saying a word. He attempted to raise his hands above his head. Before he could get them up, an officer forced him on the floor face down.

An officer said, "You're under arrest. You have the right to remain silent . . ."

Jerusalem recited the words in his head. He recalled the words from his first arrest. He knew the Miranda rights by heart.

A year later . . .

The courtroom was filled to capacity. Reporters, politicians, law enforcement agencies, and the public were all eager to find out Jerusalem's fate. During his trial he'd been found guilty on all accounts of racketeering, money laundering, conspiracy, and drug trafficking. The D.A. did his best to make Jerusalem out to be a heartless monster and a gangster and thug who preyed on and killed innocent people. Celebrities from all forms of entertainment and people from various communities spoke of Jerusalem's generosity.

Jerusalem, wearing a gray Italian made suit, walked into the courtroom with his head held high. He hadn't shaved or gotten a hair cut in over a year, so he looked different from his normal clean-cut, shaven image. He noticed some familiar faces in the crowd. He made eye contact with Egypt right before taking his place next to his three black lawyers who were on the Black Senate's payroll.

A white, sixty-year-old judge entered the courtroom. Everyone stood. The judge said, "You may be seated."

The judge looked at Jerusalem. "The State of Illinois has found you guilty of drug trafficking, racketeering, conspiracy, and money laundering. Do you have anything that you want to say?"

Jerusalem responded, "Yes, I do."

"You may stand," the judge said.

Jerusalem stood up and looked at the judge directly in his eyes without flinching. "I just wanted to say that I know I was thought to be guilty from the moment I entered your courtroom, but am I really guilty? Am I guilty for taking back what was mine? Coming from where I come from. The gutter of America. Where the forgotten and the hopeless walk. Where you don't have many paths to choose from in order to make it out of this jungle that this country has made for us. This isn't who I am. This is what you made me. This isn't who I'm supposed to be. This is who I became."

No sounds emitted from anyone in the crowded courtroom. Jerusalem had a captive audience. "Am I guilty for wanting more for me and my people? Am I guilty for wanting to be more than a second class citizen here in your country? You stripped me of everything and act like you haven't done a thing. I know some may say I'm acting like you owe me something. Well, I think you do. You stripped me of my name, my God, my language, my ancestors' ways and my religion and act like I should be okay with what you have done. Am I guilty, or are you and your people guiltier than I am? With that, I would like to say that only God can judge me because he judges a man's heart and not his actions. So fuck you and your courts. You can't do any more than what you have already done to me."

It was so quiet that you could hear a mouse run across the floor. The judge was stunned and for a few seconds remained quiet. He pulled himself together and said, "With that being said, we are ready for sentencing. Jerusalem Rasheed Williams. For the reasons stated earlier, I sentence you to life without the possibility of parole."

The courtroom was in an uproar at the verdict. Pinky, Egypt,

King Geoffrey, Anna Marie and Mama Sherry left the courtroom with tears in their eyes.

Jerusalem just smiled his signature crooked smile. The judge left the courtroom first. The officers handcuffed Jerusalem and led him out through a secure exit into a waiting black SUV with several armed officers. They transported Jerusalem to a maximum-security federal penitentiary.

The warden, afraid of Jerusalem's influence and power, housed him in a cell in the basement of the prison instead of putting him in general population with the rest of the prisoners. Jerusalem wasn't allowed to have any communication with the outside world and that included no visitors, no letters, or phone calls. The authorities were relieved to know that the leader of the Black Senate was tucked away in the basement. They were determined to break him.

Anyone looking at the cell would think it was a cage meant for a wild animal instead of another human being. Whenever a guard came in to check on Jerusalem, they would find him sitting in the middle of the cell with his legs crossed in an Indian style as if he was in deep meditation. Jerusalem would only eat one of the three meals brought to him. He only saw the outside of his cell for ten minutes a day and that was only to shower. This was the routine the warden set up for Jerusalem Rasheed Williams to follow for the rest of his natural life; until he took his last breath.

THE END

EPILOGUE

Shirtless, Malachi sat in the front room of his project penthouse in a chair that looked like a throne. He'd removed all of his jewelry and hung them across the arm of the chair and on the floor around the chair. He drank from a bottle of cognac and smoked a blunt, trying his best to drown out the sorrows of losing Jerusalem to a life-long prison sentence.

His pit bulls, Mae West and Capone sat on each side of the chair. Pinky and the gutta girls sat around the room smoking and drinking their sorrows away. Pinky felt helpless because she'd never seen Malachi like this. He'd never let anything get the best of him, but the loss of YaYa to the streets and Jerusalem to the system weighed heavily on him.

They all sat in silence and in a daze. Someone knocked on the door. It got everyone's attention.

Apple walked over to open the locked door. She turned and looked at Pinky, China Doll, Luscious, and then Malachi. Malachi became fully alert. With his dreads swinging, he reached beside his chair and retrieved his machete. Pinky and the gutta girls pulled out their handguns and stood up.

Apple slowly opened the door. Haitian Black entered first and right behind him King Geoffrey and Egypt walked in. Apple closed the door.

They all stared at one another for a few seconds. Egypt stood in the center and said, "So what are we going to do to get him out?"

BIO

Zaid Za'hid is known for sharing his deepest thoughts, struggles, and stories of the ghetto in the rhythm of poetry. He expresses political views showing his outspoken courage, voicing his passion in its truest form that is amazing and phenomenal. Zaid Za'hid is planting his seed as a ghetto storyteller and a teacher giving us his life and spirit in the most powerful, and original style that has ever been heard. He is the author of the poetry book, *Manifestation of a King* and the novel, *The Black Senate.*

To learn more, please visit him on Facebook:

www.facebook.com/zaidzahid07.

Discussion Questions for *Black Senate*

1. Do you think that it was Jerusalem's pain and suffering that life brought him that made him the man he had become?

2. Do you think that Kaleef was wrong for still dealing drugs inside of the penal system when he was given life for dealing drugs?

3. Do you think that Jerusalem was wrong for using the $50 million that Kaleef gave to him to rise in the drug game as a drug lord?

4. Do you think Jerusalem was wrong for selling his people dangerous drugs?

5. Do you think Ya Ya was wrong for not telling Khadijah about his lifestyle from the beginning of their relationship?

6. What would you have done differently with the $50 million to change your involvement?

7. Do you think Pinky should have told Jerusalem how she truly felt about him, no matter how Jerusalem felt about her?

8. Do you think that Malacia was a noble king?

9. Do you think Jerusalem was in a delusional mind state, thinking that he could build a black nation of his own here in America's ghetto?

10. Did you like Jerusalem's character, and do you think that there's a time to kill?

CPSIA information can be obtained
at www.ICGtesting.com
Printed in the USA
LVHW02s0840281017
554098LV00008BA/77/P